Revenge with a Side of Bacon

A NOVEL BY

DODI WILLIAMS

Cover Illustration by Jason McCormick

Night of Right Series

Book One

ISBN: 0-9985500-0-0
ISBN-13: 978-0-9985500-0-8

DEDICATION

To my loving husband Vince and my boisterous boys Evan and Alex for keeping it real.

To my nurturing parents for their endless encouragement to pursue that which makes me happy.

CONTENTS

Acknowledgments   i

Chapter One   3

Chapter Two   6

Chapter Three   11

Chapter Four   23

Chapter Five   29

Chapter Six   33

Chapter Seven   37

Chapter Eight   43

Chapter Nine   47

Chapter Ten   51

Chapter Eleven   57

Chapter Twelve   64

Chapter Thirteen   69

Chapter Fourteen   75

Chapter Fifteen   78

Chapter Sixteen   81

Chapter Seventeen   87

Chapter Eighteen   91

Chapter Nineteen   97

Chapter Twenty   101

Chapter Twenty-One   108

Chapter Twenty-Two   113

Chapter Twenty-Three   117

Chapter Twenty-Four   121

Chapter Twenty-Five   126

Chapter Twenty-Six   130

Chapter Twenty-Seven   135

Chapter Twenty-Eight   139

Chapter Twenty-Nine   144

Chapter Thirty   147

Chapter Thirty-One   150

Chapter Thirty-Two   154

Chapter Thirty-Three   158

Chapter Thirty-Four   161

Chapter Thirty-Five   165

Chapter Thirty-Six   171

Chapter Thirty-Seven   175

Chapter Thirty-Eight   178

Chapter Thirty-Nine   182

Chapter Forty   185

Chapter Forty-One   190

Chapter Forty-Two   195

Chapter Forty-Three   200

Chapter Forty-Four   205

Chapter Forty-Five   212

Chapter Forty-Six   218

Chapter Forty-Seven   223

Chapter Forty-Eight   229

Chapter Forty-Nine   236

Chapter Fifty   240

Chapter Fifty-One   246

ACKNOWLEDGMENTS

Many thanks to my cousins, sister, brother, and parents for the encouragement to continue writing and offering their advice and time.

It's amazing what can be accomplished when I have friends that patiently scrutinize my work, even if they only made it to the end of the first chapter.

CHAPTER ONE

Life is not always solved with a chocolate fudge cupcake with peanut butter frosting. After twelve years of loyal service to Remco, Allison Black was being escorted out the door by her manager, Todd Whitt. In a disappointing and shocking meeting several minutes earlier, Allison was told by Todd that her job had been eliminated. She was expecting a small confrontation, but a full dismissal came as a shock and was a serious blow to her ego. Now as she passed by the familiar people who had become her second family, the reality of finality was sinking in like a dead weight in the pit of her stomach. She passed by the work stations of people she had shared lunch, jokes, and her life with for many years. Allison almost choked on the unbearably thick air surrounding her departure when suddenly her walk of shame was interrupted by a loud laugh somewhere down the hall. Unsettled that someone could find humor at a time when her world was crashing down, Allison frowned, reminded that hardly anyone knew what was going on with her employment status.

Allison would miss many of the people, but some more than others. As she passed by Gloria Beason, Allison caught her eye and whispered, "Bye. Take care."

Gloria only nodded and slightly waved, perplexed as to why Allison was leaving. With her photo of her parents and other personal possessions in a box weighing down her arms in front of her, her arms were not free to wave back or to offer a parting hug or hand shake. She noticed a few others, mostly men, kept their heads down and completely missed her awkward exit. The ability to hold back tears were one of Allison's strong points, but leaving behind everything she knew was stretching that ability to the breaking point. Not wanting to be seen as a weak female, she shook off the creeping emotions, took a deep breath, and held her head high during her indignant parade through the office, past the maze of cubicles, toward the door.

She could already hear some whispers behind her back as she made her way past the last of the desks. Susie asked, "Is Allison leaving?" "What happened?" "What did she do?"

Todd opened the door for her and followed her through. He was the last person she wanted to talk to or see as she made her way through the final door and down the sidewalk. Now that they were past all the curious on-lookers, Todd tried to make small talk with Allison. "I wish you the best," Todd said.

Allison kept walking without saying a word. There was nothing she could say at this point that would change her circumstances or reconcile any differences. Any words that came out of her mouth would be condescending or politely fake. She wasn't sure either of those was appropriate so she clamped her mouth shut. The song *Take This Job and Shove It* popped into her head suddenly and she wished she had thought about downloading it to her iPhone so she could hit play as her answer back to Todd.

Instead, she fumbled for her keys to her car in silence, while trying to balance her box of belongings in one arm. Todd felt the need to fill in the deafening silence, "Keep in touch with us. Let us know how you're doing."

Allison picked up her walk a little faster to her car, her box of personal items with her picture frame, a candy dish, and other nondescript desk items she had accumulated over the years rattled with each quick step.

Trying to escape an already uncomfortable situation, she flippantly told Todd, "Yeah, okay." Eloquent words failed her as to what she was supposed to say in a situation like this. "Tell everyone I said bye," Allison said. She hated that she did not get a chance to say good bye to all of her friends she had made over the last twelve years, but honestly, she didn't want them to see the raw emotions on her face as she had to explain why she was leaving. Many of her co-workers would be shocked to learn of her fate. The gossip train in the building was already on its way to most of the departments, working its way through each cubicle to rest on eager ears.

"Okay," Todd said, "I will." Todd stood nearby in his beige pants and navy Polo shirt, watching as she climbed into her deep red Jaguar F-Type and slowly shut the door. Allison gritted her teeth as she put the car in reverse, trying with all her might to not run over Todd in the process. She slowly backed out of her parking spot, her parking spot. The one she parked in every morning for the last twelve years. She might have changed cars a few times over the years, but her parking spot stayed the same. Her salary had finally afforded her a luxury car that she paid off last year; a car that she only dreamed about in college. Todd lifted his hand in a final farewell gesture. It made her angry to think of all the wasted time and effort she spent to do her job well, not to mention the numerous cupcakes and cookies she fed Todd and the other managers like him. She had loved practicing new recipes and bringing in the results for her coworkers to try. Look where it got her: out the door without even a good referral to send her on her way. As much as she wanted to give Todd the one finger salute, Allison kept both hands firmly on the steering wheel of her sporty Jaguar and left her corporate dreams and financial stability in a haze of unanswered questions.

What happened? Why me? Why wasn't Joe terminated instead of me? These were the questions going through her mind. The most compelling questions, however, were the ones related to her most recent findings. *What will the company do with the critical information I uncovered? Was my job eliminated because of what I found? Will they suspect I made a copy of the information on my jump drive dangling on my key ring?*

Preoccupied with her own musings, Allison did not see the man standing on the sidewalk watching her car drive away from Remco. The slight, cool breeze mussed his light brown hair, which had hints of red that were highlighted as the sun shone down on him. His eyes squinted to avoid the sunlight and then frowned as he saw a familiar black car follow Allison's Jaguar out of the parking lot. He stepped out into the parking lot, making quick strides toward his own car.

CHAPTER TWO

Twelve years earlier Allison was wrapping up her senior year at Tennessee Technological University in Cookeville, Tennessee. Serving as President for her chapter's sorority during her senior year and making the Dean's List during all four years in college were accolades she was immensely proud to list on her resume. With a fresh degree in Computer Science, the whole world was her oyster and her possibilities were endless. She was hand-picked by one of her favorite professors, Doc, to apply for a job at a prestigious company called Remco. Being privately held, there was little information on Remco available. The mystique of a manufacturing company tied directly to the military made for an interesting prospect for Allison. Doc had vouched for the company, telling her they were one of the best college recruiting companies that came to town, always hiring Tech graduates at top rate salaries for beginning positions in the company.

Slightly heavy set with a trim, white beard, Doc was well liked by all the students. His litany of humor was limitless, constantly keeping those around him in as jolly a mood as he was. Many would say he did not have much of a filter before words flew out of his mouth and into the air, but he was honest to a fault, often remarking on topics that were beyond the scope of the average university professor. His jubilant and friendly behavior belied the fact he always kept a firearm tucked neatly beneath his sweater vest, secured tightly to a strap on his hip. Doc had a knack of keeping up to date with the current trends, as well as being concerned about his students' welfare. One of his favorite past-times, other than riding shotgun with the local sheriff's deputy, included computer forensic research. No company or individual was overlooked if Doc wanted to know their deepest, darkest secrets. In fact, one of Allison's best friends, Brianna DeVoe, studied under Doc for several years, learning some of his computer forensic trade secrets. Computers often told the hidden story of most guilty parties, so he was often consulted by the local law enforcement for special cases where detectives had little evidence. If he asserted that a company was decent and worth pursuing, it was in one's best interest to apply for a position.

With Doc's strong endorsement, "You're a perfect fit for Remco," and her resume in hand, Allison applied for her first corporate America job.

Remco was located in a small, mill town in Morgan, South Carolina. They specialized in making electronic parts used primarily in military vehicles. Two weeks after applying for a starting position as a junior programmer, Allison was flying down in her second best interviewing suit (her first best suit reserved for the following day). Her Remco contact picked her up from the airport for her whirlwind tour of the city. Her host for the evening was a quiet girl named Renee.

Renee had shoulder length light brown hair and kind blue eyes. "How was your flight?" Renee asked.

"It was fine. The flight was not overly crowded so I had a row to myself," Allison replied.

Renee smiled and said, "I'm glad it was a nice trip. We are pleased you were able to come down and interview on such short notice. I made reservations at Callaway's Steak House for dinner. Are you hungry?"

Since Allison loved steak she replied, "Yes, that sounds right up my alley." The girls chatted at dinner about the surrounding town, attractions, and shopping centers. Allison felt at ease and comfortable with Renee, despite being nervous about the big interview scheduled for the next day.

After dinner, Renee drove Allison around the quaint town, pointing out certain landmarks that were unique to the area. "We are close to many larger cities such as Asheville, Charlotte, Atlanta, and Charleston," Renee stated. "You can drive to all of them within a couple of hours," she said.

Being from a small city in Tennessee, Allison liked the small town feel, but would definitely enjoy a weekend excursion of shopping or playing tourist at some of the cities Renee mentioned. Feeling comfortable with Renee, Allison asked her, "What do you like best about Remco? Is it a good company to work for?"

Renee replied, "I like the people the best. It is a great company to work for. They seem to care about me and if I'm working in an area where I'm happy. Plus the pay can't be beat for starting right out of college." Renee gave Allison a slight smile, knowing that salary was a touchy subject for most people, but she had touched on Allison's unasked question.

"Thanks," Allison said. It was nice to hear someone acknowledge the fact that the starting salary was substantially larger than other company offerings, especially for someone straight out of college. "Is there anything I should be aware of for tomorrow's interviews? Any hints or suggestions?"

Renee had a slight smile on her face when she said, "Be yourself. You'll do fine."

The interview was grueling, consisting of five different interviewers drilling her about her abilities, personality, and willingness to learn. Being a people person and having a sharp technical wit, Allison excelled at the interviews. It came as no surprise that in less than three days after interviewing at Remco, she was offered a permanent position in a company she knew little to nothing about, which was over six hours away from her family, friends and life as she knew it back in Tennessee.

As a charming southern girl with a candid charisma, at first glance, no one would know that logic and math came easily to Allison. Being of petite stature, her size four stylish frame stood at only five feet two inches tall. Her long blonde hair, hazel eyes, and cute southern accent were a refreshing change to the other geeks in the computer industry. When shown a concept or theory, she was able to tackle most mathematical problems with a logical ease that impressed most everyone around her. Her uncanny ability to solve issues with such smooth finesse and funny wit made her stand out in the crowd of otherwise dull computer techies. She liked to think she was both left and right brained, marrying her creative side and her analytical side together to form a complex, bright-minded woman who liked her high tech devices, designer shoes and gourmet taste in food.

Her keen sense of fashion and love of chocolate led people to often confuse her with a mindless southern belle, rather than the mentally sharp analytic whose mind was constantly counting numbers and solving theorems. Of course, those theorems also involved coming up with a recipe for the best gourmet cupcake.

Allison did love food. As much as she loved consuming edible delights, she also had a knack for baking them. Her love of baking and many of her recipes came from her Granny, her grandmother on her mother's side. Granny was known by all of her family and friends for her chocolate fudge, peanut butter chocolate balls she referred to as buckeyes, and white fudge known as divinity. Years of helping Granny in the kitchen led to Allison's passionate culinary hobby. Baking brought back many fond memories of her Granny and Allison cherished each one every time she opened her antique recipe box. Most steps and ingredients of a recipe were simply suggestions for Allison. Although she favored traditional recipes, nothing made her happier than when she combined the most unlikely ingredients to come up with a fabulous new recipe that would please the pickiest of palettes. This keenness for cooking was one of the sharpest tools in her belt, a tool she used wisely.

During college, she quickly learned while at her part-time job at Frank's Computer World that the best way to a computer geek's mind was through his stomach. At the beginning of her junior year at Tennessee Tech, she started working evenings for Frank Connors, learning about software research. Some of the software vendors would drop by the store to demonstrate their latest version release. Whenever she needed access to certain security codes or a quick response from a software vendor, food allowed those doors to open swiftly and smoothly. It was incredible how quickly a chocolate fudge cupcake could gain access to a pilot software program that took others months on a waiting list. Good old Frank stayed impressed with Allison's ability to gain insights on the latest electronic trends far ahead of his local competition.

Frank allowed Allison the opportunity to install her own software in his store as part of her senior programming project at Tennessee Tech. Her software was a perfect fit for his store, allowing him to run simple computer queries and pull up information he needed in half the time. After a few years of working in the evenings at Frank's, Allison knew she picked the right field for her career. She hired on at Remco with a solid launching pad and firm recommendation from Frank.

Now, twelve years later, that career was fast sliding into an ever burning inferno of no return. How would she survive such a blow to her ego and her career? Since Frank's was a part-time college job, Remco was the only company she truly had real experience with after college. Twelve years of experience with corporate America was quickly going down the drain.

Allison needed a Plan B, and the jump drive on her key ring was going to help kick start this plan in motion.

CHAPTER THREE

Allison Black was befuddled thinking about how her day, and career, had ended. A chill had settled in the air, as well in in Allison's own temperament. Starbuck's was on her way home, and nothing could go down faster than a tall cup of hot chocolate with a hint of toffee nut. Following this whim and without signaling, she turned sharply into the parking lot of Starbuck's. Being preoccupied with her own thoughts, she failed to notice the black Mercedes that had followed her since she left Remco. The Mercedes drove slowly past the popular coffee shop and pulled over to wait in the parking area of the strip mall next door. Allison ordered her drink and cautiously drove away from the popular coffee shop while she held her hot cup of hot chocolate in her right hand.

As she turned onto Main Street, sipping her hot chocolate, Allison contemplated the first question that she pondered: *Why me?* Or better yet, *why just me?* She had been working on a project with Joe, who was clearly the weaker wingman. Allison had run the project successfully, dragging Joe along as best she could. He had not been blessed with natural logical instincts and so each day had been a struggle. It had not been the first time she had been on a project with Joe and honestly, she wondered why he stayed in the computer field as long as he did. Their latest project had been to make revisions to the human resources system, upgrading the software package in order to best track associates' ratings and reviews as well as salary. She was under the impression the installation was a success until this morning's meeting.

Unable to hold in her frustrations much longer, she grabbed her cell phone and dialed one of her good friends, Jane King. Other than being born the same year, Jane and Allison had little in common. Opposites attract was never a more accurate a statement about their solid friendship. Where Allison was level headed and career-minded, Jane was flighty and quirky, with an emotional temperament of a wet cat. The phone rang four times when a breathless Jane picked up, "Hey, what's up chica?"

Allison rushed to get the words out before she choked on them, "I was fired from Remco today. Todd walked me out to my car."

"Oh my word! Are you kidding me?" Jane exclaimed. "What happened? Tell me everything. Are you okay? Do you want to come to my place? What are you going to do?" Jane rushed on with her questions. Allison was grateful Jane was on her side.

"I'm not exactly sure what happened. I'm trying to figure it out," said Allison in a weary low voice.

Jane told her, "You need to come to my house immediately -

right now. We need to talk this through. Where are you now? " Allison looked around and noticed she had been driving aimlessly on auto-pilot without a thought of where she was going.

Where am I going? "I'm on Washington Avenue near the park," she replied. "Why don't you come here and meet me at Washington Park? Maybe we can talk and then go to dinner somewhere afterwards," Allison said.

"I'll be there in ten minutes," Jane replied. After disconnecting, Allison knew she had at least twenty minutes to kill before Jane arrived. Her estimated time of arrival never accounted for the time it took Jane to actually drive somewhere, only how long it took her to get ready.

Although the temperature was cool, the sun was shining and a few children were playing on a nearby swing set. Allison parked near the other end, away from the happy laughter, not ready to be cheered up by the frolicking youngsters. She took one last sip of her drink and returned the empty cup to the cup holder. Exiting the car, she spotted a bench nearby with several flowers beginning to bloom beside it. She sat down and rested her head on the back of the bench, closed her eyes and absorbed the sunshine.

The man's hand on her arm came out of nowhere.

Startled, Allison almost screamed when he said softly, "I'm not going to hurt you." He let go of her arm and continued talking, "Do you mind if I sit down?"

Allison was hesitant. She looked up into the eyes of the most gorgeous man she had ever seen. As much as she enjoyed the company of a good looking man, she was uneasy by the sudden way in which he had approached. She had not heard him approach, but looking around, she saw another car was now parked beside hers.

In a serious, business-like manner, he sat down before she could reply and said, "I know you don't know me, but I was at Remco earlier today. I saw you leave this afternoon." His face was remarkably pleasing to look at with intense blue eyes, and deep, engaging dimples.

Allison didn't know who this man was, but she was not ready to end this conversation yet. "How do you know me? Why did you follow me here?" she asked. Wow. He was captivatingly gorgeous. His bold confidence and calm nature put Allison quickly at ease after her startling awareness of him.

This stranger had obviously walked off a photo shoot for some magazine, probably called *Modern Cowboy*. The crisp, black button-up Oxford shirt had the top two buttons undone, revealing a black t-shirt underneath, all tucked neatly into the perfectly fit designer jeans which he wore with a comfortable ease. The leather belt looked hand-carved with intricate designs, most likely a one-of-a-kind from an Italian leather smith. His cowboy boots were of soft, butter leather with a unique alligator print. His blue eyes were searing into hers as he spoke.

"My name is Jack. I didn't mean to sneak up on you. I thought you heard my car pull in, but maybe you were in a zone," Jack stated.

Allison nodded, "Yes, I was. I didn't hear you." She was definitely in a zone as her own thoughts were louder than any car engines these last few days.

"Do you see that Mercedes on the other end of the parking lot?" Jack asked. Allison turned her head toward the direction indicated and saw a car idling across the way.

"Yes," she replied. "I see it."

Jack said, "That car followed you here from Remco. Do you recognize that car?"

While focusing on her own self-pity party, she had missed not one, but two cars that had followed her from her very recent past employer. She glanced nervously at the key ring in her hand. Clutching the jump drive tightly in her grasp, she answered, "No. Who is it?" Allison began to feel apprehensive about her decision to take the information that was now firmly hidden in her hand.

"I'm not sure," Jack stated. "I saw him follow you from the parking lot at Remco and decided to try and intervene before he caught up with you."

"Um, thanks, I think," Allison said. "Why is this guy following me?" she asked.

"Well," said Jack, "He must have gotten word you were being dismissed and has been lying in wait for you to leave."

Allison was confused and slightly alarmed. How would anyone besides her immediate managers know she was being terminated today? The mystery man sat in his idling car, watching their conversation from a distance. Allison was getting a creepy feeling about this unknown guy.

"Why would he care if I was terminated today?" Allison asked.

"Probably the same reason I care," Jack stated with a deadpan look on his face.

Allison wasn't sure what to think. "Why would you care?" she asked. Her nervousness showed in the way her eyes kept glancing back and forth from Jack to the black car, "Who are you again?"

"I apologize," Jack explained, "my name is Jack. I'm a private investigator. I do odd jobs for people around town. I also tend to notice when things look suspicious, such as a car following you from Remco." He continued, "I wanted to make sure you were okay." Jack looked back at the Mercedes and whoever was in it must have decided their cover was blown and started to drive away. They both watched the car exit the parking lot and drive away in a quiet hum.

Allison could feel the heat radiating from Jack's thigh resting against her own. She stared down at the connection then snapped her eyes back to his as his introduction registered. He had not explained why he or the other man had followed her or how they knew she had been fired. In fact, his response reminded her of a politician who always gave vague answers as to keep all the constituents at bay.

"Am I being investigated?" she asked, turning the car keys over and over nervously in her hands.

"No," Jack replied, "I had some complaints about the guy in the Mercedes harassing other associates that had been let go. I was at Remco trying to gather more information about recent terminations, when I spotted you being walked out to your car. I assumed from the way you were being walked out and the box you were carrying that you had been dismissed. I then noticed that car followed you as you drove out of the parking lot."

That explained why Jack knew she was let go, but Allison wasn't sure why anyone would harass someone who had been recently fired.

Isn't being terminated harassment enough? She shifted on the bench away from Jack's touch. "You're right, I was let go today. Do you know who was in that car?" she asked.

"I'm working on it," he answered, "but I thought I'd make sure you were safely away before I continue that part of the investigation." Allison was grateful he had intervened, but her curiosity was now piqued as to who the mystery driver was that followed her. A part of her wished Jack had let the man approach her so she would know exactly what he wanted, but another part of her was thankful for the handsome interruption. Jack had a calm nature about him that put Allison at ease.

She involuntarily started talking, needing to decompress from the prior events, "You know I didn't know I would be terminated today until my manager called me in for a meeting this afternoon. It didn't sink in until he followed me to my desk and helped me pack up my belongings. I guess I'm confused on how anyone else would know about my circumstances, especially someone from outside the company."

Jack watched Allison's mouth as she spoke, seeming genuinely interested in her plight. "I'm sorry you were caught off guard. I guess there's no easy way to alert someone that their job is ending," he said compassionately.

"I guess not," she replied. "I feel like such a failure." Her blonde hair fluttered in the cool breeze. The wind picked up the hem of her dark brown skirt, and Allison watched it tease Jack's leg, ruffling against his calf. *Why am I telling this stranger about my situation?* She suddenly felt as though she was one of those people that said too much, like the ones who tell their entire life story in about five minutes. Jack's sympathetic hand landing on her shoulder was too much. She looked up and saw the pity in his eyes. Allison did not mind throwing her own pity party, but did not need pity from a man with so much potential. Why is it she finally meets the man of her dreams at the most inopportune time, under the worst of circumstances, and she tells him she's a failure? *I need to think more before I speak.* Clearly, she wasn't thinking. Allison was usually cool around men, not one to bluster about her own incompetence as she was doing with this handsome stranger.

A month earlier on her last date, she had met Tom on-line using a popular dating web site. Allison had agreed to meet Tom for drinks and dessert after exchanging numerous emails with him. Tom seemed like a nice, professional guy who had a great job as an accountant and decent looking profile picture. However, when Allison arrived at the coffee shop, it was evident Tom had not updated his picture within the last ten or fifteen years. In fact, she almost would not have recognized him, if he had not called out her name and waved her over to his table. The grey-haired, balding Tom appeared to be at least fifteen years older than his younger, thinner on-line version. Allison thought he had gained about thirty more pounds than in his picture, and wondered if he hadn't been honest about his picture then what else had he lied about?

Not wanting to seem judgmental, she sat down across from Tom, ordered a slice of apple pie and a Coke. She chatted politely with him, interchanging information as one does on a first date. She learned Tom had been an accountant, but had quit his job several months earlier due to incompatibility with a co-worker. Trying to seem sympathetic, Allison listened until he revealed the incompatibility was another female accusing him of sexual harassment. Although she did not feel any instant attraction toward Tom, whom she learned was in his fifties, the nail in his coffin was when he revealed he still lived with his mother, and in fact had never left home in all his years. Allison thanked Tom for the pie and excused herself from the date earlier than usual. The single saving grace from the blind date had been the hot apple pie. She could still taste the light, buttery crust and the perfectly coated apples with a hint of cinnamon and brown sugar. Thinking back to Tom, Allison knew Jack was a far cry from the fifty year old, unemployed sexual predator who lived with his mother. Her recollection of past dating failures brought her back to the current situation with a jolt.

Allison stood up suddenly. *Where is Jane?* This entire situation was becoming improbable. She needed to be rescued, although she wasn't yet sure from what she was being rescued or from whom. Who exactly is this Jack guy, besides being the best looking entity she'd seen in several years? And who was this other fellow who had hovered in his dark car across the parking lot? Jane needed to be here and fast. Jane was the one who loved drama, not Allison. In fact, drama usually followed Jane King wherever she went. Allison was usually the level-headed friend who looked at the realistic point of view and held a steady job. Well, until today, that is. Jane had been divorced twice and had a new job every six months. Jane went through boyfriends like most people went through a hot container of fresh French fries. Not seeing Jane's car anywhere, Allison felt the need to rescue herself.

Clenching her keys tightly to her chest, Allison stated, "I need to go. My friend is expecting me." She backed away from Jack toward her car.

Jack's demeanor suddenly changed as his lips pursed together and his eyes narrowed. "Wait, let me help you," he said. Jack stood and walked quickly around Allison, grabbing her elbow and blocking the path to her car. She stumbled into him as she was suddenly halted from her escape. Towering over her at six foot two inches tall, he was an impressive blockade.

Allison said firmly, "I'm fine! I do not need any help." Jack remained unmoved. His hovering persistence set off an internal alarm in Allison that Jack might not be as safe as she thought. She had let her guard down too quickly with this new male specimen. Allison's stomach was full of butterflies, but she wasn't sure if they were from his extreme nearness or the fact that someone this hot was concerned about her well-being. He sure smelled good.

What kind of cologne is he wearing? She thought briefly of performing Tai Kwan Do on him in order to get past him, remembering basic moves from a survival class she once took. Instead, on some deep subliminal instinct she automatically reached up with her free hand and pulled his face down to hers, planting a solid kiss directly on his firmly closed lips. Shocking them both, Jack let go of her arm and stood agape. Taking the opportunity of his sudden stupor, and embarrassed by what she did, Allison bolted for the safety of her car.

Did I kiss a perfect stranger on the mouth in a public park? Allison jumped into the driver's seat and jammed the key into the ignition, locking the door with her left hand. Backing out of the parking spot, Allison noticed Jack was standing where she left him with an astonished look on his face, his hair being tossed about by the cooling wind. She could look at those dimples all day long, but the embarrassment of the situation kicked her into overdrive. Her car rolled up to the stop sign and after looking both ways, Allison peeled out onto the street as Jane's car was turning into the park. The look on Jane King's face as Allison was speeding away was of acute bewilderment.

As Allison drove madly away from the park, she couldn't help but constantly look in her rear view mirror to see if anyone was following her. She thought she glimpsed the black Mercedes several cars back, so she turned quickly down a side street, going through the back roads to try and lose him. She contemplated driving directly to a police station, but what would she tell them? *I got fired, some car followed me, and then I kissed a perfect stranger in the park.* Allison started questioning her sanity. She quickly turned again onto another side street and then pulled into a small parking lot of a local church that had a large dumpster near the back of the building. She carefully backed her car between the dumpster and the building; hiding it from the street view should anyone drive by the church.

In her haste to get away, Allison did not even notice the kind of car Jack drove. Only that it looked like a dark blue SUV, similar to half the cars on the market these days. Her expertise was not in cars, much less the make, model or year of one. She did not have a license plate number for either the SUV or the Mercedes. Nor did she know Jack's last name. Currently, her two pursuers knew more about her than she did about them. The odds were not in her favor. *I need to be more observant*, she thought. Allison had been hiding in her car for a good ten minutes when a vibration near her leg made her fast beating heart stop as she nearly jumped out of her skin. Her phone which had been left on vibrate mode was ringing. Taking a deep breath, Allison took the call from Jane.

"Where are you?" Jane asked. "What is going on?" Allison was glad to hear her friend's voice.

"I'm sorry," Allison replied. "It's been a crazy day." That was an understatement. Allison continued, "Some guy who followed me from Remco approached me at the park. He made me extremely nervous so I left."

Jane sighed, talking to someone on the other end of the line, "She said you made her nervous."

Allison stopped cold. "Jane, who are you talking to?" Allison asked.

Jane answered in a cheery voice, "Jack. He's right here in my car." Of course he was. Jane was not one to turn away a hot guy. Allison could picture Jane flirting with him and putting her hand on Jack's leg as she spoke, the same leg her skirt had brushed against earlier.

Allison asked the question, already dreading the answer, "Jane, why is he in your car?"

Jane replied, "When I saw you leaving, I was going to follow you, but then I saw Jack standing there. We talked after you left and he was worried about you. I told him we were meeting for dinner and I offered to bring him along to join us."

Allison shook her head. Only Jane would talk to a perfect stranger, well besides Allison, but at least she didn't let him sit in her car to talk. Jane thought too much with her heart, and not with her head. Her friend craved attention from men, to the point of ignoring warning signs that most normal people could see. "Jane, do you think it wise to let a stranger in your car?" Allison chided.

"Oh, he's okay. Jack doesn't look strange to me; besides, he's going to drive separately. We were sitting in my car to stay out of the cold wind," Jane countered, "so where would you like to eat for dinner?" It was typical of Jane to try and bring a date to dinner even though they were going to discuss the downfall of Allison's entire career. She wondered what Jane would think if she knew Allison had kissed Jack first?

Now she was expected to eat dinner in a public restaurant pretending that the most awkward moment of her life had not happened. Allison answered, "Um, Jane, I don't think I'm up to eating out tonight. I might go home and rest for a while."

Jack mumbled something to Jane, but Allison could not hear what he told her. Jane said, "We don't think that's a good idea. You should be with friends tonight."

Friends? Jack was a stranger that Allison did not yet trust. His earlier antics in the park had her on edge; it was hard to know if he was friend or foe. Jane was much more trusting of the male species, especially if the male species was a tall, handsome man with a charming smile, dimples, and beautiful blue eyes.

Allison told Jane, "I'll call you later tonight and let you know what happened today. I don't think I'll be pleasant to be around in mixed company. You and Jack go to dinner without me. Don't worry about me. I'll be fine."

Jane hesitated for a moment, "You shouldn't be alone after what you went through today. Do you want me to meet you by myself?" Allison could tell that Jane wanted her to say no. In fact she could almost hear Jane saying *please say no, please say no.*

"No," Allison replied. "You two go have a nice dinner." Maybe Jane would learn more about this Jack guy and let Allison know the details. She suddenly didn't seem to mind if Jane did her detective work for her, as long as Jane kept her hands to herself.

Jane's voice sounded relieved and almost elated, "Okay, well I want to hear all about what happened at Remco later tonight. I'll call you as soon as I get home. Are you sure you're okay?"

"Yes," Allison answered, "I'm fine." She hung up the phone and thought *I'm not fine. I don't know if I'll ever be fine again.*

How could this day get any worse? She placed her phone inside her purse and glanced back up to see the black Mercedes passing by the church parking lot.

Am I a magnet for trouble today? Allison wondered if she had crossed a black cat or broken a mirror lately. With all of the bad luck happening at one time, some magical forces must be in the air. After all, if it wasn't for bad luck, she would have no luck at all today. She turned around in her seat to see if there were hidden cameras in her car, hoping this whole day might be some bad joke gone wrong. *Nope, no cameras.* Miraculously, the driver in the other car did not see her and continued driving past her without stopping. Allison waited a good five minutes, tucked her hair behind her ear, and then slowly pulled out of her hiding spot, being careful to drive in the opposite direction that the Mercedes had gone.

CHAPTER FOUR

Her stomach was in knots, churning at everything that had transpired today. Last week she had started getting strange vibes from Todd and noticed other upper level managers at Remco cutting her sideways glances when they passed her in the hall. On a whim, she made sure her resume was up to date and started looking at job postings on-line. In fact, it was this morning that she decided to download the critical information on her jump drive that now dangled from her ignition. Since she had a solid twelve years of computer programming experience under her belt at a top-rate company, she felt confident that she could apply and secure another position should the need arise. After her abrupt departure today, however, her confidence sunk to an all-time low. Allison thought she would have plenty of time to look at her options and find a replacement job in the coming months, but less than a week later, Todd had escorted her out the door in the least of ideal circumstances. If the writing on the wall had come sooner, she could have been better prepared – both mentally and financially.

Allison had been diligent to put money in savings and in her 401K account, in order to save a nice nest egg for when she retired. Only she didn't expect to retire at the early age of thirty-four. She regretted the three hundred and twenty dollar Michael Kors purse and one hundred and ten dollar shoes she bought last week. A girl has to have her fashion needs fulfilled, but not at the expense of her monthly living expenses. She wondered what the return policy was for both items. Looking down at the new black shoes, she decided that the store would not want worn shoes returned. Besides, they looked overtly stylish on her dainty size six feet. As she pondered all the ways she could make quick money, she came to one conclusion. She needed to invest in the redneck retirement plan and buy a lottery ticket…a winning lottery ticket. Allison headed for the closest gas station.

It had been months since Allison stepped into a convenient store to purchase a lottery ticket. She didn't even know what the winning amount was up to this week.

Whatever the amount, it's more than I make these days. She dug through her regretfully purchased purse and came up with sixteen dollars. She opened her car door and approached the door to the store at the same time another customer was coming out of the door. The Latino man looked to be a day laborer, most likely in the construction field of painting, judging by the paint on his pants and knuckles.

He held the door for her as she walked in the store. "Thank you," she said. He nodded and smiled with kindness in his eyes. As she approached the counter, she spotted all of the lottery tickets in a large display to the right of the cashier. There were so many to choose from at the counter, but a silver one with glitter caught her eye. It was a five dollar scratch off lottery ticket with a bold amount of $500,000 in large black lettering in the center of the ticket. *I could use five hundred grand right now,* she thought.

"Can I help you?" the young teenager behind the counter asked. He looked to be no older than nineteen.

"I'd like to buy that $5 scratch off ticket please," Allison pointed to the one in the display. "And I'd like a Mega Million ticket, too." She figured she could spend six dollars on lottery tickets, leaving her with ten dollars for a quick dinner on the way home.

"Do you want to power it up?" asked the attendant, "It's another dollar."

"No thank you," replied Allison.

The young man rang up her total, "That will be six dollars." Allison handed him the exact cash, thanked him and took the tickets. She shoved them down into the side pocket of her purse and walked back out to her car. With no rush to get back to the office, Allison wasn't sure where to go next.

With her stomach in knots, she wasn't in the mood to eat yet. To be honest, she wasn't in the mood for much of anything. If only she had booked her beach vacation for this week instead of three months away in June. Thinking of her upcoming vacation now made her sad. The trip had been paid in full and was nonrefundable. She wasn't even sure she would be able to go on that trip now. What she wouldn't give at this moment to have her toes in the sand and a nice cold drink in her hand.

Drink? Hmmm...there's a thought. Allison had never been one to go bar hopping or to happy hour like others in her office. She enjoyed an occasional drink at social gatherings, but she didn't go out of her way to drink. Now, however, that idea sounded appealing in every respect. *Gambling and drinking, why not?* She remembered the steak house she had eaten at twelve years ago that had a nice rustic bar at the front of the restaurant. The dark lighting and wood paneling in a quiet, relaxed atmosphere was sounding more appealing by the minute. What better place to end a career than where she started one.

Allison drove straight to Callaway's Steak House. She parked near the end of the parking lot; away from the other cars that had parked close together near the door. She noticed the time on the door said, HOURS: 4pm to 11pm. Glancing down at her watch, she realized she had no idea what time it was. Thankfully, it was 4:45pm.

Is that too early to start drinking? Apparently it was not. The bar was already half full with what appeared to be regular customers. That would explain the number of cars parked outside. Feeling a little out of place, Allison scanned the room and located a small, secluded booth in the corner near the door. She made a bee line for the booth and quickly scooped up the drink menu as she sat down.

The menu was unequivocally elaborate with bright pictures and details of all sorts of drinks. Allison continued reading through the list of martinis as her waitress appeared. "Welcome to Callaway's. What can I get you, honey?" Wearing jeans and a white button up shirt, the waitress had curly red hair that settled on her shoulders near her name tag, Mandy. Her blue eyes looked tired already and yet her shift had begun less than an hour earlier.

"I'll take water for now," Allison replied.

"Would you like lemon in your water?" asked Mandy. She looked to be in her thirties, maybe the same age as Allison.

I wonder if I'll be waiting tables soon. "No thank you," Allison answered. She continued reading the menu when the caption under one drink caught her eye: Key Lime Pie Martini. Always one to appreciate a fine dessert, Allison loved a good key lime pie, especially if the pie was in alcohol form and could numb the growing dread in her mind. The picture showed an off-white drink with a graham cracker coating on the rim of the glass and a lime wedge perched on the side. Since Allison was now on a permanent vacation, nothing sounded better than a drink that reminded her of the tropical vacation she might not get to take.

Allison ordered her dessert cocktail as Mandy placed her water on the table. "That's one of our best drinks," Mandy stated. "I think you're going to like it." The waitress turned and walked over to the bar to allow the bartender to fill Allison's drink order.

As she waited, Allison pulled out the scratch off ticket and found a quarter in her wallet. She read the instructions and scratched off the area that indicated the winning numbers to be matched. All she had to do was scratch off a fifteen or a four and she would win the amount indicated under the winning number, up to five hundred thousand dollars. She scratched the first of five areas and uncovered a six. She took a deep breath and scratched off the next two numbers, twelve and twenty. Allison looked up and saw the waitress was occupied at another table across the room. Allison scratched off the next number, eighteen. There was one number left. She scratched off the last silver coating and uncovered a four.

Hey! I got one! She quickly scratched off the hidden area under the four to reveal the amount won. Her jaw dropped as she kept scratching off zeroes, uncovering five hundred thousand dollars as the prize won. Allison was stunned.

I won! I won five hundred thousand dollars. Oh my stars, I won five hundred thousand dollars! She glanced up nervously, almost giddy; and then noticed Mandy working her way over to her table with Allison's martini in her hand. Allison quickly put the winning scratch off card securely inside her purse and zipped it up, wiping the silver shards quickly onto the floor. With one hand clutching her purse in a death grip, Allison took the drink from Mandy with her free hand.

"Enjoy," said Mandy.

Allison almost choked on her response, "Thanks." She could not believe how her luck had changed in a few short hours. This is one drink she could enjoy slowly, as she sat in utter shock in a bittersweet mood mixed of elation and depression, Allison contemplated how best to use her newly found winnings. As with all persons of wealth, Allison knew her money could be used for good or for bad. The question was which method was in Allison's better interest. She suddenly heard an all too familiar giggle from across the bar at the table in the opposite corner. One person she knew had a giggle like that. *Jane King.*

Mandy was leaving their table, revealing Jane and Jack seated in the corner booth, heads close together in what appeared to be an intimate discussion. Once again, Allison's luck had shifted. Of all the places she picked to go to, Jane had picked the same place. She slouched back in the seat and brought the martini to her lips. As much as she loved Jane as a friend, she was not in the mood to chit chat, especially not in front of the new guy, Jack. Narrowing her eyes, her decision had been made. There was one satisfying way to spend this new found money. Allison's plan A for her life had been abruptly halted when Todd walked her out of Remco earlier that day, causing her to think of another plan. Now her plan B just got formed and funded.

CHAPTER FIVE

"How did you like the drink?" the waitress asked Allison.

Allison replied, "It was absolutely perfect. I truly enjoyed it. Please thank the bartender for me."

Mandy asked, "Would you like another one?"

Allison declined, "No, thank you; one is enough." Allison needed to be clear headed in order to put her plan in motion.

Eager to please and earn her tip, Mandy said in a sugary sweet voice, "I'll leave your check here for you. No rush, sweetie. Let me know if you'd like anything else." Allison left her ten dollars on the table to cover her four dollar drink along with leaving Mandy with more than enough tip money.

As she rose and walked toward the exit, she looked back and accidently caught Jane's eye across the room. "Allison!" Jane exclaimed. Now there was no escape. Feeling the need to meet the situation head on, Allison walked over to their table. Allison noticed Jack's astonished expression as she approached.

"What are you doing here? Do you want to join us?" Jane asked with a slight slur to her speech. The booth was clearly meant for two, leaving no room for an additional intruder. She could tell from the empty glasses that Jane had imbibed in one drink too many, in an extremely short period of time.

"Please, join us," Jack added, almost pleading.

"No thanks. I wanted to apologize to you, Jane, for leaving the park abruptly before you arrived. I need to get home and take care of a few things," Allison explained. "Like I said earlier, I wouldn't be good company tonight. Have a nice dinner. Jane, I'll call you later, okay?"

Jane looked pleased, smiling broadly and already dismissing Allison to focus unsteadily on Jack, "Okay, talk to you later."

Jack was not brushed off quite as easily. He quickly rose up from the table to follow Allison to the door. "Allison, please wait!" Jack remarked. Allison was embarrassed from her behavior at the park earlier, but with her Michael Kors purse clenched tightly to her side, she now had a bold determination as she turned to face him. It was fascinating how money could boost one's confidence, even if she had not cashed in on her winnings, yet.

"Jack, I apologize for my behavior at the park, but I do need to get going. I have a lot of things that I need to sort through right now."

Jack was not deterred, "Do you need to wash your hair, too?" The joke was somewhat lost on Allison as she reached up to touch her hair, until it dawned on her that he was teasing her.

Unable to contain a nervous laugh she said, "No, it's been a long day. Please make sure Jane gets home okay. She doesn't look like she's in any condition to drive home." Jack looked miffed. Allison was sure that being stranded with an inebriated woman was probably not how he wanted to spend his evening. "Bye, Jack. It was nice meeting you," Allison smiled smugly as she breezily walked out the door into the cold evening air.

An older man with white hair and a three piece dark grey suit stepped out of the driver's side of the Mercedes parked next to Allison's car and patiently waited for Allison to approach. The air turned bitingly cold outside now that evening was approaching. Allison shivered, not sure if it was from the cold air or the fact she had been found by her earlier pursuer. The designer suit he wore fit him with the precise measurements of someone with unlimited income resources. As he walked closer to her car, she noticed his shoes were polished to a sheen so much so that the setting sun was reflecting off of them. She hesitated, not sure if she wanted to go back in the restaurant and face Jack again or stay and finally get the impending encounter over with this stranger.

Deciding on the latter, she neared him and asked the man, "What do you want?" She looked him squarely in the eyes.

"Allison Black?" questioned the older gentleman in a cool, clipped tone.

"Yes," she answered hesitantly, "who wants to know?"

"Charlie Ponder, attorney at law," he placed his hand out front for a handshake. Allison warily placed her hand in his firm grip and shook hands. "My client is very interested in talking with you," he stated.

Client? "Am I in some sort of legal trouble?" she asked.

"Not at all," he replied. "In fact, my client and I think we have some important information that you'll find extremely enlightening." Allison paused. She had never met a lawyer that claimed to enlighten her. In fact, the only lawyers she knew were the ones on TV asking if anyone had been injured in an accident. Mr. Ponder did not appear to be the same type of ambulance chaser as the other lawyers she had seen on TV, but he had been chasing her all afternoon so her curiosity was piqued.

"Do you mind coming to my office first thing in the morning to discuss the matter? The information is quite extensive and I realize it's getting late. I don't want to take up your time this evening." Charlie Ponder said. "Here's my business card with my address and number on the front. You can reach me on my cell phone listed. My office opens at 9:00am." For someone that had behaved all day as if he was a stalker, the invitation was actually formal and business like.

"Can I ask you a question?" she asked as she ironically realized she had already asked one. "What is so important that you needed to track me down?" She did not know how he found her again so quickly.

"All will be explained in due time, Miss Black," he replied. "Will I see you in the morning?"

"Um, sure, I guess so," she answered. Thinking at first she wanted to go cash in her lottery ticket first thing tomorrow, she decided it could wait until after the ambiguous meeting. Curiosity won her over.

"It will be well worth your time tomorrow," Mr. Ponder said encouragingly. "Have a good rest of the evening," he nodded as he dismissed himself. Charlie Ponder carried himself in a confident manner as he walked back to his car, opened the door, and climbed in the driver's seat. His car purred to life, and he drove out of the parking lot in a soft murmur.

Allison now had more questions than she had answers. *I wonder if it will be worth more than $500,000 of my time.*

Allison entered her Jaguar, wrapped her hands around the cool leather steering wheel, and contemplated the dramatic events of the day. She looked over and noticed Jane's bright yellow Volkswagen Beetle parked next to a dark blue Toyota Highlander. *That SUV must be Jack's car.* Deciding not to wait around to find out, she turned on her heated seats, put her car in drive and headed home, but not until she memorized the license plate number of the Highlander, just in case.

CHAPTER SIX

Discarded piles of clothes accumulated on her closet floor as Allison contemplated outfits to wear to the mystery meeting with Mr. Ponder. She finally decided on grey dress slacks, a light blue, cotton button-up blouse and a navy sweater vest with grey striping around the collar and hem. She paired the outfit with her black, Cole-Haan pumps. At first she thought about wearing red, as it was one of her favorite power colors, but decided that this was not an interview. At least she didn't think it was. The business casual look she devised was polished and comfortable, something she could easily wear from the lawyer's office to the lottery office. She curled her long blonde hair into soft ringlets that draped softly past her shoulders. Her make-up was artfully applied and surprisingly enough, her eyes did not need much concealer, considering the lack of sleep from the night before.

Allison had been restless all night due to anticipating the excitement and the uncharted territories her day would bring. Her thoughts ranged from happiness due to the lottery ticket to anger at her former employer. She finally rose out of bed at 4:00am and started baking, putting her expendable energy to good use. One of her favorite breakfast muffins was a pumpkin chocolate chip muffin with black walnuts. The ingredients sounded like an unlikely trio, but the taste was phenomenal. As an avid baker, she kept her pantry well-stocked with all sorts of items, never knowing what she might need for the next desired recipe. She packed up the perfectly baked confections in a box made specifically to hold twelve cupcakes. She wasn't sure who this "client" was that wanted to meet with her, but it never hurt to bring something sweet to the mysterious meeting. She wondered over and over whom the person was behind the stalking attorney.

Allison had been stalked once before when she first arrived in town so she was a bit on edge. Eager to meet friends in a new town, she had joined a local book club that met monthly at the Café Au Latte. It's quaint atmosphere and cozy chairs, along with their incredible hot brownie dessert, made for the perfect book club setting. It wasn't until she started receiving anonymous letters that she realized another patron had been watching her. The letters included sexual comments about the outfits she wore, drinks she consumed, and other details of her coffee shop visits, along with his admission of his unrequited love. She would find a letter addressed to Allison Black tucked into her windshield wiper of her car, or in her chair when she arrived to sit at her usual table.

After careful observation, Allison concluded that the stalker was a mousy fellow that sat in the corner of the café. He would arrive long before Allison's group would arrive or stay for a while afterward. The poor man was a lonely desperate guy looking for love in the wrong manner. She procured his name and information from the coffee bar owner and filed a complaint at the police station, obtaining a restraining order. Her last letter from her offender was a sincere note of apology, declaring his innocence and explaining that all he had wanted was a date. Thankfully, she never saw him again.

Oh no, I hope the "client" is not that stalker guy from the coffee shop. More and more Allison began to feel a little paranoid. Maybe taking muffins was not a good idea. She did not want to encourage that type of behavior in any way. She needed a second opinion, and one that was not hung over from the night before. Jane was a great friend if you needed a shoulder to cry on, but logical thinking was not her strong suit, especially if she imbibed too much several hours earlier. Brianna DeVoe was Allison's best friend since their sorority days back at Tech. Brianna followed a similar path as Allison, being one of the few females at the time to pursue a degree in Computer Engineering. Both had the logical ease to be in the computer field, but Brianna was more of a free spirit. Although she pledged the same sorority as Allison, she did not fit the typical sorority girl mold.

On their first spring break together, at Panama City Beach, Brianna got her first tattoo, a black scorpion with blue eyes down low on her left hip. Shortly thereafter, she added more tattoos and even body piercings to her human art collection. Whereas Allison followed the career path of Corporate America, Brianna ventured out on her own, creating her own small computer consulting company, focusing primarily on web design. Brianna DeVoe also specialized in a lesser known field of computer hacking. It was not a skill that Brianna advertised openly, but had a certain clientele base that thrived on this area of expertise. Being her own boss allowed her creative freedom and the ability to take long, exotic vacations around the globe.

Knowing that Brianna always rose at dawn to meditate and practice yoga, Allison knew she could call her before 9:00am. Allison could hope that this was not the week Brianna was heading to Africa for her annual lion safari.

Please pick up. Allison patiently waited as the phone rang for the fourth time.

"Namaste," answered Brianna.

"Oh Bree, I'm so glad you're there. Did I catch you at a bad time?" asked Allison.

"No, I finished tweaking a design for Fairway Auto Mart's web layout a few minutes ago," Bree replied. "What's up?" Allison wasn't sure where to start. She decided to cut to the chase and give Bree the basics before getting to the meat of the discussion.

"I lost my job yesterday. Todd escorted me out with little notice. But before you ask, no, I'm not looking for a job, at least not yet."

"Geez, Louise," Bree exclaimed, "what are you going to do?" Allison knew that Brianna DeVoe was the right person to help her get her plan B in motion, but she needed to get through this morning's meeting first.

"I have a meeting with a lawyer this morning," Allison began.

Bree interrupted her, "Oh good, you sue them for everything they've got!"

Allison chuckled, "Actually, it's not my lawyer; he's an attorney that approached me yesterday in an odd way. In fact, he sort of chased me down and asked me to meet with his client this morning."

"That sounds suspicious," Bree stated. "Do you know what type of law he practices, or who his client is?"

"No," Allison answered, "only that he seems to be well off. He drove a Mercedes, and I'm pretty sure he was wearing an Armani suit. He said he would explain more today, and it would be worth my time. What do you think, Bree? You don't think it's that stalker I had from years ago do you?"

"Well," replied Bree, "you said the lawyer was well off, and I honestly don't think that loser could afford an attorney that expensive. Maybe you have a long lost relative that died and left you some money, and this lawyer is in charge of dispersing the assets from the will." Leave it to Bree to think of a more reasonable answer. Allison's paranoia had gotten the best of her and had allowed her imagination to run wild.

"Oh, that's one interesting theory. You've put my mind at ease some," said Allison, still leery since Jack had told her the lawyer seemed to be directly connected to her termination, and she didn't know of any rich relatives that would be leaving her money. She still wasn't exactly sure which theory to believe.

"Well let me know what happens and what you decide to do. I can always use another web developer, if you're interested," Bree offered.

"Thanks, but I think I have something else in mind. Are you going to be around this week? I'd like to run some ideas by you," said Allison.

"I have a few meetings this week, but nothing major. My advice is always free for you. Call me back soon; I'm curious to know how it goes," Bree replied.

"Thanks, Bree, you're the best! Take care," Allison said.

"Bye," Bree said as she disconnected the call. Breathing a sigh of relief, Allison decided that she would indeed take the pumpkin chocolate chip muffins to the lawyer's office. After all, if she was about to inherit a large sum of money either from a dead relative or some other means, she would want to thank the participating parties properly. Speaking of large sums of money, Allison checked her purse to make sure the lottery ticket was tucked away in the side pocket. She zipped up her purse, not wanting to risk a chance of the winning ticket falling out and into someone else's greedy hands. She grabbed her black pea coat, purse, box of muffins, and then headed out the door early, needing to make a quick stop on the way.

CHAPTER SEVEN

Allison was not one prone to violence, but after the previous day's events and not knowing what the future would hold for one that would be soon falling into a hefty sum of money, she felt the need to protect herself with something that would make her feel less vulnerable. Her first line of defense was conveniently located near the check-out counter at the front of the nearby sporting goods store in an assorted display of brightly colored cases. Mace was the quickest defense mechanism she could think of that would not need a concealed weapons permit; she would work on obtaining her concealed weapons permit in the near future. She chose the standard black case, not wanting to draw attention to it, if the need should arise. Allison purchased the mace and tucked it gently into her purse, then made her way out to her beloved Jaguar and on to her anticipated morning engagement.

Perched on a slight hill, Mr. Ponder's office was located downtown, directly off Main Street in a completely renovated early 1900s two-story house. The large white columns supported the covered porch befitting the entry way in a grandiose manner. Allison climbed the few steps to the landing and opened the over-sized front door. Everywhere she looked screamed high end finishes, from the hard wood floors with an intricate grain, to the light fixtures with LED lighting, raw stone walls, crown molding and antique cherry desk planted in the middle of the foyer. A polished young man dressed in a modern, yet professional, suit and tie sat behind the desk. "Good morning, Miss Black. Mr. Ponder has been expecting you," he stated in a slightly effeminate voice. "May I get you something to drink, coffee or water perhaps?"

Allison was taken a little off guard. *Does everyone in this town know who I am?*

"Water, please," she responded.

He rose and offered, "May I take your coat for you?" She placed the box of muffins on his desk while she shrugged off her coat, handing it to his outstretched arms. Picking up the container, she turned and watched him hang her coat then he said, "Please follow me. You'll be meeting in the front conference room today." She followed her host to a large, exquisitely decorated room down the hall to the right. A carved, oval table dominated the center of the room, surrounded by six padded wing chairs. The area rug under the table was a plush, antique Persian rug with hand woven blue and green peacocks. Sconces hung on the wall to reflect a soft and inviting lighting, along with fresh cut flowers in a crystal vase in the center of the table. Lacking in the field of art, she assumed the paintings on the walls were probably timeless pieces done by well-known artists. This was unlike any conference rooms at Remco, which usually focused more on the high tech feasibility of conference phones and overhead projectors. Allison was accustomed to dangling cords draped across plain white tables, uncomfortable chairs, and fluorescent lighting. In fact, this room rather reminded her of an upscale funeral home, but without the lingering smell of the recently embalmed.

Allison placed the box of muffins on the table, chose a seat facing the doorway and placed her purse on the table in front of her intended chair. Not wanting more unexpected surprises, she preferred not to have her back to the door, but instead she wanted a clear view of anyone coming into the room. The assistant soon returned with Allison's water, which was served in a crystal goblet and placed on a leather coaster on the table in front of her.

"My name is Anthony should you need anything else. Mr. Ponder will be in shortly."

"Thank you," Allison murmured. She picked up the heavy crystal glass, noting that it was most likely Waterford crystal by the carving and weight of the glass. Even the water tasted purer, not exactly the tepid tap water she was accustomed to. *Mr. Ponder has expensive taste.*

She was staring at a painting that had melting clocks draped over a tree branch when Charlie Ponder walked in. "Salvador Dali," he stated.

"Excuse me?" Allison asked.

"The painting you're admiring is an original work by Salvador Dali, one of my favorite artists," Charlie Ponder admitted.

"Oh, it's interesting," Allison said.

Mr. Ponder steered the conversation away, "Since you're not here to discuss my art collection, let's get down to business. Shall we? Thank you again for coming in this morning." Charlie seated himself at the head of the table, near Allison, and placed a leather bound portfolio on the table. Her eyes were focused on the elusive paperwork when her peripheral vision caught another movement at the door. A tall handsome man entered the room as Allison looked up and made eye contact with him.

"Jack!" she exclaimed. *The mystery client is Jack?* Allison was confused, and the expression must have shown clearly on her face.

"Ah no," stated Charlie, "Let me introduce you to Mr. Austin Roman."

Charlie continued his explanation, "Austin is Jack's twin brother. They have been silent partners in the firm since their uncle, Clifton Remco passed away six months ago. Mr. Roman here is concerned about your well-being and would like to offer you a substantial package in lieu of your recent misfortune."

Misfortune? Is that what they call it these days?

Austin extended his hand in a formal greeting, "It's nice to meet you, Miss Black." Allison, not wanting to be rude, hesitantly shook his hand and nodded, speechless. Austin folded his large, muscular frame into the wing-backed chair across from Allison, keeping his eyes focused on hers while he settled into his seat. Unlike Jack's more casual dress, Austin wore a custom grey suit with a dark red silk neck tie. His hair was neatly trimmed and styled in a business manner, whereas Jack's had been a little more mussed when she last saw him. The similarities were remarkable, since typically when twins grow older their appearances change with weight or lifestyle. There were some subtle differences now that she could focus on Austin, but with a quick glance she didn't think she would be able to tell them apart.

Austin started speaking, "It's come to our attention that some recent actions of certain department leaders at Remco are not in line with our future goals for the company. We understand you recently uncovered some information that is crucial to our success as a top-rated ethical company. Unfortunately, that information was highly sensitive and poses a risk, which in turn led the management team to feel it was in the company's best interest to let you go. We would not want the sensitive information accidently leaked or shared with other company associates, so I apologize that we had to meet off site like this. We do, however, appreciate your involvement and wish to show our gratitude. Mr. Ponder will go over the specifics of our offering, and we hope you find it agreeable."

The cocky manner in which Austin delivered his well-practiced speech unnerved Allison. She turned toward Mr. Ponder as he opened the portfolio and pulled out several legal-sized papers. He presented his documentation in a firm, professional tone, "We would like to offer you a severance package of $10,000 to ease your transition until you find another job. We are also making services available from a local job placement firm, in order to help you locate a position in the industry of computer programming at another organization. They will help you with interviewing skills and resume development."

$10,000? Not a bad offering. She wondered what the catch was but did not have to wait long to hear it.

Mr. Ponder continued, "All we need you to do is sign a waiver that you will not pursue a legal course of action against

Remco as retaliation for your recent termination. We would also like to remind you of your confidentiality agreement you signed each year as a condition of employment." Charlie Ponder smiled. "Do we have an agreement?" he asked. She glanced at Austin, who had a smug look on his face, one that bespoke of a confidence of someone that had had delivered this familiar edict many times before with favorable success.

How is Jack involved in this? Were they working together to get me to sign this asinine agreement? This whole happenstance was indeed related to her recent termination. There would be no inheritance from a rich relative, just a rich jerk...or two.

Or maybe not...Allison smiled smugly back at Austin, "Mr. Ponder, Mr. Roman, although your tactics are a bit obscure, you both have presented to me a fair offering. It would be silly of me to turn it down." Charlie smiled, passed the papers toward Allison, and handed her a Montegrappa Italian fountain pen with which to sign. She admired the pen, turning it over in both hands before speaking, "But," she began. Mr. Ponder and Austin both looked up nervously as she continued, "I don't think it prudent to sign anything without discussing it with my own legal advisor. I'm afraid it would not be in my best interest to agree to all the conditions outlined without extensive consideration, not to mention a good night's sleep." Allison rose from the table, regretfully laying the expensive pen back on the table. At this critical juncture, she did not want to get arrested for stealing, especially over something as trivial as a pen, even it was worth over $12,000.

She slowly placed the shoulder strap of her handbag over her shoulder and struck out her hand for a handshake from Charlie, "It was nice to meet you, Mr. Ponder." He glanced at her outstretched hand, looked over sharply at Austin, and slowly shook her hand.

"I don't think you understand, Miss Black," Austin stated with a sharp, low tone. "The terms of this agreement are not negotiable. It is in your best interest to sign the papers today."

His voice carried a definite underlying threat.

"And if I don't?" she countered.

"We don't make idle threats," Austin said; his teeth almost seething.

Not wanting to show the intimidation she was feeling from him, Allison decided to play her dumb blonde card, "I have so much to think about today, I don't think I'll be able to sign anything right now. This legal mumbo jumbo is too confusing." She smiled a soft, feminine grin and batted her eyelashes toward Austin. Not offering another handshake or physical touch of any kind, she concluded, "Mr. Roman, Mr. Ponder, have a nice day. Enjoy the muffins." She strode out of the room with an aggravated kick in her step and retrieved her coat from the coat rack in the front room, where Anthony had placed it earlier. Anthony barely glanced up from his desk as she sailed out the door and down the steps. Allison Black was eager to get started with the next phase of her life.

CHAPTER EIGHT

What a waste of a perfectly baked batch of pumpkin chocolate chip muffins. Allison had plugged in the address to the lottery office in her GPS system and was navigating her way there. *I hope he chokes on every walnut.* Her mind was racing, not sure what to make of the fact that Jack had lied about being an investigator and that he had conveniently left out his last name and connection to Remco when he had introduced himself. *They must have practiced this good cop, bad cop routine for some time now.* The thoughts rolling through her mind were not pleasant, at least not towards the handsome duo. All of the scenarios she worked through her mind had the twins ending with tormenting pain.

Although she knew that money could not buy happiness, she sincerely hoped that her impending windfall would somehow boost her mood considerably. Having already encountered the aggressive nature in which Remco tracks down associates, Allison knew that Austin's threat was a real one. She did not know how Mr. Ponder had found her the night before. She wasn't sure how far Austin would take the threat or what exactly her consequences would be for walking out of the earlier meeting, but she knew he would not take it lightly. Thankful for her earlier morning purchase, her mace still resided in her purse close by in her passenger seat.

After working at Remco for all these years, she knew it was a privately held company that had many secrets, but she did not know that the elder Mr. Remco had passed the company along to his nephews. Allison knew there was a board of directors, but she thought they had assumed ownership until a new director could be found. Little did she know the new owners were already in place and running the company. The subtle changes she had noticed in her manager's behavior and in others around the computer department were now beginning to make a little more sense. She wondered how much they knew about their new owners and the fast and furious methods they employed in order to squelch any possible litigation against them.

"Turn left in two miles onto Stone Avenue," the lady on the GPS machine stated. Her heart rate began to beat a little faster as she realized she would be cashing in on a large lottery ticket in less than ten minutes. If not for her unfortunate circumstances, she might have taken a long vacation from Remco without telling anyone of the winnings and gone on a glorious shopping spree in Paris, France. However, in lieu of recent events, Allison would be investing this money in a cause that now would carry more importance than she initially thought last night at the steak house. She knew that in the business world, and after taxes, $500,000 would not last as long as she would hope. This entire business plan would need to be evaluated and budgeted to make these newfound dollars stretch in order to make the biggest impact.

Allison parked her Jaguar on the street directly in front of the South Carolina Education Lottery office. As she stepped out of her car, she observantly looked around to make sure no one had followed her. The streets had hardly any traffic during this time of the morning, as most people had made their way to work by now. She locked her car and strode up to the door, which rang a small bell announcing her presence as she opened it. The office was small with posters on the wall depicting the different lottery games available and what the estimated winning amounts were for each one. The clerk was standing beside the Mega Million poster, changing out the numbers as Allison approached her. The brunette lady wore glasses and appeared to be in her fifties. She was dressed in a turquoise blouse with ruffles around the neckline and black pants. She turned around slightly when the bell rang and said, "Good morning, I'll be right with you."

"Take your time," Allison replied.

The lottery official finished correcting the poster with the new estimated winning numbers and turned around, smiling, "How can I help you?" Allison took out her scratch off ticket and held it in her hand. She had signed it the night before, but wasn't sure what else she needed to do in order to cash it in.

"I'd like to claim the prize on this ticket, please."

"You don't waste any time!" exclaimed the lady as she made her way around the counter to the ticket machine. "We knew someone in the area won yesterday, but usually with a jackpot this large, it takes a few days for the winner to come forward."

Allison handed the clerk her scratch off ticket, with a look of confusion. "Oh," said the lady, "I thought you were cashing in on the Mega Million prize. The winning ticket from last night was sold yesterday here in town."

Allison laughed, "That would be nice; but I would like to collect on this scratch off." The kind woman took her ticket and ran the barcode under the scanner on the lottery machine.

"You're a winner," the machine announced.

"Wow!" exclaimed the lady, "That's the grand prize for this scratch off game. I'd say you did quite well." Allison smiled broadly, sharing in the excitement.

The clerk continued, "Let me get the paper work started so we can cut you a check. I'll need to see your ID if you don't mind." Allison removed her wallet from her purse and took out her driver's license.

She spotted the Mega Million ticket inside her purse. "Do you mind checking this one for me as well?" she asked.

"Sure thing, it never hurts to check," answered the woman as she took the Mega Million ticket from Allison's hand.

She scanned it under the electronic reader as the machine said again, "You're a winner!"

"Oh my God," the lady looked like she had seen a ghost, "you won two tickets in one day."

"That's great!" said Allison. "How much is the Mega Million worth?" Even twenty dollars would be nice to add on to her large prize from the scratch off ticket.

The astonished woman looked up at her and stated, "Two hundred and thirty million dollars." Allison almost fell over. Shock waves were coursing through her entire body. She had never fainted before, but felt sure she was about to.

The clerk screamed for joy and ran around the desk and gave Allison a huge hug. Allison didn't know if it was to keep her upright or to touch someone on the verge of being famous. "Congratulations, honey! You hit it big time. We've never had a winner this big at this office." Not having anyone else to share this sudden thrill of elation, Allison hugged her back.

They stepped apart and Allison started giggling uncontrollably. Her mind refused to form intelligent words and for the first time in her life, Allison did a jig with a complete stranger in the middle of a downtown office, laughing hysterically and smiling like the cat that caught the canary. This game suddenly took on another whole dimension. Allison wasn't thinking about the lottery game, she was thinking about her future, or better yet, her game of revenge.

CHAPTER NINE

Allison considered herself well-educated so had never had her own personal financial advisor. She kept a basic retirement account, checking account, and savings account. Having merely one W-2 and a small house, she filed her own taxes each year and made sure to keep up with the ever-changing regulations by purchasing a comprehensive software package that led her step by step through all the tax rules. She had arrived at her bank right before the lunch crowd clinging tightly to her purse, which had two extremely large checks made out to her name. The chair she sat on in the lobby was firm yet cozy, as she waited to see the next available manager.

After being greeted and escorted into his office, she sat down across from his desk and pulled out the checks. "I need to make a deposit," Allison said, handing him the two checks from the lottery office. She managed to calm down considerably since leaving the lottery office minutes earlier. Allison forced herself to maintain her composure and play the part of the competent customer. The manager's desk plate indicated that his name was Mark Walling.

Mr. Walling glanced at both checks with a rather good poker face and then glanced back up at Allison. "Thank you for choosing our bank, Miss Black. We would love to help you make the best financial decisions with your winnings. Would you be open to a financial advisor? Sums this large are usually invested as opposed to depositing in a regular checking account. It's completely up to you, of course."

Allison considered the offer and decided it was in her best interest to speak with an advisor. Mark Walling brought in his senior advisor, John Bridges. He introduced him to Allison, and after a few hours of financial planning, proceeded to make the single largest deposit to his bank in history. Knowing it would take several days for an amount that large to clear, the bank manager released a large amount of funds for Allison to use until her assets were firmly in place.

Allison had held in her excitement for too long. She took care of her financial business and after making sure she wasn't dreaming, she placed a call to update her friend, Brianna. She dare not tell Jane, as she did not want the entire world to know she had won the lottery. Allison had heard of horror stories where lottery winners had been robbed or threatened by greedy psychopaths, not to mention all the long lost relatives that would be climbing out of the woodwork to claim their piece of the pie.

Part of her paperwork at the lottery office included an anonymous form, where Allison stated she did not want her name shared with the public. The public did not include the best confidant a girl could have, Brianna DeVoe. She placed the call but had to leave a message on Bree's voicemail. "Hey Bree, it's me. I have some interesting news to share. Call me back A.S.A.P." Allison could not keep the excitement out of her voice and was hopeful Brianna would return her call soon, as she didn't know how much longer she could keep her emotions bottled up.

She also needed to download the information from her jump drive onto a safe back up disc, away from threatening former employers. She felt sure that Bree could help arrange a safe alternative for the information she had obtained illicitly. With all of her running around, Allison suddenly found herself hungry. *When is the last time I ate?* She recalled the liquid dinner consumed the night before and decided it did not count as a meal. Going on two o'clock in the afternoon, she had built up quite the appetite. *What do rich people eat?* She thought of caviar and champagne, neither of which sounded the least bit appetizing. Only one thing sounded good to her, bacon, and lots of it, piled high on a big juicy cheeseburger.

Sitting in a booth alone at Bubba's Burgers, Allison took a big bite of her juicy, delicious burger. The bacon was cooked well and had a smoked flavor in it that enhanced the flavor of the burger richly. The sharp cheddar cheese was melted with enough heat that the entire ensemble was a picture of perfection. It was times like these that Allison missed her parents tremendously. They had been killed in a small plane crash several years earlier while on vacation in Canada. Allison's dad could grill one of the best burgers east of the Mississippi. Her mom would always prepare the bacon in the oven on a large sheet pan, baking it to a firm, meaty consistency before dressing the burgers after they came off of the grill. Being an only child, the three of them had been close. It had been hard on Allison to move away from Tennessee to go to a state many hours away from her parents. They had stayed in touch, visiting each other often, until the fatal plane crash took them from her early.

Allison was not too sure her parents would be proud of some of her recent decisions, such as taking information from her former company. However, she did know they would encourage her to do what's right and not settle for a meager pay off to keep her silence. In the middle of a huge bite of her burger, her phone rang. It was Bree returning her call. "Helloof," Allison mumbled with her mouth full.

"Hey," said Bree, "give me the scoop. What happened at the lawyer's office this morning? Are you rich now?"

If only she knew, thought Allison. She chewed quickly, swallowing the bite of food before answering, "Bree, I have to talk to you, in person. Can I come see you this evening? I can leave soon and be there in three hours."

Allison had begun to get paranoid about phone taps after the way the lawyer had found her last night.
If they were able to chase her down, then their prying ears might be listening to her phone conversations as well. She did not know what manner of tactics the despicable twins were capable of doing.

Bree answered, "Are you okay? Nothing's wrong is it?"

Allison replied, "Everything's great. Wait until you hear what happened today. I need your help on moving forward with a few tasks, but I want to tell you in person." DeVoe's carefree spirit prevented her from prying too much at this point. She always rolled with the flow and knew that Allison would reveal the whole story in her own time.

"I'll be here. Come on over anytime," Bree invited.

Allison paid for her burger with cash, newly drawn from her bank account, not wanting to leave a credit card trail for anyone to follow. Her paranoia was creeping in on her, not sure if anyone at Remco would be interested in her money trail that involved bacon cheeseburgers, but her sixth sense refused to let her use her credit card to pay for her meal. She left Bubba's, constantly scanning the horizon for any familiar cars. Arriving at home, Allison hurriedly packed a few clothing items and necessities in a large bag in case of an overnight stay. Mapping out her future goals would take careful consideration and she did not want to rush them. She was eager to rush out of town, away from prying eyes and ears, ready to embark on her exciting new life. She threw her bag in her car and was backing out of her driveway when her phone rang. *Jane.* This was one conversation she was not looking forward to.

CHAPTER TEN

"Hi Jane," Allison answered the phone, deciding it was best to get the awkward phone call over with now; plus she wanted to make sure her friend made it home okay last night.

"Hey," Jane said, "I'm sorry I didn't get to talk to you last night. I must have fallen asleep as soon as I arrived home. Are you doing okay? Tell me everything."

Allison knew Jane had most likely passed out, as opposed to falling asleep, but did not feel the need to correct her. Jane was referring to Allison's job dismissal. She had missed out on the latest crucial life changing events of the last twenty four hours.

"I'm fine," Allison replied. "I've decided to take some time away from the corporate world and consider some other options. I'm going to go see Bree in Atlanta and get away from it all for a while." *Crap. Why did I tell her where I was heading? What if she tells Jack?* "Don't tell anyone where I am, okay? I want to be left alone for a while," she amended.

Jane said, "Okay, tell Bree I said hi. You missed a good dinner last night. I wish you would've stayed."

Knowing that staying was the last thing that Jane had wanted Allison to do, she smiled. "I'm sure you and Jack had a nice time without me," Allison said. *As nice a time as one can have with a lying snake in the grass.*

"Jack's a super nice guy, but I don't think he's into me at all," Jane admitted. "He couldn't stop asking questions about you the entire night."

"What did you tell him?" Allison said warily, hoping Jane had not revealed anything that the hot twin could use against her.

Jane replied, "Oh, nothing much. I told him that you were sad you had lost your job, but that I didn't get a chance to ask you about it. He seemed worried about you losing your job and asked what you did at Remco. I told him you liked computers and worked for some jerk named Todd. Are you interested in Jack?" Jane asked the last sentence in a sing-song voice that reminded Allison of that song about two people k-i-s-s-i-n-g.

"Not at all," Allison replied definitively.

"Oh, too, bad, he's really cute," Jane said as if the answer to all dating dilemmas was a guy's appearance. Comfortable that Jane had not gotten far with Jack and glad her friend had made it safely home, Allison felt a small relief of tension leave her body.

Allison entered the on ramp for the interstate that would take her straight to Atlanta. She chatted briefly some more with Jane about Todd, the jerk of a manager at Remco, but left the details of her dismissal out of the conversation. Seemingly satisfied that her jobless friend was indeed okay, Jane wished Allison a good trip and offered to take her for a pedicure when she returned to Morgan.

As one last parting note, Allison told Jane, "Don't talk to Jack anymore, Jane. I don't trust him." She did not want to tell Jane his true identity, but wanted to make sure she at least warned Jane to stay away.

"I don't think that's a problem," Jane replied. "I don't even have his number."

That's a good thing. They said their goodbyes then Allison turned her XM radio up loud to her favorite pop channel, ready to sing along all the way to Georgia. She was ready to celebrate her winnings in style with one of her most favorite people. She hoped Bree DeVoe was up for the challenge.

Being in a car for several hours allowed Allison to reflect on how quickly her circumstances had changed since she went to work yesterday morning. It seemed like a life time ago, and yet it was only the previous morning that she had gone to work as usual and then lost her job. She had not talked to any of her co-workers since leaving and knew they were probably sitting at their desks today talking about "poor" Allison. Poor could no longer be used to describe Allison now, and behind a desk staring at her computer was the last place she wanted to be any more. She had several close friends at Remco, but none that she wanted to share her breaking news with anytime soon. Being on high alert, she did not know who might be spying for whom at her old company and did not trust anyone with news of this importance.

Allison arrived in Atlanta right after the sun had set, creating an orange glow around the city. With Brianna being into nature and all things Zen, it surprised Allison that Bree remained in the congested city among the congested traffic and obnoxious noise. Bree's creative genius thrived on all sorts of various stimuli, but

Allison wasn't sure how Brianna did it in the amount of ruckus the big city offered. Allison assumed the buzz of the city encouraged her gifted friend and visionary. In fact, Allison was counting on Bree's introspective nature to help her get her own idea off the ground. Allison's red Jaguar purred to a stop in front of Bree's town home. Set in a trendy new neighborhood, Allison was grateful for the gated community, giving her a sense of protectiveness that her own house in South Carolina had not provided. Bree buzzed the gate upon her arrival and had left the front door open to welcome Allison to her home.

Allison knocked gently on the door and pushed it open further. Brianna DeVoe decorated her house with more throw pillows than Allison had ever seen for sale in a single Pier One Imports store. All sizes, shapes, and colors were strewn about the couch, chairs, and empty floor space. Other than the cluttering of pillows, her house was impeccably clean and had a certain feng shui charm to it, with candles and books placed neatly on the end tables.

"Come in," yelled Bree from somewhere in the back of the house. Allison placed her overnight bag on a nearby chair and walked toward Bree's voice.

"It's me," stated Allison. Bree entered the room in a long yellow cotton skirt and black tank top. She looked comfortable, more so than Allison who was wearing her same dress slacks from earlier.

"I've been waiting all day for this big news of yours. Let's get some popcorn and Skittles and you can tell me everything," Bree offered, assuming that Allison also enjoyed the sweet and salty combination, and continued, "but first, let me see if I have something to make you more comfortable. Just looking at you is making me itch."

In a few minutes they were settled onto the floor among the pillows with Allison wearing borrowed yoga pants and a comfortable t-shirt. While eating popcorn and Skittles with Bree,

Allison knew she chose the perfect way to kick off her celebration of becoming the richest person she knew. "First, you know that Todd walked me out yesterday without much explanation," began Allison. "You also know about me meeting a lawyer yesterday, but what you don't know is that the lawyer works for Remco. In fact, the meeting was about them trying to get me to sign a waiver stating I wouldn't file a retaliation claim against them for my termination, and in return they would quietly give me a meager severance package."

"Those jerks! I hope you didn't sign it," said Bree.

"No, I didn't. In fact, you should've seen the look on Austin's face when I told him I wouldn't sign," Allison replied.

Bree looked confused and asked, "Who's Austin, the lawyer?"

Allison told Bree all about Jack and Austin, the best looking twin brothers and their evil agenda to try to silence Allison. She even shared the part about kissing Jack in the park. "I don't know how to take their threats, or I should say, Austin's threats, but he seemed pretty genuine," Allison explained.

"You're smart not to take any threats lightly," added Bree. "People with authority tend to get a little big for their britches sometimes."

Allison nodded her head agreeing. "Bree," she started hesitantly, not sure how to say the next words, "I need to let you in on a fairly big secret. Something happened to me last night, well today actually, and I need you to swear not to tell anyone about it."

Bree's eyes grew large and Allison could see Bree's brain trying to come up with all sorts of crazy assumptions that would need her sworn secrecy. Bree nodded her assent, "Yes, I swear. What is it?"

Allison blurted it out, "I won the lottery, twice! I don't mean like twenty dollars, I mean big time! Last night I won five hundred thousand dollars on a scratch off ticket. When I went to the lottery office to claim my prize after I left the lawyer's office, I had the clerk verify my Mega Million ticket, and it was a winner, too!"

"Geez Louise, Allison! Are you serious?" questioned Brianna.

"Two hundred and thirty million dollars serious," replied Allison.

Bree shouted out loud and hit the bottom of the popcorn bowl with her hand, spraying salty popcorn in the air all around them. She rolled around on her back, kicked up her legs and pounded Allison on her back in a friendly excited way like a puppy would pounce on its owner after being away all day. "Whoop whoop!" Bree yelled, "My friend is rich!" Allison almost choked on a Skittle during the chaotic celebration.

Seeing the need for something stronger than seltzer water, Brianna broke out some wine glasses and poured them the white wine she had on hand. "What in the world are you going to do with all that money?" Bree asked after calming down from her earlier excitement.

"That's where I need your help," responded Allison. "I met with a financial advisor today at the bank, so I have a plan for how to invest it all, but I need your help on executing a business plan I've been working on." Allison laughed suddenly, "In fact, I'd like to hire you as my first employee. I don't know your job title yet, but I can guarantee a hefty salary for you. How would you like to be my partner and put Remco in their place at the same time?"

Bree agreed eagerly, "I'm in. What plan did you have in mind?"

CHAPTER ELEVEN

Allison had not stayed up all night brainstorming since her college days when she worked on final exam projects. She slept fitfully with much on her mind and woke in the morning to the smell of coffee and the sound of loud classical music being played in the den. She retrieved her jump drive from her key ring and walked out of the guest room to greet Brianna with her valuable data file.

"Good morning, sleepy head," greeted Brianna. Bree was on the floor of the den, with the pillows pushed back out of the way, and the floor was clean of all traces of last night's scattered popcorn. The angle of Bree's body was in a contorted yoga position. Allison thought Bree would never be able to unravel from the awkward pose. Bree took a deep cleansing breath, and unrolled her legs into a sitting position.

She makes that look so easy. Impressed, Allison smiled and said, "Good morning. I wanted to share something with you. I didn't get a chance to show you this last night."

Allison held open her hand and showed Brianna the jump drive. Allison asked, "Do you have a computer that can download this?"

"Sure," Bree jumped up lithely and walked over to the dining room table, retrieved her laptop computer, and plopped down in one of her thick cushioned chairs. Allison handed her the jump drive and waited for Bree to download and open the file. "What is all this?" Bree asked, while looking at names, dates, and what appeared to be dollar amounts.

"This is black mail," Allison replied.

"Allison, you are full of many unusual secrets lately. Is this a list of everyone's salary level at Remco?" Brianna inquired of the first file she opened.

"Yes," Allison replied. She was leaning over Brianna, looking down at the computer screen, "in fact it shows that every female was paid much less than every male counterpart in the same position for years. It also shows termination dates of every employee and their real reason for termination. I assume my name will be added to this file shortly."

"Wow," Bree breathed a heavy sigh, "no wonder they wanted to keep you quiet. Do they know you have this information?"

Allison looked at her friend, "No, I don't think so, but they know I discovered it when I was working on a system change for the human resources manager, Mr. Tomlinson. It was a locked file, but I was able to unencrypt it purely by accident, or perhaps you could say by curiosity. I notified Todd of the file, but did not tell him exactly what I knew was on it, only that I had come across a suspicious file that he needed to be aware of in the system."

Brianna then noticed a second file on the drive. "What's this one?" she said as she clicked on the file to open it.

Allison took a deep breath, "That first file was interesting, but this one could be the nail in their coffin." Brianna stared at the computer screen in awe, reading some of the information streaming across the page. "After Todd started acting funny, I decided I needed to protect myself a little bit more. I put my thinking cap on and did a little Bree DeVoe action myself. I know that Remco primarily manufactures electronic parts for military vehicles. In the past, I didn't care what kind of parts or what type of customers Remco had, but I knew that much of that information was confidential and available on a need to know basis. With all the new government regulations, companies are now required to list their customers in order to verify they aren't selling to terrorists. This file was buried in the server under *International Regulations.*"

Allison told her, "I had to unencrypt the file using some questionable software I downloaded on my work PC so I could read it. I knew if it was that hard to open, it must be something good. I didn't know how right I was."

Brianna turned to stare at her friend in amazement, "You have guts! Did you leave a trail?"

Allison sighed, "I hope not because I was pretty careful and uninstalled the encryption software immediately after I made a copy of the file on my jump drive. I didn't notice any strange spy ware on my computer afterwards, but two days later Todd walked me out to my car."

Brianna leaned back in her chair, and raised her legs to sit cross-legged with her laptop perched in her lap. "Do you mind if I make a copy for safe keeping?" asked Brianna.

"By all means, please do," Allison quipped with a stoic grin on her face. "Oh," she added, "I also happened to leave a small hole in their firewall before I left, in case I needed to get back in from the outside."

Brianna was so in awe, she patted her friend on the back and said, "I should be the one hiring you. You go girl."

Twelve years earlier, Allison had been impressed with her own starting salary for a girl right out of college. What made her angry now, with the acquired information now securely stored on Bree's private server, was the knowledge that every male college graduate had been offered ten percent more than every female. And that had only been the beginning of her findings. The second file showed that Remco had been playing dirty for a long time and not just towards women. While Remco boasted about their strong ethics and support of the United States military, they were selling to questionable customers. This file could be extremely dangerous if put in the wrong hands. The names of certain clients alone were enough to make anyone nervous. Brianna and Allison had a long discussion on how to rectify this situation, both legally and somewhat illegally. Knowing that they both were now privy to classified Remco information, their safety was at high risk. If the government found out Remco was selling to third party companies that potentially funded terrorists, Remco could be fined heavily or even shuttered completely. The two sorority sisters knew Remco would not want this information revealed and would not let it go without a fight.

By late afternoon, the computer techies had had enough of scheming and plotting and decided to escape to the big city for a bite to eat and to let Allison spend some of her new money burning a hole in her pocket. Brianna had called and canceled her conference calls that had been scheduled for the next few days, then they dressed and drove to eat at one of Allison's favorite Asian restaurants in Atlanta, Chang Lo's. After parking Brianna's Jeep near the entrance, the ladies entered the restaurant with an appetite to match their purse strings. Allison's habit of eating junk food or hardly any food the last couple of days was taking a toll on her body, and she was more than ready to remedy this fault. Ordering the chicken lettuce wraps and crispy green beans were the starters for Allison, followed by the Mongolian beef, while Bree imbibed in her favorite sushi. Not wanting to appear to be pinching pennies, and not wanting to share dessert, Allison and Brianna each ordered their own chocolate melting cake, Allison's treat of course. The friends enjoyed the meal thoroughly; all thoughts of revenge, money, and men were dismissed for the time being.

Feeling more relaxed than she had in the past two days; Allison treasured her time with her sorority sister. Atlanta offered many benefits for the recently wealthy, one of which was a person with certain anonymity. With so many shops available, it was easy to spend freely without having to constantly look over her shoulder to make sure she was not recognized, as she would have had to do in her small town. Jane used to tease Allison about seeing someone she knew everywhere they went, whether at their small shopping mall or a local restaurant. Her ability to purchase big ticket items without raising a red flag gave Allison a certain thrill that can only come with the knowledge of having unlimited funds. Not that she had purchased anything too large. After all, she had to wait for her assets to clear and be routed in the correct accounts, but she was having a great time shopping for the first time in her life without worrying about the sale rack.

Brianna and Allison made their way to Lennox Square Mall in the Buckhead area of Atlanta, after satisfying their hunger for food. Her hunger for materialistic items was not as great but more of a lingering itch she couldn't wait to start scratching. Allison purchased a new Burberry coat even though warmer weather promised to be on the way soon. She could not resist getting two pairs of Prada shoes and another pair for Bree, after all, what girl didn't love new shoes. They made their way through the popular accessory stores and found themselves at the jewelry counter in Cartier. Even in the digital age of cell phones and iPads, Allison wore a watch every day. She felt lost if she could not look down at her left wrist and immediately see what time it was.

"I've never owned a real Rolex watch," Allison told Brianna. "The closest I ever came was that fake one that I bought at the straw market in the Bahamas when we went on our cruise our first year out of college."

Allison remembered how she and Bree, along with two other sorority sisters, Krista and Meredith, carefully planned a reunion cruise one year after they graduated from college. The four young ladies had been close all through college and had pledged together in the same sorority during their freshman year. Each of them had gone their separate ways after earning different degrees but remained in touch over the years, especially Allison and Brianna. Allison recalled roving through the straw market for the perfect souvenir, deciding on a Rolex watch for a measly forty dollars. It had lasted almost two months before the silver paint started flaking away, revealing a lack luster metal underneath.

Brianna laughed, "I told you that was a fake!"

Allison smiled. She glanced down at the genuine luxury watches under the freshly polished glass and pointed at one with a bright blue watch face and said to Bree, "That one is so pretty. I can almost hear it calling my name."

Bree admired the time piece as she continued to peruse the jewelry laid out intricately, catching the light faintly enough for each piece to sparkle. "Nothing's holding you back. You should get it," Bree quipped.

"I think I'll wait at least another week anyway, until the majority of my funds have settled" whispered Allison. She was not ready to break out the credit card, yet. She had used some of the cash she procured from the bank the day before for her purchases at the other stores, but with a price tag the size of a Rolex she would have to use her credit card and was also hesitant about leaving a money trail.

Passing on the watch purchase, they continued to leisurely walk through the mall stopping in to admire a skirt here or a blouse there, until she stopped cold in front of her favorite store. Allison knew instinctively that Williams-Sonoma would be her biggest spending weakness. She might not spend more money than she would on a Rolex, but she could definitely see herself buying one of everything in the entire store. Brightly colored cookbooks with delicious looking pictures caught her attention as soon as she entered the store and slowly looked to her left. Lined up in pristine order, Allison began to have visions of a cookbook library in her own home. No, wait, in a new home, one she had not even purchased yet but would design completely around her kitchen. Her eyes were suddenly opened wide as she began to think of all the new changes her new lifestyle would bring. "Oh gosh, Bree," Allison sighed, "which books do I buy first?" She pulled one off the shelf that displayed a decadent mouth-watering six-layer chocolate cake on the cover.

Brianna chuckled and headed over to the knife section, while Allison remained fixated on the cookbooks. Allison sat her shopping bags on the ground near her feet and proceeded to clear off a space on the table behind her by removing the sale sign of the featured Belgian Waffle Maker. Allison began stacking her intended books on the table space she had cleared.

After narrowing down her book selection to four, Allison made her way around the rest of the store, adding unique cutlery and kitchen gadgets to her already vast collection. Upon exiting, she spotted Bree sitting casually on a bench in front of the store, patiently waiting for her friend by checking her email on her cell phone.

Allison approached her, "I don't think my arms can carry much more. I need a personal valet if I buy one more thing. Do you mind if we head out to the car to drop these bags off?"

Bree smiled and offered to take a few bags from Allison. "You know," Bree stated as they walked toward the mall exit, "I know a lot of different people that could use a job like that. You know, like a personal assistant or something. Would you like for me to ask around quietly and find someone trustworthy? I have a feeling we're going to need a lot more help."

Allison looked thoughtful and answered, "Bree, I knew I came to you for a reason. You're right. I'll want someone that can be my buffer to the outside world. The vultures will be swooping in once word gets out about me. I won't be able to keep low once we start putting our plan in place." They loaded the numerous bags in the back of Brianna's Jeep, climbed in, and headed back to Bree's town home. Brianna's suggestion was the catapult that Allison used in order to get her wheels spinning. The more she thought about it, the more she wanted to help other competent people that found themselves unfairly without a job, much like Allison's own situation. Allison Black had to think about a lot.

CHAPTER TWELVE

Spending two days in Atlanta gave Allison the time she needed to get some of her rambling thoughts organized. With the help of her confidant and partner in crime, Allison had a tentative agenda of top priority items she wanted to accomplish within the next few days. One of the first tasks she completed included making a list of the army of people she would need to expedite her plans.

Allison thought as she pulled into her own driveway, *who better to use than some of the women that Remco brushed callously aside?*

She unfolded her legs from the car and grabbed her purse and new coat, leaving the remaining items to unpack later. The back door gave way too easily. It was slightly open. Knowing she had dutifully locked up her house before leaving a couple of days earlier, Allison's stomach began doing the kind of flips that normally come when anticipating the free fall from a large roller coaster. She hesitated and wondered if the trespasser was still lurking inside. Feeling uneasy, Allison slipped her hand slowly into her purse and clutched tightly the mace she had thankfully purchased a few days earlier. She paused, listening for any suspicious sounds; after several minutes of silence, Allison decided to enter her own house.

It was trashed. Not the kind of trashed that teenagers or college dorms reminded her of, but the kind of trashed where wild starving raccoons were let free to upend any and everything looking for a crumb to eat. She knew this was not a random act of perpetration.

Remco! She was livid. Her neck and cheeks giving away her seething mood by turning a shade of pink she had not turned since she once caught an ex-boyfriend making out in public with another girl. She wondered what it was with men that could make her so mad that her blood boiled in such an obvious display. This time around, it was Austin and Jack; neither were ex-boyfriends, but she was convinced they had a part in this breach of her private domain.

So Austin's threats were valid. Allison looked around at her once cherished possessions, zoning in on her kitchen, her previous place of quiet contentment where she had so lovingly created some of her favorite baked confections. Walking around pots and pans scattered on the floor among broken dishes and discarded dish towels, she made her way to the sideboard that once housed all of her treasured cookbooks and recipes. Her grandmother's hand-written recipe cards were scattered across the floor in front of the cabinet, but thankfully, still intact. She found the old tin box the recipe cards had been kept in, now sporting a dent in the side of it, and she started placing the carelessly tossed cards back inside. Once she completed sorting the cards she pulled out her cell phone and placed a call to the local police.

Detective Steve Lumon arrived within an hour, giving Allison time to walk through the rest of the house before his visit, careful not to touch any door knobs or surfaces that might contain incriminating fingerprints of the assailant. Her initial assessment was aggravated chaos, not finding anything missing at first glance. The entire house had been rearranged in a less than desirable decorative style. Nothing appeared to be stolen or taken except for her laptop, which did not surprise her given that the one component they might have been looking for was the computer file. Luckily it was securely located on her key chain in her direct possession. Detective Lumon surveyed the house and had it dusted for prints, finding none of course. He recorded her vague statement of which she offered none of her own conclusions and chalked up the event to a random home invasion, most likely spurned by rogue drug addicts looking for items to pawn. She decided not to tell the detective about the missing laptop.

"Since they didn't take anything, they must have been scared off by something or someone," he concluded. Allison knew better. This was no random act; it was a clear and deliberate warning.

Sitting in the front driver's seat of his dark blue Ford Taurus, the investigator perched his clipboard on the steering wheel while one wide leg rested on the ground outside the open car door. His extra-large white Polo shirt had the sheriff's office emblem on the front left chest, identifying him easily as an officer of the law. From his large girth, she could tell he had been at a desk job for some time, not having much exercise in the field as of late. He appeared to be comfortable in his beige chinos and black loafers, probably preferring this line of work over his counter parts that had to chase down criminals physically, rather than on his elected paper.

His shaded eyes looked up into Allison's face as he offered his kind condolences and advice, "You will want to contact your insurance company immediately, if you feel the need to file a claim for any damages or losses. If you do not feel safe staying alone here, do you have somewhere you can stay tonight?"

"I'll be fine," she answered. "Thank you for your time detective."

Going through the proper motions, Allison next called her insurance agent, but not to file a claim. She simply reported the incident, and then requested a face to face consultation for some immediate additional coverage she would need on substantial upcoming purchases, the first of which would be proper, secure housing. Anticipating a hefty kickback for new coverage, her agent, Sarah McQueen, agreed to meet with her the following morning in the lobby of the Marriott at ten o'clock. Allison had one more person to call before the end of the day, Ashley Porter.

"Hello." The phone had been answered barely before the first ring, somewhat catching Allison off guard.

"Is this Ashley Porter?" she asked.

"Yes it is. How can I help you?" replied Ashley. Her perky voice could be heard through the line in a firm, yet friendly tone.

Allison, taking her cue from Ashley, cut straight to the chase, "My name is Allison Black, and I'm looking for a real estate agent, someone that could help me find something rather quickly. I understand you have several listings in Morgan Country Club Estates for sale. Would you have time to show me a few of them on short notice, say this afternoon or this evening?"

Allison had found Ashley's name on the list of associates that had been terminated from Remco. She had been a top performer in their customer service division before being superseded by a new young recruit by the name of George Zimmer. Ashley had rebounded by becoming the top real estate agent in the area within five years, focusing on high end listings and having the assertiveness of a bulldog.

"You caught me on a good day. With it being a week day, I'm wide open this afternoon. Do you have a certain property in mind?"

Ashley asked. "I need something move in ready," replied Allison, "and money is no object."

Ashley chuckled softly, "Well I have two properties that are vacated, so the owners are motivated to sell. One of them comes fully furnished, and the other listing is a clean slate. I can show you both of them if you'd like."

Allison confirmed the showings and planned to meet Ashley at the first listing in about an hour. Having liked Brianna's gated community, Allison had already looked up similar neighborhoods in Morgan on-line before she had driven back home. Now that her current house had been vandalized, her motivation to move to a more secure place increased tenfold.

She walked around her mess of a house once more, straightening a few pieces of furniture and gathering essential items that she might need later. It would take hours to put her home back in order, if she had to do it alone. Reminded once again that she could help someone else out by hiring them to do the job instead, Allison stopped sorting and focused more on making a mental catalog of all the amenities she would want to take with her to her new house. Her next order of business was to call Brianna to see if she had made contact with Allison's future new assistant. She also needed to bring Bree up to date on the recent violation by Remco.

She dialed Brianna, and then rested her phone on her shoulder as she waited for Brianna to answer. She placed the recipe box, a few pictures and other sentimental knick knacks in a tote bag so she could keep them in her car for safe keeping. She opened her back door to walk out to her car and slammed head first into a solid, unyielding person blocking her way.

At the same time, Brianna answered her call, "Hello."

Allison looked up, stunned, "Jack," she said breathlessly into the phone.

CHAPTER THIRTEEN

Allison could barely discern the fact that Brianna was talking to her through the cell phone. She had to clutch the phone with her free hand before it dropped off of her shoulder.

Staring daggers into Jack's deep ocean blue eyes, she jerked the phone up to her ear, "Hey, Bree, let me call you right back." She hung up without waiting on a response and turned back around to shut and lock her back door. "Did you miss something the last time you were here?" she asked him, dripping with sarcasm.

Jack Roman looked unapologetic, "I've missed you, but I don't recall being here a last time."

"You missed me? You don't even know me," she said and then quickly amended, "or do you? I know who you are Mr. Jack Roman." Allison emphasized his last name with a sneer and added, "I don't appreciate being played. It was bad enough that you and your despicable cohorts fired me; I don't need your conniving lies and scare tactics as well." Allison walked around him to her car, opened her trunk and placed the tote bag in alongside her overnight bag.

Jack looked thoroughly confused, "Scare tactics? I might have embellished my role at Remco a bit if you want to call that lying, but how is that scary? You might not believe me, but I had nothing to do with your recent termination. I was honest about investigating the matter and concerned about you and others like you."

Allison thought, *good cop, bad cop. Jack is trying to play the good cop again.* "Does your brother Austin know you've come to pay me a visit? Is he the one that wrecked my house earlier?"

Jack glanced back at her house, "Wrecked your house? What are you talking about? Someone wrecked your house?"

Allison was seething. *He truly is good at playing dumb.* "Yes, my house is trashed. Thanks to you and your brother I no longer have a job and my house was ransacked. Your games won't work on me. I'm not signing any documents for you."

Allison opened her car door and sat down in the driver's seat, slinging her expensive purse and phone into the leather passenger seat.

Jack grabbed her open door before she could close it and bent down until he was eye level with her. "I don't know what documents you're referring to, and I'm confident Austin would never step foot in your house." His nearness was consuming her senses. His tanned, strong arm was close to her cheek as he placed his arm on her headrest to further trap her attention. His eyes had a genuine concern in them, but Allison couldn't tell if it was for her well-being or his brother's. He continued, "Did you meet with Austin? Is that why you've been hiding for the past few days? What did he tell you?"

Allison shoved his arm away from her as she bitingly replied, "Ask him yourself! And I haven't been hiding. I've been on...a vacation." She grabbed the door handle, "Tell Austin he's not going to intimidate me!" She slammed her door shut. She backed out of the driveway, spotting his vehicle parked on the road in front of her house. Once again she drove away from Jack, leaving him standing silently, breathing in exhaust fumes from her crimson Jaguar.

At least I didn't kiss him this time.

Before she could pick up her phone to call back Brianna, it rang. "Hey, Bree, sorry about that. Jack showed up at my house as I was calling you."

Brianna sounded concerned, "Are you all right? What did he want?"

Allison answered, "I don't know why he was there. I came home and found my house had been broken into by someone. I think he or Austin sent someone over to either scare me into signing their legal agreement or look for the file I have. I had to meet with the police as soon as I discovered the break-in, but I didn't tell the police about Remco being involved or my missing computer. Jack said he didn't know about my place being ransacked, but I know he's lying. My whole house was turned upside down."

"Geez, Louise," said Bree. "Are you going somewhere safe now? Do you want to come back to Atlanta?"

Allison dismissed her suggestion, "No, I'm going to meet with my new realtor. She's the one I found last night on-line that used to work at Remco. She said she had a couple of listings I could view today. I'm going to stay at the Marriott until I can get my living arrangements finalized. I need to play it cool and not let on that I might have information they need. If I run, they might get more suspicious. Hey, were you able to get a hold of that personal assistant that you had in mind for me?"

Brianna had found a local assistant near Morgan for Allison; one who would be more than capable of keeping and handling Allison's confidences. "Yes, her name is Gwen Brewer and she is raring to go. I'll text you her contact information now because I think she's excited about working with us."

Allison let out a heavy sigh. She knew her to do list kept

growing longer by the minute, and she was ready to pass along some of the work to an assistant. "I'll call her as soon as possible. Thanks Bree!"

"Anytime," DeVoe replied. "Send me some pics of your new house when you decide on it."

The gate house at the front of Morgan Country Club Estates was manned twenty-four hours by a paid security guard. All vehicles and persons had to be cleared in order to enter the upscale neighborhood, which checked off one of Allison's must haves, security. Allison announced her name and intentions of meeting Ashley Porter for a house tour. She gave the guard the addresses of the houses. The guard then gave her a visitor's pass, and Allison was waved through the gate and directed to follow the road around to the right to the first listing. Each lawn was magnificently manicured to perfection in order to enhance the property of each estate. It was clear she was going to need to add master gardener to her growing list of employees. She found the first address easily enough and pulled into the long, curved driveway up to the front entrance of the house. *To call this a house is an understatement.*

Her eye caught the intricate brickwork around the grand entrance way, starting from the pavement, up the sides, and arching over the top of the door. Standing in the driveway, waiting for Allison to exit her car, was a slender, light-skinned black woman. She was in her mid-forties with short black hair, a hot pink business suit, and black heels. Allison had parked behind her white Lexus and smiled as she drew close to her new real estate agent, stretching out her hand in greeting, "Hi, I'm Allison Black."

Ashley took Allison's hand in a warm grip and welcomed her, "Ashley Porter. It's nice to meet you. I'm so glad you called me today. I can't wait to take you inside and show you your new dream house."

Having a fully furnished house would have many perks, Allison thought. She would not have to take the time to pick out furniture that might or might not fit; however, she would also miss making the home truly hers by selecting each piece of furniture by hand. The first house had all the rooms and furnishings she would ever need, including some rooms she did not think would ever be used. Having five bedrooms and five and a half baths for one person seemed absurd until she thought of all the fun she could have throwing parties and hosting guests.

This huge brick estate included a media room with all the latest movie viewing equipment and six custom recliners, a fitness room that had cardio equipment, a weight bench, and a ballet bar along a mirrored wall, an unbelievable cave-like wine cellar with temperature controls that could be adjusted by an application on her phone; and a large library with floor to ceiling windows and custom built in bookcases surrounding a large stone fireplace. Ultimately, she knew her decision would come down to the kitchen layout. This home had an enormous appliance pantry set off from the kitchen that could house all of her baking supplies and kitchen gadgets, affording her a luxury she did not have in her current living situation. With dark cherry cabinets raised to the ceiling, she worried about needing a step stool to reach them all because of her petite height. Ashley was pleased to show her the engineering feat of a rolling ladder that slipped in a side cabinet out of sight until needed. It slid on a hidden track near the ceiling all the way around the kitchen, affording Allison easy access to any height of any kitchen cabinet she needed. She was speechless.

The second listing was a beautiful home with a stucco appearance as opposed to brick on the previous home. The layout was open and modern with a touch of cool sophistication. The stark white kitchen cabinets and travertine floors were pristine, but did not provide the cozy creature comforts and storage space Allison had in mind. It lacked the warmth of the first home she had toured and her decision was made. After placing a call to her banker, Allison took less than an hour to sign a contract for one point two million dollars on her new brick manor. She thanked Ashley for her quick response and promised to be in touch with her as soon as the funds had been cleared. Breathing a sigh of relief, Allison sat in her car in the driveway of her future home. They had driven back to the first listing, so Allison could walk through the perfect house one more time; then Ashley left to file the paperwork at her office and to notify the owners of the impending contract. *What a rush!* Never in her life had she moved forward so quickly on such an important investment.

Feeling the need to decompress after all the events of the day, Allison decided to call Jane. Jane picked up on the third ring, "Hey Alley cat, how are you?"

Allison knew she would have to tell Jane eventually some of the happenings that occurred in the last few days, before she heard it elsewhere through the grapevine. "I'm doing fine, and I'm back in town. How would you like to get that much needed pedicure tonight?" Allison asked her friend.

"Welcome back. That sounds great to me. I've been on my feet most of the day and could use some pampering," Jane replied. Allison agreed to meet Jane at their favorite spa where appointments were not needed, and walk-ins could choose one of twelve pedicure chairs to rest their weary feet. After all, Jane would need to be sitting when Allison dropped the bomb shell on her.

CHAPTER FOURTEEN

"Why didn't you call me earlier? I can't believe someone broke into your house. Talk about a bad week. Do you want to stay at my apartment tonight?" Jane rambled on, somewhat concerned, but mostly morbidly excited about her friend having more drama in her life. The friends were seated side by side, soaking their feet in warm, bubbling water, waiting on the next available pedicurist. Allison could tell that Jane was anxious about what had happened to her friend.

"No thanks, I'll be fine. I'm going to stay at the Marriott until things get settled," Allison was glad her friend expressed concern about her well-being, but wasn't sure how she would handle Allison's other news. She tested the waters, slowly, dropping her voice to a quiet hum, "Jane, I wanted to let you know that I've had a few investments that paid off recently. In fact, I've come into a bit of money lately. I don't want a lot of people to know so I hope I can trust you to keep it quiet."

Jane stared at her friend, her expression almost blank, "What kind of investments? What kind of money are you talking about Allison?" Jane's voice dropped to a whisper, "Are you doing something illegal? It's not drugs is it?"

Allison laughed out loud. "No, it's not illegal. I invested wisely and now I have a hefty nest egg. I don't want all the vultures swarming in trying to take it from me, so I want to keep it on the down low." Jane looked skeptical, not sure how to take Allison's news of a mystery investment.

Allison continued, "I'd like to start sharing my wealth by treating you to this pedicure. I would also like to tell you about my new house that I'm going to buy."

Jane's surprise was evident, "You've got enough to buy a new house? How much money are you talking about?" Allison smiled slightly, leaned back in the comfortable chair, and clicked on the massage button to activate the rollers that slid over the tense muscles in her back.

Allison answered Jane's question, "Enough money to keep me from having to work at a place like Remco ever again."

Allison said good night to the bewildered and excited Jane after their much deserved pampering. Allison then drove to the hotel for the night. Not knowing how long she might be displaced, Allison had reserved a suite with full amenities for the entire week. Her first order of business tonight was ordering room service to abate her gnawing appetite. Throughout the day she had snacked on some breakfast bars she had stored in her car for emergencies because there had been no time to sit down and eat a proper meal since she had been dealing with the detective and then the real estate agent. The soft knock on the door was a welcome relief. She grabbed her wallet and found several dollars to provide tip money for the delivery staff, opened the door and welcomed the warm steak and baked potato.

Melting into the pillow-top mattress and down comforter, Allison thought how easy it would be to relax in comfort and order room service every night, without any other care in the world. *I could get used to being rich.* She snuggled into the ultra-soft pillows, burrowing her face down inside the most comfortable bed she had ever slept in during her entire life. Her last thought before she drifted off to sleep was yet another task she needed to add to her growing list. *I need to make sure I get one of these mattresses for myself.*

Allison was sleeping so soundly, she barely heard her phone ringing. Pushing the covers aside, she turned over and read the digital clock on the side table. It read 9:02am. She could not remember the last time she slept so deeply. Feeling revived, she sat up and located her phone plugged in and lying beside the lamp on the table. The display showed one missed call with a number she did not recognize. A few seconds later, her phone beeped and indicated voice mail.

A frown appeared on her face as she listened to Charlie Ponder's voice, "Good morning, Miss Black. I hope you have had time to review the documents we discussed earlier this week and are ready to move forward by signing them. I look forward to hearing from you at your earliest convenience." Her earliest convenience would not be today or any day in the near future. Instead, she ordered room service.

Motivated by a good night's sleep and a hearty breakfast of bacon, hot buttery biscuits, and a hard-boiled egg, Allison placed a call to her future assistant, Gwen. Gwen had not been an employee of Remco, but she had suffered a similar dismissal experience to Allison's from a company that practiced the good ole boys' rules. Brianna and Gwen had become fast friends several years earlier, after having met at a technical conference in Las Vegas. To Allison's benefit the two women had stayed in touch, since Gwen resided in South Carolina near Morgan.

The quick phone interview took mere minutes to ensure that Gwen was more than capable of handling Allison's pressing needs. Gwen could be at the hotel lobby to meet her new employer within the next hour. This suited Allison fine seeing that she needed to get ready and dressed for her meeting in a few minutes with her insurance agent. Hopefully Gwen would arrive in time to be able to meet Sarah McQueen and take over some of the mundane tasks from Allison, such as working with her insurance agent to get a quote on insurance for her new property. This chapter in her life was keeping her way too busy, hardly leaving any room for the celebration a lottery winner truly deserved.

CHAPTER FIFTEEN

The lobby of the hotel was set up in a comfortable, open style manner, yet offered areas of cozy grouped seating, creating a sensation of a more private nature. Sarah arrived minutes after Allison made her way downstairs, staking claim to a charming cluster of chairs near the beautifully lit fireplace. She thanked Sarah for coming out on short notice and gave her the address of the house she put a contract on yesterday. Sarah had come prepared, opened her laptop, and assessed the property within a matter of moments. The ladies were gazing intently at the numbers on the screen when Gwen arrived.

Allison stood and greeted Gwen with a heartfelt handshake, "Good morning! It's so nice to put a face with a name. Bree has talked about you often and don't worry, it's all good."

Gwen smiled and firmly returned Allison's handshake. "I'm happy to be here, Miss Black," Gwen said.

Allison corrected her, "Please, call me Allison." Gwen sat opposite of Allison and Sarah. Allison introduced the two women. "We started on some basic insurance information for a house I am planning to purchase for my personal use," Allison stated. "I'm hoping you can listen in and offer any advice for me, and then work directly with Sarah on our upcoming business plans." The ladies worked through the numbers and discussed additional insurance endorsement clauses that would need to be added on a house of significant worth.

After Sarah McQueen left, Allison invited Gwen up to her hotel suite in order to discuss their business arrangement privately. "I guess Brianna filled you in on what I'm looking for," Allison said as they sat down at the small table in her hotel room.

Gwen nodded, "She told me the basics. I think what you two are planning is awesome. I can't wait to get started. Let me know what you need for me to do first."

Allison took out the list of names she had jotted down, next to open positions she had available. "I need you to get started by contacting some of these people. Make initial contact with each one and see if they're receptive to coming on board with us. I am also going to need retail space for a business. We can sit down and discuss the design and layout for the space this afternoon, so you can get a feel for what size space is needed. I can give you Ashley's information for finding the space we need. She is my new realtor and should have some good leads for us, without you having to start from scratch."

The two ladies continued talking, getting to know each other and taking notes as ideas emerged for their growing plans. Since Allison wanted the three of them to be a strong, cohesive unit, they conferenced in Brianna a few times to get her opinion on some of the technical aspects of the business. Needing to take a break and get some fresh sunshine, Allison treated her second full-time employee to lunch outside of the hotel. The weather was starting to warm up the last few days, so they walked a few blocks downtown to a local bistro called Sizzle.

The ladies were seated at a quaint table for two perusing the menu when Allison turned toward a heated conversation on the other side of the restaurant. Two men were raising their voices in an almost shouted whisper. What a surprise to see Jack and Austin seated nearby, obviously not in agreement about something.

Allison turned back to Gwen and said, "Follow me, Gwen. I'd like to introduce you to someone." They stood and Gwen followed Allison to the twins' table. Allison was wearing a bright green and white checked skirt with a white cardigan. Her white sandaled feet quietly approached the men at the nearby table. Both men stopped bickering and looked up in alarm at the ladies looking down on them. "Gwen Brewer, I'd like to introduce you to my nemeses, Mr. Jack and Mr. Austin Roman."

Jack smiled showing off his deep dimples, while Austin's face took on a sinister sneer. Jack recovered first, stood up, and put his hand out in greeting for Gwen to shake, "Nice to meet you, Gwen."

Allison spoke in a very sweet, high sing-song voice, "I didn't mean to interrupt your important conversation. By all means, please carry on. Were you perhaps discussing me?"

Jack sat down, replied quickly and was kicked under the table by Austin, "Yes. Ouch! Yes we were as a matter of fact." Jack rubbed his shin under the table.

Austin finally spoke, "Hi Miss Black. We were having a private conversation. If you'd like to discuss any matters relating to Remco, I'm sure Mr. Ponder would be happy if you called him directly."

I'm sure he would. Allison missed the blatant dismissal cue on purpose and replied, "Unfortunately, I don't have any reason to talk to Mr. Ponder at this time, but it was nice seeing the two of you here."

That was an understatement, seeing as how both men were equally the most gorgeous male specimen in all of Morgan, South Carolina. Today Jack wore a red button up collared shirt, neatly tucked into his blue jeans; Austin had traded his suit for a more casual couture appropriate for any golf course. She continued, "Seeing as I missed your house call earlier this week, Austin, I hope that Jack passed along my message to you." Austin and Jack traded glances as though that was exactly what they had been discussing.

Austin took a deep breath and slowly replied in a smooth voice, "I don't know what you're talking about Miss Black; I've never been to your house. I'm sure it's a lovely place, but I wouldn't know."

"Yes," Allison said with a hint of sarcasm, "I'm sure you

don't. Well, in any case, I hope you enjoy your lunch." Allison and Gwen slowly returned to their table, sitting down long enough to see Austin rise up and leave the restaurant abruptly. Jack smiled sheepishly, placed money on the table, and followed his brother out the door.

"Wow," said Gwen. "Brianna didn't tell me how fine they were."

Allison snickered, "Bree has never met them. They are both a piece of work. Now, let's talk about this business I'd like to start. I'm hoping with you and Brianna's help, we can kill two birds with one stone. The first is creating a respectable place of business where everyone truly is treated fairly. The second is watching Remco choke on it." The two ladies proceeded to have an enjoyable lunch as Allison shared her vision for a company the three of them would soon have in place.

CHAPTER SIXTEEN

Morgan Country Club Estates had never seen so many cars lined up and down the streets for one private house party. Three weeks had passed since her last encounter with the Remco owners and since then several milestones had happened. First and most important being the money from the lottery finally cleared and her finances were firmly in place. Second, the closing on her new house had been finalized. Allison now employed a full-time master gardener and a maid; both of which were recruited from the list she took with her from Remco. The master gardener had been a man in his fifties that had been forced to take early retirement allowing his department head to hire cheaper, younger labor. Although he did not fit the female profile that Allison had first contemplated using, his similar circumstances and love of all things outdoors put him at the top of her list for lawn maintenance. He and his son had started their own landscaping business after he left Remco, and Allison wanted to make sure she invested in the local small business.

Her new maid, Mitzie, had been down-sized from Remco as well, when the cleaning staff had been traded in for a third party company that Remco hired in order to not pay benefits to those employees. Mitzie polished and cleaned the new estate before Allison moved in, making Allison's transition an easy one. Mitzie's cousin, Ava, was a whiz at organization, so Allison had utilized her abilities during the move, allowing her to unpack and stow away dishes, clothes, and other household items. Ava had sorted her closet in color order, pairing outfits together in an efficient and remarkably simple manner. Her kitchen had never been so organized, having everything accessible in an easy to find layout.

Allison spent much of the last week refining recipes in her kitchen and learning to use her new appliances in her state of the art kitchen. She was thrilled to have two convection ovens along with a six-burner gas stove. The light-colored marbled, granite counter space was more than enough to hold the numerous batches of cookies, pastries, cupcakes, and cake pops she had prepared in anticipation for tonight's event. The hired caterers artfully displayed her confections on platters throughout the downstairs rooms, next to the warm finger foods they had prepared on-site. Allison had never paid anyone to prepare food at her house, but having white-coated staff seeing to each detail and restocking food was a pleasant experience. It gave Allison plenty of time to enjoy mingling with her friends and showing off her new luxurious accommodations.

Not only had she invited Brianna, Gwen, and Jane, but she also included many of her new acquaintances such as Sarah McQueen, her insurance agent and Ashley Porter, her realtor.

Allison also reached out and invited many of the local politicians and city management, hoping to build up a network of contacts for her future business. At a last minute suggestion from Gwen, she invited several non-profit directors of local agencies, so she could get a feel for how she might distribute monies to worthy charities. Her main focus was on the many guests that had been displaced by Remco. Allison invited them in order to have an informal interview of sorts to see what positions some of the ladies and a few gentlemen might fill in her new, upcoming business venture. Conversations were kept casual and open, with Allison speaking to each person individually, before moving on to the next person.

The decision to have an open house party had been a tough one. On one hand, Allison wanted to remain reclusive and hide away in her new gated community, keeping her newly acquired financial status to herself. Brianna pointed out that a bolder commanding stand might prove to have more benefits to help their cause. By providing an invitation-only private party, the ladies would be able to rub elbows with the movers and shakers in town and introduce Allison to the societal elite. It reminded Allison of when young ladies were presented at debutante balls, marking them as eligible for marriage; except in her case, she would be marked as eligible for business.

As each guest arrived, Gwen or Brianna greeted them at the door and ushered them into Allison's house, gathered their name and a few details about each person, and introduced them to Allison. Some of the guests seemed a little confused as to why they were invited to such an elaborate affair or what the purpose of the party was. None the less, most were excited for being included in such a high profile event. Each person on the list arrived dressed to impress, not wanting to miss an exclusive party at Morgan Country Club Estates. Brianna and Gwen highlighted Allison's culinary abilities and invited the guests to tour her new house, which currently housed two open bars along with bartenders eager to serve.

Mayor Glen Ross approached Allison while she was standing

near two ladies in the library. "You have a beautiful house, Miss Black," he stated.

"Please, call me Allison," she replied.

He continued, "Thank you for inviting me tonight, Allison. I thoroughly enjoyed the scrumptious red velvet cupcake. I understand you did most of the baking."

"Yes," she answered, "I did all the desserts for tonight's party. I'm so glad you liked the cupcake. Make sure to try one of my signature cookies as well. I think you'll like them."

The mayor said, "Oh, I will. Do you mind if I take some goodies to my wife? She was not feeling well and unable to attend tonight."

Allison smiled, "Please do. Take as many as you like. In fact, one of the catering staff can box some up for you if you ask them."

One of the ladies to Allison's right remarked after the mayor stepped away, "Allison, what kind of business are you going to be starting? I understand from Brianna that you'll be investing in the community soon by bringing in a new business with potential job opportunities here in Morgan. She said you wanted to get to know some of the local people that might be able to help contribute to this new venture."

Allison nodded and smiled at the lady, remembering her name from an earlier introduction as Faith Bradley, alongside her friend, Lorraine. "Well Faith, we're still working on the details but hope to have an announcement ready soon. I'm counting on finding some strong resources such as yourself and Lorraine to possibly help me out." Allison glanced at Lorriane and noticed she was listening intently to Allison's answer, hoping to solve some of the mystery surrounding the night's event.

Faith and Lorraine both nodded. "We'd be happy to help in

any way we can. Did you have something specific in mind?" Faith asked as she kept trying to dig out more information from Allison.

"I hear you are good with numbers; you have an accounting degree, correct?" Allison inquired of Faith.

Faith nodded, "Yes, that's right."

Allison continued, "I'll need someone to help lead up our accounting department starting next week as our store gets underway. Do you think you might be interested? If so, maybe we can set up a meeting with Gwen next week to discuss a permanent position."

Faith smiled, "That sounds like quite a job. I am definitely interested."

Allison turned to the other lady and said, "Lorraine, I'll need someone that has a strong background in marketing. Would you like a similar opportunity in our marketing division?"

Lorraine looked visibly stunned but recovered quickly, "Yes, I'd love a chance to do marketing again. Since I left Remco, it's been difficult finding a similar position without having to leave Morgan to go to a bigger city."

Allison seemed pleased that she had shored up not one, but two essential positions needed to get her new business plan off the ground. "Let's go find Gwen and set up a meeting. Be sure and grab one of those cake pops on your way," Allison said, leading the ladies into the large, open den to search for Gwen. Reluctant to share her business plan openly, Allison kept the details vague and the intrigue high.

The rest of the night passed quickly as the ladies continued to establish a presence among the various Morgan constituents. The hour grew later and soon only Allison, Brianna, Gwen and Jane remained, having seen the catering staff pack up and drive away moments earlier.

"I'd say this night was very successful," Bree stated as they made their way into the den to sit and discuss the event in comfort.

"My feet are killing me," said Jane, kicking off her shoes and tucking her feet underneath her as she settled on the soft leather couch. Allison had brought Jane in on their business plan last week, deciding it would be best to have another person help work the crowd at their coming out party.

Gwen said, "I have so many meetings lined up for this next week; we might have to call the caterers back to feed us, since I don't know when we'll have time to eat."

Allison smiled. She looked around at her friends and new assistant and said, "Well, I had a great time! Thank you all for helping me tonight. I think it was a great success for us and our future business."

Brianna quipped, "It was fun to see so many people trying to figure out exactly what business we're starting. The mysterious business of one Miss Allison Black has certainly created a buzz of excitement."

Allison laughed. "In due time, ladies, in due time. I can't wait to unveil our plans next week. We're going to turn this town upside down. I can't wait to bring home the bacon! What do you say we all adjourn to the hot tub?"

CHAPTER SEVENTEEN

"Bacon?" Jack confusingly asked Austin. "Why would you get a pack of raw bacon in the mail?"

Austin frowned at the package wrapped in brown paper sitting on his desk that had been delivered by courier moments before. "I don't know," he replied, irritated that he did not know the answer.

"Does it say who it's from?" asked Jack.

"No, the card says *for the two biggest pigs in Morgan.* I bet it's from your girlfriend, Miss Black," Austin said sardonically.

Jack smiled tentatively, "She's not my girlfriend, but you could be right about her sending the bacon. I wonder what she's up to now. Exactly how much money did you offer her? I hear she bought a new house and is opening a business soon."

Austin retorted, "It's not from our money. She refused to take it. I'm not sure who is funding her. " Jack Roman paced around in front of his twin brother Austin's desk in his designer blue jeans and crisp, light blue, button-down shirt. The blue hue of his shirt highlighted Jack's eyes, which had a hint of amusement in them.

"I can't believe you tried to bribe her to keep quiet. You should have offered her the severance package with no strings attached. " Jack stated.

Austin had an air of arrogance about him and definitely was not willing to concede defeat, "Well she hasn't sued us, yet, so it might have worked after all and saved us ten grand to boot!"

"You were playing with fire by having her place ransacked," Jack said.

Austin grimaced, "My intention was to give her an incentive to sign the agreement, not cause a war."

Jack shook his head, "I never would've believed my brother was capable of such low-down methods."

Austin Roman looked at his brother squarely in the eyes, "Our necks are on the line here. Uncle Cliff left us in a bad situation because the way he ran this business was completely unethical. I'm surprised Remco hasn't been sued before now. I'm trying the best way I know how to clean up the mess he left us."

Jack broke eye contact and kept pacing, "He was old school alright. But I don't agree with how you handled Allison."

Austin said, "What would you have me do, send her flowers? Not everything can be polished over with a little flirting, Jack."

Jack's tone was clipped, "I wouldn't call expressing concern flirting. She deserved to keep her job. That human resource director Tomlinson needs to go. His corrupt tactics are what put her on the chopping block to begin with. I talked to Todd Whitt personally and he said Tomlinson wanted her gone after a salary file was exposed during some routine software maintenance. Allison was a good worker. The salary file would not have been anything to worry about, if people had been paid fairly."

Austin looked over at the picture of Clifton Remco on the office wall. He picked up the bacon, and threw it in the trash can. "Well she should have kept her nose out of places it didn't belong," retorted Austin.

"That's just the beginning of our problems, brother. I talked to Brian Cooper in the shipping department this week. We have bigger issues on our hands than some computer programmer that was terminated. Do you know those parts that we ship to Turkey for the military radar equipment? Well, according to Brian, the end customer is questionable. Some of those parts are ending up in Kosovo, being used against our own military personnel. I have him following up with a shipping agent at the border. If the wrong people find out, it could mean trouble." Austin sighed heavily under his breath, "We better hope this gets fixed soon. Otherwise, Miss Black will be the least of our problems. Do you think it is possible Allison knew about these customer accounts?"

Jack answered, "She's a smart cookie. If she was feeling threatened, she might have acquired some information before she left as collateral. I spoke with our senior sales agent, Martin Kowzalski, in that division last week. Martin assured me that those customer accounts have since been closed and no new shipments have been sent to them in the last few weeks. I hope Brian can tie up all the loose ends over in Turkey," Jack stared at the bacon in the bottom of the bin. "I might go see what our little gift giver is up to these days."

On the other side of town at their newly renovated building, Brianna DeVoe was laughing out loud, "You sent them a package of bacon? That's classic Allison. I must say, I didn't see you as the antagonist type. I bet that was a nice surprise."

Allison smiled sheepishly, "Well, the idea occurred to me as we were mocking up our business flow the other day. What better way to remind them that I'm still around? They need to be reminded that they can't treat women like they treated me, not in this day and time. Two can play this game. Besides, I'm not over them trashing my other house." Allison had her previous house cleaned and loaned it to one of the charities in town that needed housing for displaced families. Her ego still smarted from the callous way her termination and severance offering had been handled.

"Well, they are pigs," said Bree, "and how appropriate a gift for them with our new business launching this week."

After several weeks of dedicated planning and tiresome

working, Allison and Brianna were ready to open the doors of their new joint venture. Gwen had scheduled the unveiling for Friday morning; she arranged a press conference shortly afterwards. Allison was happy to be providing over thirty jobs to the small town of Morgan, South Carolina. She hoped this was merely a start and soon the business would thrive, possibly even expand into other cities.

Ashley Porter had procured the perfect retail space for their company, which shockingly did not require much transformation on the outside. The inside was a completely different story. Most of the remodeling had been electrical, with a bit of cosmetic additions. The electrical remodeling had been extensive, including the top of the line security systems, numerous additional outlets, and all new LED lighting. The building was located in the middle of downtown, in a large brick two-story building convenient to all residents of Morgan. The building had housed many businesses in the hundred years it had stood, the latest of which had been a bookstore.

With Jane's help, Gwen had managed to order all the computer equipment needed and set it up in the new office space ready for installation. The kitchen area of the new building had been expanded from a small kitchenette to an industrial-sized operation, complete with stainless steel appliances and shelving. It was located on the ground floor, toward the back of the building. The kitchen contained two floor-sized industrial mixers, a jet air oven that could bake up to thirty-two pans of cupcakes at one time, a gas range with eight burners, an over-sized walk-in refrigerator, and a walk-in freezer.

Storage room space was located off the kitchen and would serve as a pantry as well as hold boxes and other miscellaneous supplies for the bakery part of the business. Allison had brought in an interior designer to help her new marketing manager, Lorraine Phillips, design the décor of the new customer space. She created a bright, creative atmosphere for the customers, which would be downstairs near the front of the building. Glass display cases would showcase the available confectionery selections, many of which were photographed and put into large prints around the customer area.

Allison and Brianna were currently upstairs in the employee office space, which would house several open desk areas including a space for their new accountant, Faith Bradley, as well as desks for Lorraine, Allison, Brianna, Gwen, and Jane. Jane had been hired on to be the customer support liaison. With her bubbly personality, it was a natural fit for her to be the face of the company, circulating among customers and talking with the public. Gwen Brewer would assume the role of general manager, hiring employees and keeping items stocked, basically overseeing the day-to-day operations. Brianna and Allison would provide the brains of the operation, specifically the computer analysis and the confectionery delights, along with a host of additional resources.

All the pieces were falling into place quickly to start their new venture, Computer Forensics & Bacon Confectionery. Allison had taken her top three loves and combined them into one company offering: her love of computers, bacon and all things sweet.

CHAPTER EIGHTEEN

As with any small business, Allison knew she was taking a risk, especially with a niche marketing item such as bacon. Her clientele would be two fold, those seeking technical help and those seeking a unique bakery experience. She was counting on many of those customers crossing over into the other category. To appease the morning crowd, she would cater to breakfast items, such as maple French toast bacon muffins, bacon breakfast quiche with mascarpone and eggs, bacon apple crisps, bacon cinnamon rolls, banana bread mini loaves with bourbon candied bacon toppings, and apple bacon cheddar crostini. The specialty morning drinks would include bacon infused mocha cappuccino or hot chocolate, apple cider with a bacon garnish, and bacon flavored lemonade.

For the afternoon and evening crowd, her offerings would include confections as well as afternoon specialty drinks. The daily bakery items would be dark chocolate bacon cupcakes, bourbon cupcakes with maple glaze frosting and bacon sprinkles, bacon herb quiche with peppers and green onions, beer cheese cupcakes with bacon cheddar cream cheese frosting, candied cayenne bacon cake pops, bacon caramel popcorn, bacon brittle, loaded baked potato cupcake, bacon peanut butter banana cupcake, bacon apple pie, and chocolate bacon truffles. The cocktail drink menu would offer a bacon chocolate martini, pig on the rocks, bacon bloody Mary, and a seasonal bacon and eggnog cocktail.

Allison had hired several bakers to work with her on fine tuning the recipes and offerings. She would provide a few non-bacon items throughout the week, but her main focus would be on all things bacon. The unique atmosphere combined a coffee shop motif married with a brightly lit bar that had room for laptop computers and tablets at each seating area. Brianna and several of her new technical recruits would provide the computer support for individual clients who would need help with basics such as resumes and web design, as well as the more intricate work of computer forensic research. These research consultants would be available to businesses at their site as needed or locally within the Computer Forensics and Bacon Confectionery building.

The press release was being fine-tuned by Lorraine for Friday's grand opening. What it would not state was the underlying secret mission of Allison's business. Only Allison and Brianna knew what was at the true core of their new company. In their technically savvy world, Remco would feel some pain. Leaving the back door open to Remco's firewall was a convenience that Allison had provided for a professional hacker such as Bree DeVoe. Brianna's ability to penetrate firewalls was almost legendary in the small underground society of hackers. Having a quaint store front property would be the perfect ruse to hide the true nature of their business.

A knock sounded on the front door downstairs. Allison looked up at Brianna and asked, "Were you expecting anyone today?"

"No," replied Brianna. "Were you?"

Allison shook her head no and stood up. "I'll go see who it is. It could be UPS delivering more bakery boxes." As she made her way down the winding staircase, she glanced out the large glass windows in the front and frowned. *Jack Roman. What does he want?* She had not seen Jack in the last few weeks, but turned her frown to a smirk as she thought of the bacon she had delivered that morning. *He must have received my gift.* She unlocked the door and pushed it open, allowing him to step into the store.

"Hello, Allison," Jack greeted her with a warm smile.

Allison replied, "Jack, what do I owe the pleasure? We're not open for business, yet. You're here a little early."

Jack walked in and looked around at the work in progress. He noted the coral and black floral print on the padded chairs at small round tables with a hanging modern light fixture over each one. He saw the mirrored bar along the right side with the large chopping block bar top and the top shelf liquors lined up behind the cappuccino makers. Each bar stool had coral and black striped fabric that complemented the dining chairs. The small round tables were a light oak wood that had been fitted with charging stations in the center of each one.

93

"Are you opening a coffee shop?" he asked Allison.

Allison answered, "Not exactly. It's more of a unique bakery. We'll be releasing the press announcement at our grand opening this Friday."

Jack turned to look at Allison and said, "I hope it goes well. I've been thinking about you lately."

Allison almost choked on her reply, "I bet you have. Speaking of business, how is Remco doing these days? Have you and Austin laid off anyone else lately?"

Jack looked sincere as he said, "I'm truly sorry, Allison. You were not treated fairly. I wish I could have prevented that from happening."

Allison looked in his ocean blue eyes and wanted to believe him. She couldn't look away, "Well, everything happens for a reason. So what brings you by today? Were you in an apologetic mood?"

Jack Roman seemed to be looking straight into her soul. "No," he said, "I mean, I did want to apologize, but that's not why I'm here. I wanted to make sure you were doing okay." Allison hesitated, not sure what to make of Jack's unexpected visit.

"Well, as you can see, I'm doing just fine, no thanks to Remco," Allison stated as she caught a movement at the top of the stairs. Brianna was at the landing, looking down at Allison and Jack.

Brianna motioned with her hands and mouthed, "Are you okay?"

Allison nodded to her. Jack noticed Allison's attention had been diverted and turned to see Brianna upstairs, leaning over the handrail. Brianna was wearing a grass-green maxi, pleated skirt with a billowy tan top. Her feet sported light tan sandals with her unpolished, but well-trimmed toes.

Jack called up to her, "Hi."

Bree answered, "Hey yourself." She started walking down the spiral stairs to see this fine specimen at a closer angle.

Allison made the introductions, "Brianna DeVoe, may I introduce Jack Roman."

Jack stretched out his hand as she drew nearer in order to shake her hand. Brianna looked at his hand, but did not take it.

She folded her arms in front of her and said, "So this is the Jack Roman!"

Jack dropped his arm, "The one and only."

He assessed Allison's business partner and then turned back to Allison as she spoke, "Brianna is my friend and business partner from Atlanta."

Jack replied, "It's nice to meet you Ms. DeVoe. Allison, I don't want to take up anymore of your time. I wanted to stop by and wish you the best." He walked back toward the front door across the inlaid wooden floor. Allison opened the front door and waved him out the same way he came into the store. He lingered, looking her up and down, taking in her tight designer jeans and black, fitted sequined tank top, and with a hint of admiration in his voice said, "Good luck Friday."

"Thank you for your concern, Jack. Please give Austin my regards." Jack stepped out and Allison closed and locked the door behind him.

Brianna whistled after the door was shut. "Girl, he is smoking hot. If I'm not mistaken, he has a thing for you. He couldn't keep his eyes off you the entire time."

Allison stared at her friend, "What are you talking about? He doesn't have a thing for me!" She had emphasized the word thing.

Bree laughed, "Are you blind? He was boring holes straight through that shirt of yours."

Allison looked down at her shirt, then back up at Brianna. In a dismissive tone she stated, "Speaking of clothes, I need you to go with me to pick out something for the grand opening on Friday."

Brianna chuckled, "Someone is in denial." She turned and walked lithely back up the stairs to retrieve her purse from her desk.

The girls locked up the shop and walked down several blocks to a boutique owned by a local pair of sisters. With barely three days left and wanting to make a good impression for the news media on Friday, the business partners carefully selected outfits that were unique to each other's personalities, yet complemented each of them. Brianna, with her five foot six, willowy frame, selected a long one piece cotton lavender dress. She found a scarf with bright purple and chartreuse green to accessorize her simple style. Allison Black chose a pair of black slacks with a bold, dark purple fitted top with rhinestones around the scooped neckline and three-quarter length sleeves. She purchased several silver bangle bracelets for her wrist, wishing now she had bought the Rolex in Atlanta a few weeks earlier.

Besides the purchase of her house, Allison had not flaunted her newly won money. Most of her time had been consumed with launching her new business, which in turn would start her plan to get even with Remco for terminating her position and others like her. She had not had much time to focus on spending her money on frivolous items. There would be plenty of time, and money, to do that later. For now, she wanted to strike while the irons were hot. Allison settled on her newest outfit, gathered the purchase in her arms, and made her way back to the breeding ground of the biggest silent revenge the town of Morgan would ever see.

CHAPTER NINETEEN

One of the most important aspects of revenge is to affect the primary parties that deserve it, without damaging innocent bystanders. It would have been too easy for Allison to get a lawyer and sue the company based on her own disheartening experience and credible findings. That would have placated her ego but not addressed the other unfortunate women and men that had been terminated unnecessarily. She knew Remco employed over nine hundred people, mostly from the town of Morgan. If she caused the company to go completely under, many more innocent bystanders would lose their jobs. It was a careful balance of keeping Remco afloat and yet making an impact big enough to incite permanent change. Allison Black had to use her knowledge to benefit the most people, and of course teach a lesson to the ones that deserved it.

She had a feeling that Jack had stopped by the day before in order to find out more information, but with Brianna's presence his visit had been cut short. She had not had any more phone calls from the lawyer, Charlie Ponder, nor had she had any more threatening antics from Austin Roman. Her guard was up, though, not trusting him to let the issue go unresolved. She was convinced that Jack had shown particular interest in her because she was a threat to his newly inherited company.

Allison was sitting at her desk upstairs in the office area, staring at her cell phone. She had installed a new application that synced up with the twelve security cameras recently installed in her bakery. She touched the screen that showed the camera angle near the front door. *This would have been nice to have yesterday when Jack showed up.* She scrolled through each camera which focused on the exits, cash register, storage room, and customer area. It was similar to the security system she had recently installed at her new house, not wanting to be vandalized a second time.

She watched on her phone as Gwen unlocked and opened the front door. She switched cameras and followed Gwen through the customer area to the stairs.

Gwen called out as she ascended into the office area, "Anyone here?"

Allison laid her phone down on her desk, and replied, "Hi, Gwen. I'm here. Bree had to go back to Atlanta to tie up a few loose ends with her other business. She'll be back tomorrow." Gwen Brewer was slightly heavy set, leaning towards comfortable clothing rather than stylish or chic the last few days. She had donned her blue jeans and paired them with an oversized, light yellow cotton shirt and her slip on rubberized shoes. She had brown eyes and curly brown hair that came to rest on her shoulders. She was a work horse who willingly tackled any job Allison had thrown at her in the last few weeks, while at the same time maintaining a cheerful attitude and strong stamina. All of them pulled extremely long hours while getting the store ready for its grand opening.

"Do you think she'll move here from Atlanta, or keep her place there?" Gwen asked Allison.

"I don't know. I guess it will depend on how well our other computer techs can handle the work load without her being on site. I imagine she will stay here in Morgan at least the first month or so. Since she is merging her customers from her other business in with this one, I don't know if she'll need to go back to Atlanta part time or not," Allison replied.

Gwen placed her keys and phone on her own neatly organized desk and sat down. "This is all so exciting. I can't believe we actually open this Friday," Gwen breathed a sigh of relief.

Allison smiled, "Have you heard from Lorraine? Do you know if the store front sign will be delivered today?"

Gwen said, "Yes, the sign maker is bringing his bucket truck this afternoon to install it. I'll make sure it's covered well in order to keep it under wraps until the reveal on Friday." Allison was amazed again at how efficient Gwen was with all the little details. It struck her that so many good people were let go at companies for bad reasons. *Their loss, my gain,* she thought. "Thank, you Gwen. It's all coming together nicely. Jane is coming in later as well to work with the new staff on a mock run through. She's going to make sure they know how to use the coffee machines and computer register at the bar. I have a hair appointment today, but I'll have my cell, if you need me. Are you going to be okay alone until Jane gets here?"

Gwen replied, "Sure, I'll be fine. I'll touch base with you later."

It had been at least two months since Allison had her hair cut or styled, and she desperately needed it trimmed and even toyed with the idea of adding highlights to her already blonde hair. In the past she had forgone the highlights, knowing it would take an effort to keep up with the maintenance. Now that her life had taken a different path, she wasn't sure if she was ready to tackle the upkeep or not. Allison enjoyed her long blonde locks, enabling her to wear it up or down, as her mood dictated. After trying many different stylists over the years, Allison had finally found someone that she liked and trusted.

Tame the Mane was located on Fifth Avenue, far enough

from her downtown establishment that she felt the need to drive instead of walk. She pulled in front of the small salon as a silver late model Corvette was pulling out of the parking lot. She glimpsed in the driver's side window and saw a familiar face. The Corvette drove away from the hair parlor in the opposite direction that she had come. She parked her car and opened the door, watching the car speed away. It continued down the street at a fast pace, not giving Allison time to catch the license plate. She pulled open the door to the salon and saw her stylist, Brittany, sweeping hair from around her chair. Brittany glanced up, "Hey Allison, come on in," she shouted over the sound of a nearby hair dryer.

"Hi Brittany," said Allison. "Whose hair did you just cut?" Allison cut straight to the question in order to get her suspicions substantiated.

"Oh, that's Mr. Austin Roman. Do you know him?" Brittany asked, continuing, "He's a sweetie and not bad to look at if I do say so myself."

Allison had barely glimpsed his profile, but her surmise had been correct. "Yes, I do," she admitted.

Brittany stated, "Oh that's right, you do work at Remco. I guess you would know him."

Allison felt the need to correct Brittany, "Actually, I was let go from Remco. I no longer work for that company." Brittany's smile faltered, "Oh no. I'm sorry to hear that. Where are you working now?" Allison was once again reminded of how lucky she had been to win the lottery, or else her answer would be very different.

She sat down in the unoccupied chair and told Brittany, "I'm opening my own business. You should watch the news this Friday for our big grand opening announcement."

Brittany gushed, "That's great! What kind of business is it?"

Allison did not want to reveal too much before the press release, especially knowing that a beauty salon was the biggest gossip bed in town.

"It's a surprise," she said, knowing the suspense would kill someone in Brittany's industry.

Brittany pursed her lips and asked, "If I guess, will you tell me if I get it right?"

Allison laughed, "Maybe." She spent the next hour entertained at all the wild guesses from her stylist and other patrons in the salon. She decided against the highlights and settled on a layered cut that put a bounce in her freshly trimmed blonde curls.

The ladies at Tame the Mane would have to wait until Friday along with the rest of Morgan to find out about Allison's new venture. In the meantime, Allison would ponder the unique differences between Austin's choice of a flashy sports car and Jack's practical sports utility vehicle. To assuage her curiosity, Allison asked Brittany one last parting question, "Is Mr. Roman a good tipper?"

Brittany smiled and replied, "One of the best."

CHAPTER TWENTY

For two people that looked exactly alike, the Remco twins could not have been more different. From their personalities to the style of management, the brothers were like night and day. In a small town like Morgan, it was natural that Allison would continue to run into the newest members of society. She drove past the guard's gate at Morgan Country Club Estates, waving to the guard on duty. It was after ten o'clock on Thursday night, and her grand opening was in the morning. She had finally completed her last minute tasks and was eager to get home and put her feet up for a while. Ahead of her, rounding the curve, she saw the taillights of a familiar looking car. The silver Corvette passed under the streetlamp, illuminating the entire car long of enough for Allison to gasp. *Does Austin Roman live in my neighborhood?* Her curiosity was piqued. She drove past her driveway and continued to follow the sports car at a slow distance.

She watched as his car pulled into a long driveway several houses down from her own house. Looking into her rear view mirror, she saw the streets were empty and no one was behind her. She pulled over and stopped for a few minutes, not wanting Austin to catch her spying on him. After waiting what she hoped was ample time for him to have exited his car and gone inside, she drove by at a creeping pace. The garage door was almost closed, but not before she caught a glimpse of Jack's car right beside Austin's. *They both live here!* Her gated community was no longer a security blanket for her. *I guess the old adage is true: keep your friends close, but your enemies closer.* She knew where the Roman brothers lived now, and she was positive they knew she was their new neighbor.

Allison was startled awake by the loud, obnoxious alarm she had set on her phone for six o'clock in the morning. She was lying on the couch with her legs curled under her throw blanket, while her head rested on one of her new silk decorative pillows. The television was still on, having been muted during one of the commercials before Allison succumbed to sleep the night before. She stretched, wishing she had made it to bed to avoid the stiffness she knew she would feel during the day. She arose begrudgingly, turned off the television, and shuffled through the kitchen toward her bedroom. Her first order of her busy day would be to get a shower in hopes of wiping all traces of exhaustion from her body. As she pictured Brianna doing her impossible yoga moves at this very moment, she shook her head.

Her team had decided on a grand opening time of eleven o'clock, but would allow the press and other special guests to enter earlier at nine a.m. for a private preview party. Allison was dressed and ready to go by seven, giving herself plenty of time to make sure everything was in place before the doors opened. Her shop would operate two shifts for the bakery side, as well as two shifts for the computer technical support side. Brianna had personally designed and launched their website, which had gone live at midnight.

Allison's Jaguar purred quietly into the parking lot located behind the building. The downtown area was quiet in the mornings. She noticed Gwen's white sedan and several other cars that belonged to her new staff were already in the nearby parking lot. Her nerves were starting to gather in the pit of her stomach. Anticipation was building to a climax as she realized one of her biggest fantasies was coming true. *It really does take money to make money.* At least she hoped she would be making money soon, not just for her benefit, but for those she now employed. She slid her key into the back door entrance which opened into the large industrial kitchen and smelled the distinguishable aroma of bacon.

"Good morning," Allison greeted the kitchen staff as she walked in her business. *This is it. It's real.*

Several ladies turned and greeted her in response. Large muffin pans were lined up on a baker's tray, ready to be filled and then baked with the first batch of cupcakes. For the special grand opening, she would be offering everything on the menu at nine a.m., not solely the breakfast items. She walked through the kitchen, observing the ingredients and staff, certain she had selected the finest.

She asked Betty, one of her top kitchen bakers, "How is

everything going? Are we going to be ready for the crowd today?"

Betty was in her fifties but commanded a kitchen in a way that only a grandmother could. She had loving touches and a knack for multi-tasking. "We're doing great. We have all the prep bowls filled, as you instructed us yesterday. All we need to do is fill the pans and set the timers."

Allison replied, "That's great, Betty. Let's cross our fingers we have enough to last the day."

She made her way up the small, back staircase, entered the office area, and moved over to her desk. She locked up her purse and snapped her phone in its case on her hip. She could hear the voices of several people downstairs in the customer area and made her way to the front staircase and looked down. She observed Gwen and Lorraine down below in front of the bar, talking with a few of the baristas. Since many people would be sampling items at the preview party, they had decided to use small shot glasses instead of the larger glasses they would use after the store officially opened at eleven. The shot glasses were lined across the bar waiting to be filled by the concoctions the baristas were creating.

She watched as Jane unlocked and entered through the front door and waved down to her when she glanced up the stairs to see Allison. "Good morning," Allison called out to Jane. Allison made her way down the winding stairs and hugged her friend.

Jane said, "Good morning. I had to come in the front door to see what our customers would see when they arrive. It looks so good in here!"

Lorraine and Gwen joined them and nodded in their agreement. "Everything is going smooth so far. I think we will have more than enough free samples to go around for our first round of guests," said Gwen.

As the time drew nearer for the doors to open, Allison watched a couple of local news trucks pull up out front. Cameramen were taking some footage of the store front and covered sign, hopefully to be used during the newscast this afternoon and evening to bring in more business. Her team quickly assembled in their respective places for the doors to be opened. Besides Allison and Brianna, each staff member wore a coral-colored Polo shirt with the new company logo on the front left side of the shirt and black pants, which gave the appearance of professionalism that Allison had wanted. Allison sent Jane to unlock the front doors.

Each guest that attended the private opening party had been hand-picked, and a special invitation had been mailed to each one. The maximum customer capacity was eighty people, so Allison and her team had carefully chosen a meager sixty guests for the pre party. There were several journalists, two local news anchors and their cameramen, several local politicians including Mayor Glen Ross, a few corporate leaders of local businesses, and many close friends of the girls. At the same time Jane unlocked the front door, Allison had the cover removed from the large sign outside, indicating they were now open for business. As the guests filed in, Allison greeted each one warmly, "Welcome to Computer Forensics and Bacon Confectionery."

Hostesses and staff were there to greet and seat folks, but many of them chose to stand and linger around, looking at the décor and taking in the fresh smell of bacon. Allison picked two breakfast drinks to feature as the samples for the early guests, bacon infused mocha cappuccino and apple cider with a bacon garnish. These were on trays being circulated around the room by waitresses. The muffins, cupcakes and breakfast confections were on platters, available to the visitors in mini versions. Allison couldn't help but notice the smiles on peoples' faces as they bit into the savory treats.

Brianna and Gwen worked the crowd by visiting each person and handing out business cards with the new company logo, explaining how the computer side of the business would operate. The first couple of hours went by quickly. Allison gave several interviews to the local television newscasters, explaining the unique concept of her business. At eleven o'clock the sign on the door was changed to OPEN, and the business was open to the general public.

Allison stood on her feet most of the day, greeting guests and welcoming the people of Morgan to her new store. They had ordered plenty of supplies to handle the onslaught of traffic, which kept the kitchen staff busy all day. By mid-afternoon, the rush had died down to a steady trickle of people, and Allison was able to sit down at the bar next to Brianna for a few minutes.

"What a great opening day," Allison told her.

Brianna nodded in agreement, "I'm glad we ordered business cards. I think I've passed out over three hundred of them to potential clients."

"That's great," said Allison. She glanced around the room, taking in the buzz of excitement at each table. Her eyes roamed toward the front door, and she froze as her next guest walked in. *Jack.*

"Don't look now, but we have an interesting visitor," Allison told Brianna. Of course Brianna turned immediately around to see who Allison was referring to.

"Well, well, look who we have here," Brianna mumbled to Allison.

Jane rushed to greet Jack at the door and offered him a table for two that became unoccupied. Allison knew Jane did not know the whole story with Jack, but she figured the less people knew the better. She rose and drifted over to his table, watching him as he picked up the small menu and read it.

"Welcome to Computer Forensics and Bacon Confectionery,

Mr. Roman," Allison said with a fake politeness to her voice. Jack looked up, his blue eyes quickly catching her hazel ones, which had been emphasized by the dark purple top she chose to wear. The rhinestones from her neckline sparkled against the dancing ray of lights.

Jack smiled and said, "That's a mouthful. It's a pretty interesting name for a business."

Allison smirked, "Yes, well we do try to please. What would you like to try today?"

Jack broke eye contact and glanced back down at the menu. "What do you suggest?" he asked. "I've never been to a bacon confectionery before today."

Allison bit her tongue, trying to avoid any references to pigs as she offered, "The bourbon cupcakes with maple glaze frosting and bacon sprinkles is one of my favorites."

Jack laid the menu back on the table. "That sounds good," he said, "and a lemonade to drink, please."

One of the waitresses arrived and Allison gave his order to her. "Penny will be happy to get that for you. I hope you enjoy it."

He replied, "Thank you, I'm sure I will. I had to come by to see what the big reveal was for the newest store in Morgan. My curiosity was killing me."

Allison took in his broad shoulders covered by a navy t-shirt, which emphasized his strong bicep muscles where the sleeves ended on his tanned arms.

"Yes, well, I'm glad you were able to satisfy your curiosity," she said. Her own curiosity had been piqued at what he would look like without his shirt. Catching herself staring a few seconds too long, Allison sighed, "I must see to my other guests.

Enjoy your cupcake." She left, stopping at a few other tables to talk to the customers and answer questions. She stayed busy the rest of the afternoon, not noticing when Jack left but relieved that he did.

After five p.m., the next wave of customers came in, looking for a new happy hour destination. Allison saw several people from Remco that she used to work with and greeted them warmly. She wasn't sure if they came to try her confections or to see that she had made something of herself after leaving Remco. Either way, she was happy to feed them and offer her establishment as a new gathering haunt. None of the Remco associates asked why she left Remco, but some of them did have leading questions, hoping Allison would take the bait and give them answers. She evaded the questions politely and focused on her new business, not giving a shred of evidence as to her termination from her previous employer.

By closing time at ten o'clock, all of the ladies were beat. Jane, Gwen, and the rest of the staff were leaving quickly; ready to call it a day. Allison and Brianna retired upstairs to close out the books on their first successful day as a legitimate business. In due time, the secret core of their business would be underway.

CHAPTER TWENTY-ONE

After a successful first two weeks, Allison felt she had a good group of employees that would be able to do the shift work without her being there to watch over them the entire day. Brianna had successfully lined up multiple customers for the technical side of the business. Her clients ranged from the house wife wanting to track her cheating husband's internet and email chats to the local business that needed a basic web design. They had enough business lined up to keep them busy for several months, so they hired extra technical experts to be on site. Brianna was going to drive back to Atlanta for a couple of days to wrap up some loose ends with her previous customers and pack up her condo. She decided that moving to Morgan would be more feasible, since she was now a permanent partner with Allison and business was doing well.

Ashley Porter was already on the lookout for a house or condo for Brianna to buy in Morgan. She was also looking for a small building or facility that could house a large server and miscellaneous computer-related equipment. Bree and Allison had been looking at some computer code that would work within Remco's system. With the back door open to the firewall that Allison had created before she left, it was imperative that their access remain undetected. Most of Remco's security was slightly out of date and easy to penetrate for a pro hacker such as Brianna DeVoe. Decrypting some of the program files would be a little trickier as the code language was old, and Brianna was not as familiar with some of the program structures specific to Remco. Bree wanted to do the hack herself so as not to involve any third parties. This would take some time and careful preparation and planning.

Allison would help Brianna with some of the special computer code once Brianna made her way into the primary programs, since Allison knew the systems at Remco. With Allison's intimate knowledge of the custom code structure, the two would be working closely together once the hack was fully in place. Allison was eager to get started on her part of the project but needed to wait for Bree to have everything secure first.

With Brianna in Atlanta for a few days, Allison stayed busy at the store making sure business was flowing smoothly. Gwen was fast becoming less of Allison's personal assistant and more of a store manager. She enjoyed the fact that Gwen stepped so easily into those shoes and made the job look effortless. Jane took pleasure in talking with the public and being in the front of the shop, greeting customers and gathering any local scoop that she could. Allison had recently hired on a second manager that could help run the shop in the evening, for both the kitchen side of the house and the technical side. Most of the computer work would be done during the day, however, requests would be taken in the evenings as well and then assigned the next day.

The new evening manager, Katie Dorchester, had a background in restaurant management. She had started her career years ago at Remco as an administrative assistant to a manager but left when that manager preferred to have someone younger. After leaving Remco, she struggled in the restaurant industry starting out as a waitress and worked her way up to management after several years. Allison was thrilled she joined their team and could already tell she was going to be a perfect fit.

As Allison made her way home late that evening, she spotted Jack's sports utility vehicle on the road several cars in front of hers, making his way to their neighborhood. She was reminded how close he was to her every night. Her mind started daydreaming about ways she wouldn't mind him being even closer to her at night. In her fantasy, Jack was her lover, sharing her bed and creating a future together. She could picture him holding her tight at night, small kisses nipping at her neck, and sharing small talk while they drifted off to sleep. In reality, she could never have a future with Jack. The bitterness she felt toward Remco and the havoc she was about to create would be the driving wedge between them. She might have given him a chance, if only he did not have a part in the humiliation and downfall of many careers in Morgan, South Carolina.

She watched as Jack's car went on ahead, past her house to the house he shared with his brother, Austin. With her newfound millions, money would not buy her love. It would however, give her a chance to help so many others that found themselves suddenly without a job. She turned into her own driveway, parked her Jaguar in her spacious four-car garage, and made her way into her large home. She set her purse and keys on the kitchen counter then heard the doorbell to the front door ring.

Who is calling on me at this hour? Allison was hesitant to unlock the front door, so she quickly picked up her cell phone and opened the application on her phone, showing views from the cameras she had installed outside each doorway of her house. It was similar to the security system she had installed at Computer Forensics and Bacon Confectionery. As the picture from the security camera popped up on her phone, she saw it was Jack Roman standing casually at the front door, waiting for it to be answered.

Allison saw him drive past her house earlier when she pulled into her own driveway. *He must have seen my car in his rear view mirror and double-backed.* Still dressed in her khaki dress pants and dark blue blouse that she had worn to work, Allison made her way to the front foyer. Her blonde hair had been arranged in a long blonde braid down her back, making it easier to maintain when she worked in the bakery. She turned on the outside front porch light and the foyer light then unlocked and opened the door. She kept the glass screen door closed and looked Jack up and down. He watched as she took in his physique and observed him from his casual tennis shoes, past his black work-out shorts and red, sweaty t-shirt, all the way to his eyes.

Allison had never seen Jack look so casual or wet from sweat. It was evident he had come from the gym or some athletic event in which he took part.

"Hi," Jack said through the glass door.

Allison replied somewhat hesitantly, "Hi."

Jack glanced down at the locked handle, "Do you mind if I come inside?"

Allison tentatively unlocked the screen door and pushed it open for him to enter. Jack looked up at the chandelier hanging above his head in the foyer and took in some of the furnishings from his limited view point. "Nice place you have here," he said as he stepped in further and let the door close behind him. Allison watched him carefully wondering why he chose now to pay her a visit, revealing that he did indeed know where she lived.

"What can I do for you, neighbor?" she emphasized the word neighbor, allowing Jack to know that she too knew he lived nearby and then hoped her words were not misconstrued to be something other than neighborly. She quickly added in a lighter tone, "Do you need to borrow a cup of sugar?"

Jack laughed, "No, I'm not doing any baking tonight. I saw the headlights from your car pull into the driveway, so I knew you were home. I wanted to catch you before you turned in for the night." Allison wondered if he would catch her if she decided to fall for him. In her mind every word they spoke was being taken out of context. She shook her head to try and clear any illicit thoughts and tried to focus on the real reason for his visit.

Jack continued, "I know you've been overly busy with the new bakery and all, but I was wondering if you had a free night this week if you would like to go out to dinner with me?"

Allison's mouth gaped open slightly. *Did he ask me out on a date?*

CHAPTER TWENTY-TWO

Allison tried to recover, but her brain was not able to form a reply quick enough for Jack. She told herself there would never be a future with Jack. He patiently waited while the silence grew thicker between them.

He finally started talking at the same time as Allison did, "I know..."

"Did you..?" she said at the same time.

Jack stopped so Allison could finish.

"Are you asking me out on a date?" she said in an unbelievable tone. She looked down at his long, strong legs and silently admired this new part of him that she had not seen before, since usually they were hidden under his jeans. Jack grinned, showing his perfectly straight white teeth. Allison looked back up from staring at his sculpted calves and wondered if he had had braces like she did as a teenager in order for his teeth to line up so nicely.

"Yes, I am," Jack replied. He displayed a cheeky grin and added, "At your convenience of course."

Not usually at a loss for words, Allison had to process this information and the ensuing consequences in her brain if she accepted. "I'm not sure that's such a good idea," she finally told him. "After all, you were my former employer. I think it's a conflict of interest or something."

Jack took a step closer to Allison, narrowing the gap and creeping into her personal space. He stared down into her questioning hazel eyes and said, "I think if I was still your employer it might be a conflict of interest, but since we no longer have that between us, I don't see any problem with us going out on a date. After all, we are two consenting adults."

Allison shook her head slowly and retorted, "I haven't consented to anything, yet."

Jack was not giving up that easy and closed the gap even more between them. He took her dainty left hand in his large, warm hand and inquired, "What do I have to do to get you to say yes?"

Allison's heart almost stopped. The warmth from his hand radiated up her arm straight into her soul. She could smell the deep manly perspiration on him. Her full lips were partially opened in reply, when his head lowered and he claimed her mouth with his. Jack's kiss was slow and soft, melding his lips to hers, tasting her with long, purposeful meaning. Allison was pulled in by the kiss, holding tightly to one of his hands; she placed her free hand on his shoulder, drawing him against her wielding body.

Betrayed by her lack of resistance, their lips remained locked as they explored each other's mouths in a sensual, heated manner. Allison became warmer by the minute, her breathing more labored with each intensifying second. She let go of his hand in order to wrap her own around his neck, not wanting to break the urgent connection. Jack slowly walked forward until her back was pressed up against the foyer wall. One arm was wrapped around her waist, the other hand on the nape of her neck, keeping her head firmly in place for the assault on all of her senses. Her eyes had closed, focusing on the sensations of his wet, skillful tongue. Her lone thoughts were of intense physical gratification as her body overrode any rational thoughts her brain might have had.

Several minutes later, Jack slowly eased off the kiss; nipping small bites on her swollen lips until he released them at last. Clinging tightly to her, his warm breath was labored right next to her face.

He asked in a breathless whisper, "Is that a yes?" Allison

blinked in slow recognition of what she had let happen. She put her hand on his chest and pushed him ever so slightly until she had more than a whispered breath between them.

"You're a really good kisser," she said, almost shocked at the admission that was spoken out loud. Allison could not remember the last time, if ever, she had such an instant physical connection with someone.

Jack kept his hand near her plaited hair, now playing gently with the tail of her braid. "I'd like to take you out and get to know you better," he said, smiling at her admission. His hot handsome nearness was her undoing. His intense blue eyes were focused in on her own alert hazel ones, waiting patiently for her answer.

Allison had run out of excuses and could not think of another reason why she should not go on a date with Jack. She wanted to keep her enemies close, but she wasn't sure this was what she meant. In fact, she couldn't remember why Jack was her enemy. After all, his uncle had been the one to run the company in such a caveman outdated manner. She wanted to give Jack the benefit of the doubt and hoped he was not conspiring with his brother, Austin, to bend her will to match his brother's.

Allison's mind was filled with too many thoughts at once. She did not know if Jack had an ulterior motive, nor was she willing to back out of her plan to get redemption. Her final thought before answering was one of personal gratification and self-empowerment. *After all the frogs I've kissed, I deserve a date with a fine looking specimen.*

"Yes," she finally answered his earlier question, "I'll go out with you. I'll need to check my calendar and see what night I have free." Dropping his arms reluctantly and releasing his physical contact, Jack backed away slowly widening the space between them. Allison inhaled deeply, finally catching her breath while his eyes continued to bore into her own. His chiseled face had a look of satisfaction as though the cat had finally caught the canary.

His eyes glanced back down to her swollen lips and then back up to her eyes. Allison could still taste him on her mouth; her heart beat rapidly, wondering if he was going to draw her in again for another round of tonsil hockey, not sure she would be able to turn him away if he did.

He took a deep breath and ran his hand through his own hair, then took a step back towards the door. "Thanks Allison," he said. "I look forward to it."

She nodded and opened the glass door for him. He pushed it open and walked out onto the covered brick entryway.

"I'll call you later this week," she said, slowly closing the glass screen door and latching it shut. She stood at the glass and watched as his long legs strode down the walk away from her house. He turned and waved then continued to his car. She closed and locked her large front door, leaning her back against it in a wave of exhaustion. *Good Lord, what have I done? I don't even have his phone number.*

Allison knew that obtaining his private cell phone number would be a piece of cake for a certain business partner of hers. She smiled, not knowing what Brianna would say to her about her upcoming date with a certain Remco owner. However, she did know that Brianna would go with the flow since she was always one to take advantage of any self-fulfilling opportunities herself. Allison recalled a certain professor that Brianna had certain relations with simply because the professor had a brilliant mind. Brianna had wanted to test his physical assets as well, verifying that not all geniuses used their knowledge to the best of their abilities. If Brianna had not already earned a top grade on her own intellect, her side experiments would have.

Allison couldn't wait for Brianna to get back in town. The business partners had a lot to discuss, not the first of which was the launch date of the new program that would soon be installed on the unsuspecting Remco server. Allison contemplated her new circumstances and the impact it might have on her decision making capabilities. If Jack did not think they had a conflict of interest, then Allison would need to keep Jack separate from the company, Remco. Analytically, she had no problem doing so; she hoped her pounding heart would comply.

Her last thoughts of the day focused on Jack. She saw him in a different light tonight, picturing his fine muscular legs that tapered down to his athletic shoes. Allison tried hard to not think about the upper part of his legs that disappeared under his shorts. As she slipped off her shoes and out of her work clothes, Allison Black wondered if Jack Roman was taking a cold shower to bring his blazing temperature down, as she would be doing shortly.

CHAPTER TWENTY-THREE

Looking back over how well her business had progressed in such a short time, Allison was surprised no one had questioned her ability to fund such an operation. It was well known that an anonymous winner from the area had won one of the largest jackpots in the state, but yet she was able to somehow slip under the radar as one of the prospects. In fact, she had a few people bring up the fact that her parents would be so proud if they could see her now. They had assumed that Allison's money had come from her parents' estate after their deaths. She had collected from a small life insurance claim but used most of the money to pay for their funerals, leaving little discretionary funds. She sold their house, which had a large mortgage, and their two leased cars were turned back over to the car dealer. Her parents had enjoyed life to the fullest, leaving a miniscule monetary footprint.

The anonymity suited Allison's lifestyle perfectly fine. She had never liked the public eye much and did not crave the popularity or attention like many others did. She never chased after rich doctors or lawyers, preferring to date men that were in a similar middle class structure, focusing on the professional, white-collar worker. Allison had certainly never dated an owner of a multi-million dollar company, and a few months earlier she would have considered his type out of her league.

For the first time in her life, Allison now wondered if the person she was going out with was using her for her money, or if he was trying to get her to sign a contract so she wouldn't go after his money. She had never before worried about money as an ulterior motive before going on a date. With most other men, the ulterior motive had involved physical contact. Since Jack knew the type of house she now lived in, he would know she had to have money somehow. *Why can't dating just be fun?* She had so many random thoughts and questions running continuously through her mind.

Allison had not spent a lot of time with Jane lately as girlfriends instead of coworkers. They had been so busy with getting the store up and running that she had missed their quality girlfriend time. Jane had turned out to be the perfect fit for her store front associate and was pleased with how well they worked together. Having friends working for you can sometimes be troublesome, but in this case it was smooth sailing. Allison could not be happier with her selection of Jane as one of her employees. She had not told Jane about her latest intimate dealings with Jack or about her true source of income. As flighty as Jane was, she remained one of Allison's closest friends and Allison enjoyed spending time with her. Since she would need an outfit for her upcoming date with one of the most eligible bachelors in town, she decided to invite Jane along for the shopping spree.

The bakery slowed down after most of the downtown lunch crowd meandered back to their places of work. Many of the local companies were within walking distance of the shop, so it provided a convenience for many of the downtown employees who wanted a unique and quick bite to eat during their lunch break. By mid-afternoon, Allison was ready for a break of her own and invited Jane to stroll with her to the same boutique that she and Brianna had frequented several weeks earlier.

On the brief walk down the sidewalk, Allison told Jane, "I have a date coming up this week and need to find an outfit to wear."

Jane gave Allison a sidelong glance and said, "Oh? And who is this date? Anyone I know?"

Allison hesitated slightly and said quietly, "Jack Roman." Jane stopped walking and turned to look directly at her friend.

"Jack Roman? Is that the Jack that I met at the park that day?" Jane asked.

Allison nodded, "Yes, that's the one."

Jane had a teasing look on her face, "I thought you weren't interested in him."

Allison looked down as she replied, "Well, you could say I've found him more interesting lately."

Jane laughed softly and started walking again, then abruptly stopped for the second time. "Wait a minute. Did you say Jack Roman? Is he related to the Romans that inherited Remco?"

Allison saw the bewildered expression on Jane's face and answered her honestly, "Yes, he is one of the new owners, since his uncle passed away." Allison was surprised that Jane knew about the brothers when she had no clue. *I need to listen to the news more often.*

Jane was speechless for one of the first times in her life. Allison grabbed Jane's elbow and forced her to resume their stroll towards the boutique.

"Allison, you can't be serious. I had no idea he was part of Remco. Does that make you uncomfortable after what they did to you?" Jane finally recovered but was in shock that Allison would actually go out with someone who had been part of her corporate downfall.

Allison answered her, "I was uncomfortable with the idea of going out with him at first, but it seems to be growing on me. I think I'm mature enough to put being fired behind me. After all, Jack didn't personally fire me. That was Todd's doing, and that jerk of an H.R. manager, Tomlinson."

Jane seemed to mull over Allison's explanation and said, "Well, it's your decision. I'll support you in whatever you decide to do." She smiled at Allison as they entered the entrance to the store.

With Jane's insistence, Allison ventured slightly out of her comfort zone and purchased a form fitting dress with a hemline right above the knee. It accentuated her slender frame and small curves, giving her an appearance of a petite hour-glass figure. The hand-sewn sequins formed an intricate pattern around the neck line, embellishing the bright blue color with an elegant touch. The color reminded her of the Rolex watch she did not purchase when she traveled to Atlanta. It would have been the perfect accessory. Allison thought about calling Brianna the day before and asking her to run by the store to get the watch while she was in Atlanta, but she knew Bree would be too busy trying to pack and settle her house and business in Atlanta.

Searching for the right pair of shoes would be difficult in the small town of Morgan. Her options were limited and did not include such luxury brands as Prada or Jimmy Choo. The closest thing she had to fancy footwear was a small local shop that carried a few brand name shoes. The shoe store was located on the outskirts of town away from her downtown business. After picking out her dress, they arrived back at the bakery in time for Allison to meet the delivery truck from one of her food sources. Gwen was upstairs on the phone with another vendor, and the store front kept Jane busy with a tour group that rolled up in their Greyhound bus a few minutes earlier. With all of the activity in the store it was after five before Allison had a chance to think about shopping for shoes and by then the small shoe store had closed.

Allison had not called Jack yet to let him know which day was convenient for her. She decided to keep in him suspense for as long as she could. It had been two days since he visited her that night at her house. She remembered the feel of his warm, damp lips pressed against her own. Brianna was driving back to Morgan today from Atlanta, and Allison was eager to let her know about her impending date with Mr. Roman. All she needed were the shoes and maybe a sexy new shade of lipstick.

CHAPTER TWENTY-FOUR

Allison Black and Brianna DeVoe were alone upstairs in the shop, discussing Brianna's trip to Atlanta. In the middle of a conversation about a client Brianna was bringing onboard to the new company, Allison interjected, "I have a date with Jack!" Allison told Brianna and then proceeded to tell her the entire story. It took Brianna less than twenty minutes to procure Jack Roman's cell phone number for Allison.

"You go girl!" Brianna said. "There's more than one way to skin a cat." Allison smirked, not sure if skinning was the accurate verb for what she wanted to do to Jack.

"I actually kind of like him," Allison said, shifting her eyes downward, not making eye contact with Brianna.

Allison could feel Bree's eyes upon her and glanced up to see the slight smile on Brianna's face. "Well, well, well," Bree said. "I can't say I blame you. I always take my kicks where I can get them, so I'm not one to condemn you for your choice. Jack is a fine looking specimen."

Allison smiled, grateful for her friend's honest support. If only she could convince herself that this was the right move, especially since her plan of revenge would soon be unfolding and directly affecting Remco's purse strings.

Bree seemed to read Allison's mind and said, "I assume we're still on for the installation next week. I'm close to completing the hack into Remco so you can install your code once I breech the main program files."

Allison nodded, "Yes, all systems are go. I need to test the structure of my computer code a few more times to make sure it's performing correctly, but I'll be ready by next week."

Allison had stayed up late the last few nights working on the program that will be installed on the Remco server by Brianna. Brianna grinned and then switched back to the dating conversation.

"So what are you going to wear on this big date?" Brianna asked.

Allison described her dress to Brianna and told her she had yet to find the right shoes. She also told her that she had not exactly called Jack to let him know when she was available, but thanked Brianna for providing his cell phone number.

"I think you should go with some silver, open-toed shoes; maybe something with a sparkle to accent the dress," Brianna offered. "Do you want me to ride with you to the shoe store?"

Allison shook her head and answered, "No thanks, I might run by there a little bit later and try to get something before they close for the day."

Bree suggested, "Why don't you head out now? I can hold down the fort for a while."

Allison said, "Are you sure? I know you just got here. I don't want you to be overwhelmed on your first day back."

Brianna chuckled and said, "It's not overwhelming when you're having fun. Go on. I'll be fine."

Allison replied, "Okay, I think I will. Call me if you need anything. I'll be twenty minutes away." She logged off her computer, grabbed her purse, and made her way to her car.

With the afternoon to herself, it was the first time since she had won millions that she was going shopping on her own. Since she had been mission driven the last two months, Allison had not taken time to enjoy the benefits of having unlimited resources. On her way to the shoe store, she decided to call Jack and let him know of her availability.

He picked up the phone on the third ring and sounded out of breath. "Hello, Jack Roman" he answered.

"Hi Jack. It's Allison Black," she replied.

He must not have recognized her number for his tone suddenly softened, "Oh, hey, I was thinking about you." His heavy breathing continued and Allison's curiosity was piqued as to why he was thinking of her and breathing heavily at the same time.

"Did I catch you at a bad time?" she asked.

Jack revealed, "No, I was shooting hoops at the Y with the guys. I heard my phone ringing over near the bleachers and ran to get it."

Allison said, "Don't let me interrupt your game."

Jack's breath began to calm, "Oh no, we were wrapping up. Besides, I'd rather be interrupted by a pretty lady than hang out with some sweaty guys any day."

Allison could picture him as hot and sweaty as she had last seen him with his shirt clinging tightly to his chest and arms; his hair slightly damp and ruffled from his hand running through it. "I wanted to let you know that I'm free Friday night if you'd still like to take me out," she suggested.

"Friday is great!" he said, "I can pick you up at seven."

"Seven it is. See you then," Allison replied.

"Oh, and Allison," Jack interjected, lowering his voice, "I can't wait to see you. Have a wonderful evening."

"Thanks," she said with a slight lilt in her voice, "You too."

Allison pulled in to the parking lot of the shoe store and found a spot near the entrance. The store was set on a small hill right off the main highway. The building appeared to be an old home that had been renovated several decades earlier into a quaint shoe store that offered some brands not found in the typical small town retailers. The interior walls of the old home had been removed, making way for one large open area for the displays. Each current model of footwear was on display with the corresponding boxes of various sizes beneath them. Most of the store was arranged by color with the women's shoes located near the front of the store. The sale items were upstairs on the second floor, accessed by a narrow staircase in the back of the store, which showcased the previous season selections.

Allison made a beeline to the dress shoes on the left side of the store directly past the antique cash register. The clear and silver shoes immediately caught her eyes. The small shop offered several varieties in the preferred color choice of silver, as Brianna had suggested. Once she found the perfect shoe, it was usually an issue finding the right size. Wearing a size six shoe often proved to be difficult since that size usually sold out quickly. As she looked over the different styles on the shelves, a store associate approached and asked if she needed any help.

Allison glanced at the tall black man and recognized him from her previous visits. He always had a smile on his face and offered the right amount of customer service.

"I'm looking for a size six from your silver selection of heels," Allison said. She preferred heels due to her short stature, and Jack was notably taller.

The helpful clerk said, "You're in luck. We received a new shipment in this morning, and I think I recall seeing several size sixes in the latest styles. I haven't had time to put them on the shelves, yet. I'll run to the back and see what I can find."

"That would be great," Allison said, encouraged by the friendly sales associate. She was sitting down slipping off her right shoe, when he returned carrying three boxes. He sat them on the floor near her and opened the top box.

"This one is my favorite," he stated as he pulled out a four-inch sparkling silver, open-toed heel. It had the right amount of bling on it to attract the eye, embroidered with silver sequins on the side of each heel. It was elegant and perfect.

As she tried on the shoes and walked around the area in front of the bench, Allison looked in the mirror and immediately decided the shoes were not only attractive but also exceedingly comfortable, given the height of the heel. "I'll take these," she said definitively.

The kind clerk smiled and boxed up the shoes after Allison reluctantly removed them. "I can ring you up at the register," he said. She paid for the shoes and headed back to her house. She needed to work on the code for the program that she and Bree were installing next week. The program was complex and lengthy, needing lots of testing before it would be ready. Her desire to right the wrongs of the company were evident and she was not going to back down just because the new owner was hot for her.

CHAPTER TWENTY-FIVE

"I think we need to install some big screen TVs in the customer dining area," Gwen suggested the following morning. Allison arrived early the next morning to help the kitchen staff with some new recipes. They focused on the featured cupcake for next week.

The staff had taken a vote after tasting several different varieties and decided to go with the French vanilla cupcake that had crispy bacon dipped in dark chocolate cake batter lining the bottom of the cup, deeming it the bacon black bottom cupcake.

Taking off her apron, Allison turned to Gwen and asked, "And what brought this on?"

Gwen cheerily replied, "I have the perfect idea as to what should be played on those television screens throughout the day."

Allison was curious, "I hope you don't think we should show pictures of pigs on them."

Gwen laughed and exclaimed, "No, but you're close. We should play Kevin Bacon movies!"

Allison was amused and liked the ingenuity of the idea. "I like it," she said to Gwen encouragingly. "I love his movies and can't think of a more suitable place for his movies than in our bakery."

Gwen smiled big and said, "I knew you'd love that idea. I'll order three TVs and the movie equipment today. I think the forty-eight inch size will be best."

Allison agreed by giving her blessing, "Sounds good to me. I can't wait to see the customers' reactions." Gwen left the kitchen to go upstairs to her office and place the order for the televisions. Allison was pretty sure that Gwen was humming a song from *Footloose* as she ascended the steps.

As she exited the kitchen, she walked toward the front of the store to check on the customer flow for the morning. Jane was happily greeting folks as they entered, explaining the concept of the shop to some first time visitors. She admired Jane's enthusiasm and professional courtesy to all of their guests.

I think she found her niche. Allison looked over to the bar area of the shop and noticed one of the computer technical writers sitting with a client, discussing their findings. The client looked pleased and was nodding in agreement with the techie, showing a look of satisfaction on her face. The latest marketing pitch had brought in even more customers than expected, giving Allison a chance to silently thank Lorraine Phillips for her efforts as her lead marketing executive.

In all, Allison could not be more pleased with her staff and the smooth progress towards making a hefty profit in their first quarter. She had not opened Computer Forensics and Bacon Confectionery as a tool to make money, but was thankful for the side effect, which allowed her the opportunity to employ more of the underappreciated population of the city of Morgan. Faith had shown her the accounting books recently, and Allison was thrilled with the positive numbers. Allison toyed with the idea of giving the employees a bonus for doing so well. After her meeting with Faith, she decided to proceed with the bonus this coming Friday. She would also discuss with Gwen the need for additional staffing to fill in for vacation and sick times.

She slowly climbed the stairs, taking in the delight one can only get from seeing a well laid plan come together.

Brianna was focused on one of the three computer consoles sitting on her desk. She appeared to be deep in thought as she studied the center screen.

"Good morning, Bree," said Allison as she entered the office space.

Brianna did not look up but mumbled a reply, "Hey." Allison was curious as to what could possibly hold Bree's attention enough to block out the hum drum noises of the business around her.

Allison came up behind her and whispered in her ear, "Be careful, people might think you're actually working."

Brianna laughed and finally turned around. "Hey," she said, "I was looking at some code that I'll be using next week for a potential client." She used air quote marks when she said the word client and winked at Allison.

Knowing she was referring to the hack job they would be

performing on Remco, Allison smiled. "By all means, continue," Allison said.

"By the way I found some shoes that will be perfect with my dress for tomorrow night," Allison said out loud.

Gwen looked up from her own computer screen where she had been looking up information on televisions and sound systems. "What's tomorrow night?" Gwen asked.

Bree chuckled and answered for Allison, "Our beloved owner has a hot date."

Gwen raised her eyebrows and smiled, "Oh, do tell. Who is this date? Anyone I know?"

Allison seemed to blush and answered, "Jack Roman."

Gwen's smile faltered, "Really? You're going out with him on a real date?" Allison knew it must look bad to those who knew she had been fired from Remco because Jack was one of the new owners of the company.

"Yes, I'm going on a real date with him," Allison said. "I figured I could rise above the stigma from a few months ago and behave as a mature adult."

Gwen looked a bit skeptical, but seemed impressed, "Wow, you never cease to amaze me, Allison! Best of luck to you."

Jane chose to walk up the stairs at that moment and asked, "Why is Allison amazing?"

Gwen replied, "She's going on a date with Jack Roman. It doesn't even faze her that his company fired her."

Jane smiled, "Oh, that. You should see the sexy dress she's going to wear. He won't be able to keep his hands off of her."

Brianna laughed and added, "He won't stand a chance." Allison was getting embarrassed by the teasing as her cheeks began to get a slight pink tint to them.

Jane asked, "Where is he taking you on this date?" Allison had not thought about where they would go.

She answered with a slight shrug of her shoulders, "I'm not sure. I guess the standard dinner date to some place nice."

Brianna interjected her thoughts, "Jack Roman doesn't strike me as your standard date kind of guy. I bet he'll have something interesting planned." Allison looked around at each of the ladies from Gwen to Jane then to Brianna.

They all had the same teasing look and seemed to enjoy that Allison was experiencing some mild discomfort. "Well if he wants to go rock climbing, I'll have to wear different shoes," Allison said sarcastically. The ladies all laughed, reminding Allison that her lot in life had brought together a diverse and dynamic group of wonderful friends.

CHAPTER TWENTY-SIX

Friday was finally here, and Allison started getting butterflies in her stomach early in the day. The anticipation of the evening's event had her second guessing her attire for the evening and even the date itself. *What if he does takes me rock climbing? I need a backup outfit ready in case we do something less formal.*

She mentally walked through her closet, trying to recall each piece of her wardrobe for a suitable solution to a more physically challenging date. The last time she had done anything strenuous was several years earlier when a small group from her information technology department at Remco had gone hiking as a team building exercise. She had worn jeans that day and found them to be overly hot and constrictive. Allison did not own any hiking shorts or boots. Her athletic wardrobe was limited to yoga pants, t-shirts, and tennis shoes, most of which were worn around the house on the weekends and not for actual exercise.

Once again, she found herself needing to shop for clothes; even though she knew these clothes might not ever get worn. Looking across her desk she spotted Gwen and decided since she had previously taken Brianna and Jane, she would ask Gwen to tag along on this shopping excursion. Plus it would give her a chance to get to know Gwen in a more informal setting, not just as a business associate.

"Hey, Gwen," Allison said, getting Gwen's attention, "I need to go shopping today to find a few casual pieces of clothing. Would you like to go with me?"

Gwen looked surprised and then recovered quickly answering, "Sure, I'd love to."

"Great, I know it's early in the day, but I'd like to try and beat the lunch crowd to the store," Allison explained.

They grabbed their purses and headed down the stairs and out the back door to Allison's Jaguar. "I heard about a new outdoor store that is geared toward hiking equipment and clothing," Allison said. "I'd like to try there first. Have you ever been to that store? I can't remember the name of it."

Gwen thought for a minute and then replied, "I've passed by it. I think it's called *The Great Escape*. I've never been inside." Gwen settled into the passenger seat, admiring Allison's choice of car.

Gwen remarked, "I don't think I've ever sat inside a Jaguar."

Allison grinned, "I think we're both doing a lot of firsts these days."

The girls arrived at the store as a man was unlocking the front door and turning the closed sign over to show that it was now open. He grinned and opened the door for them saying, "Welcome. Come on in." He appeared to be in his thirties and remarkably fit. After glancing around the store, it was evident he was wearing some of the merchandise as a form of advertisement. His khaki shorts came to his knees and had several pockets, while his grey t-shirt bore the logo of the store. The hiking boots he wore were dark brown with black trim and came slightly above his ankles, showing thick grey socks that were made for comfort and warmth.

"Can I help you find anything in particular?" he asked with a cheerful attitude and big grin.

Allison thought that he reminded her of a Cabbage Patch Kid, with his short blond hair, large brown eyes and round face. His torso was lean and fit though, not quite matching the soft curves of his cheeks. Gwen was staring at him, clearly taken in by his physical appearance.

Allison answered him, "I'm looking for some clothes that I can wear hiking or rock climbing."

"Our ladies outdoor wear is right over here," he said, leading them in the direction of middle of the shop past the displays of camping gear.

"Thank you," replied Allison. "Is it alright if I try on several items in your dressing room?"

He nodded his head and said, "Feel free to try on as many

things as you like. My name is Ben, if you need anything." Ben left the two ladies to browse the clothing racks, while he attended to the front counter in order to ready the computer register for the day.

"Wow," Gwen whispered to Allison. "Ben is pretty fine." Allison smiled and continued to sort through the clothing racks, moving the hangers of each garment to see the one behind it. She selected several shirts from the hanging rack and turned to spot the shorts on a display shelf.

"I'm going to try some of these clothes on. I'll be back in a few minutes," Allison said.

Allison emerged from the dressing room several minutes and many outfits later, spotting Gwen Brewer near the shoe department. Ben and Gwen were laughing together as he was helping her try on a pair of waterproof hiking shoes. He touched Gwen's calf as he helped glide the shoe in place on her right foot. Allison could sense something brewing between the two of them. She hung back for a minute and watched the playful flirting from both parties. It was refreshing to watch a relationship form in a natural easy manner, unlike her recent relationships lately.

Clearing her throat as she approached Ben and Gwen, Allison neared the couple with a huge smile on her face, clearly showing her approval. They both looked up startled and embarrassed from being caught in such an intimate, yet innocent moment. "Are you getting some shoes?" Allison asked Gwen.

Gwen was slightly blushing and replied, "I might. What do you think of these?" Allison liked the style of shoe and sat down in the chair next to Gwen, laying her garments across an empty chair.

"I love them," Allison said, "I may try on some as well. Do you have them in a size six?"

Ben let go of Gwen's leg by that time and stood up answering, "Yes, we do in the tan and blue colors."

Allison said, "Perfect." As soon as Ben had disappeared in the back room of the store to find the shoe, Allison encouraged Gwen in a soft voice, "He's cute, Gwen. You should get his number."

Gwen's jaw slightly dropped and said so low that Allison could barely hear her, "Really? Do you think I should?" Allison felt a bit like Brianna as she said, "Sure, what's the worst that can happen? You're already not dating him, so if you continue to not date him, the status quo remains the same. Go for it!"

Gwen smiled and whispered, "We'll see."

Ben returned with the shoes and helped Allison try them on her dainty feet. She liked the fact that the shoe had open holes throughout and yet provided comfort like a tennis shoes. It was water proof and considered fashionable for the outdoor girl. "I'll take this pair," Allison said, "and these clothing items."

Ben nodded and said, "I'll take them up front for you." He turned to Gwen and asked, "Did you want to buy those shoes as well?"

Gwen nodded, "Yes, thanks." He boxed up both pairs of shoes and grabbed Allison's clothes, carrying all the items to the front register.

Allison was rung up first and upon completing the transaction stated, "I need to go make a phone call. I'll meet you in the car, Gwen." She winked at Gwen as she grabbed her bag and left the store, giving Gwen her privacy with Ben.

Several minutes passed as Allison waited in the car until Gwen showed up and entered the passenger side of the red Jaguar. "Well?" Allison asked.

Gwen smiled coyly and pulled out her cell phone, "We not only swapped numbers, but we're going out tonight for a late movie."

"Wow!" Allison exclaimed, "You work fast! Way to go, Gwen." Gwen smiled and looked down, staring at her cell phone at Ben's number.

She dropped Gwen off at the shop and told her to call if anything should come up that needed her attention. She was going to see to a few more last minute details before her own date that night. Reflecting on the budding romance of a new couple, Allison's spirits were emboldened as she contemplated her own potential liaison with Jack Roman.

CHAPTER TWENTY-SEVEN

It had been ages since Allison had had a pedicure and since she was wearing the stunning silver shoes with an open toe, she wanted her feet to look nice. One of her last minute tasks included a stop at the local nail salon. With her toes polished to a deep, glossy red, Allison had a fresh kick in her step on the way to the last stop on her agenda. The lingerie store in the mall carried everything from bras and panties to the exotic and revealing nightgowns and teddies. It always amazed Allison how expensive the items were that had the least amount of material. With her bank account status now greater than ninety-nine percent of the people in the state of South Carolina, Allison no longer had to look at the price tags.

Being logically minded Allison did not go straight for the frills and fringes of the sexy lingerie. She opted for the simple and comfortable matching sets of underwear that would flatter her figure and be attractively stylish. Even though people did not see the lingerie under her clothes, it always made Allison feel a little prettier and confident knowing that she wore beautiful undergarments. She wanted to look and feel her best for tonight's date. She spotted a beautiful silk nightgown near the register in the back of the store. It was a long deep red, sleeveless nightgown with beading around the plunging neckline. Most of her nightgowns consisted of the cotton variety, with little emphasis on flair. As a last minute splurge, she bought the beautiful item along with the many matching sets of unmentionables she had picked out from the front of the store.

With her task list completed, Allison headed home to get ready for her big night, whatever that might entail. As soon as she entered her house, she threw her newly purchased undergarments and hiking clothes in the washing machine then hit the shower, washing her long blonde hair and shaving her short sculpted legs. She followed up the shower with a long lavender-scented bubble bath soaking in as much relaxation as possible, since the tension and anxiety had been building all week. She gently dried off after the relaxing soak and threw her clothes in the dryer when her doorbell rang.

She froze then looked at her clock in a panic. It was only six o'clock. *Surely Jack is not an hour early.* Allison wrapped her hair in the towel and grabbed her robe, cinching the belt tightly around her waist. She picked up her cell phone and opened the security icon to see who was at her front door. *Brianna.* Allison let out a huge sigh of relief and ran to the front of the house to open the door.

"What are you doing here?" Allison asked as she let Brianna in the front door. Brianna smiled and brought her hands from behind her back, revealing a small wrapped box with a tiny silver bow on top.

"I thought you could use this for tonight," Bree said, handing her the gift. Allison took the small box and walked over to the sofa so she could sit down to open it. Bree sat beside her and watched in anticipation.

"What did you get me?" Allison asked, unpeeling the last of the tape to reveal a jewelry box from Cartier.

Bree smiled and commanded, "Open it." Allison cautiously lifted the top of the box to reveal the coveted Rolex watch with the bright blue face and white gold band that she desperately wanted from Atlanta. The four small diamonds set within the watch face twinkled with the catch of the light.

"Oh wow!" Allison exclaimed. "I can't believe you got me this watch. I absolutely love it."

She held the watch box with one hand and wrapped her other arm around Brianna's neck. "You're the best! I'm in shock. How did you have time to get it?" Allison inquired.

Brianna's face was bright with the pleasure she received from surprising her friend. "I called ahead on my way to Atlanta this past week, and the sales associate had it wrapped up and ready to go when I arrived. Do you like it? I thought it would go perfect with your blue dress you're wearing tonight."

Allison sat back and stared at the watch again. "It's perfect. Thank you so much. I owe you big time," Allison told her sincerely.

"Have a good time tonight, get it? Time?" Bree chuckled at her own joke. "Don't do anything I wouldn't do."

Allison laughed and told her, "There's not much you wouldn't do, so that leaves me a lot of options."

Bree said, "That's true. Have fun. Be yourself. I'll talk to you tomorrow."

She rose and walked toward the door. "Thanks again," Allison said, "I'll be at the shop tomorrow, so I'll fill you in on all the details."

Allison let Brianna out the front door, locked it, and ran back to the master bathroom to continue getting ready for her night out with Jack. She blew dry her hair and rolled it in long soft flaxen curls down her back and brushed her straight white teeth. She rubbed lotion all over her freshly washed body, making her skin silky smooth. She carefully slipped into her new blue strapless bra and the matching, "no show" bikini panties that were warm from the dryer. As she applied her make-up, she was reminded of the countless formals she attended in college with her sorority sisters. The girls always wore beautiful dresses and had their hair and make-up flawlessly applied. Although this wasn't a prom or formal, Allison had the same butterflies of anticipation as she did during other significant events.

She donned her beautiful blue dress and once again admired the sequins that outlined the rounded neckline of the dress. The sequined pattern was about one inch wide and swirled in different directions, creating an eye-catching effect so she would not need a necklace to embellish it. She slipped the beautiful Rolex on her left wrist and snapped it in place. It hung slightly loose on her arm much like a bangle bracelet and had already been set to the right time. *I might have to resize it to fit tighter when I have time.* For now, the watch would do wonderfully, and it perfectly accented her stunning bright blue dress. She selected diamond studs as her earrings, keeping them simple as to not detract from her watch. At five minutes before seven, Allison slipped on her new silver shoes and applied a rose shade of lipstick.

She grabbed her silver clutch bag that had seen many formal events and put her license, phone, credit card, and lipstick inside. Her doorbell rang for the second time that evening. This time Allison did not check her phone, being sure it was Jack at the door.

CHAPTER TWENTY-EIGHT

Jack cleaned up strikingly nice; however, he almost reminded Allison of his brother Austin, in a grey Brooks Brother suit, dark blue patterned tie and black, lace-up dress shoes. His white collared, button-up shirt was neatly pressed and she glimpsed a cuff link peeking out from beneath the jacket sleeve. The one give-away that this was Jack and not Austin was his hair, slightly ruffled, most likely from a nervous hand gesture that he used when running his hand through his hair. His hair showed more of the natural red highlights with the setting sun behind him as he filled up her front doorway. The man truly was a work of art.

"Hi," Allison greeted him, as she opened the glass screen door for him to enter. Although she had the more casual outfit picked out in case it was needed, she was so glad she had chosen the more elegant blue dress to wear. By the look on Jack's face, her suspicions were confirmed.

His mouth hung slightly open as his eyes grew large. "Wow," he said, "you look gorgeous." His eyes roved up and down the full length of her petite frame several times, not able to take in all of her at once. His wide blue eyes were a darker shade of blue against the twilight sky. Allison noticed that his eyes kept stopping at her neckline, where the sequins played next to the skin of her chest, pulling his vision toward her bosom like a magnet. As a true gentleman, he quickly recovered and brought his enchanting blue eyes up to meet the sharp gaze of her eyes.

"You look pretty nice yourself, Jack Roman," Allison stated, clearly impressed with this side of Jack. As he stepped into the foyer, the full-length glass door shut softly behind him. She appreciated a man being on time and even more so the effort he spent getting ready for the date. She was glad she was not the only one that went out of the way to look extra special for this evening. His suit coat was a perfect fit, yet it managed to enhance his broad shoulders, reminding Allison of his tanned strong arms hidden beneath the sleeves. After eyeing each other for several moments, Jack stepped forward and bent down to greet Allison with a kiss. She was caught off guard and wasn't expecting an intimate moment so quickly into the date and turned her head at the last moment, causing Jack to connect his lips with her cheek.

Already the date was off to an awkward start, slightly embarrassing Allison for being so demure. "So, um, what are the plans for tonight?" she asked, stumbling around to find the right words to ease the situation.

Jack put his hands in his pockets and cleared his throat, giving himself time to collect his thoughts and regain his composure. The move prevented him from touching her any further. She had clearly set the boundaries, and he did cross over them. "I made reservations at The Palmetto Club," Jack answered. "Have you ever been there?"

"I didn't know you were a member there. I'd love to go to The Palmetto Club!" Allison responded enthusiastically.

"My uncle joined years ago, so Austin and I took over his membership when he passed away. I've been there for a couple of business luncheons during the day, but I haven't tried their dinner courses, yet. I've been told they're amazing," Jack replied.

"Let me grab my keys to lock up the house," Allison said, walking back toward the kitchen counter where she had laid her keys earlier. Jack waited patiently by the front door and then opened it, stepping out onto the brick landing. Allison followed him out the front door, closed it, and locked it with her house key. He offered his arm to her as they strolled to his awaiting

SUV.

He unlocked his vehicle with his electronic key fob and walked her to the passenger door, opening it for her to enter. Gone were the days of leaning over to unlock the driver's door, so Allison waited while Jack walked around and let himself in the driver's side. His car had been recently cleaned and a new car smell lingered in the air. She gave him a few more imaginary points for taking the time to have his ride detailed for her benefit. As far as first impressions on a first date, Jack was pulling out all the stops. Allison hoped it was truly for her favor and not for an ulterior motive.

The Palmetto Club was set back away from the main street to allow for a large parking lot and adjacent church building. The outside reminded Allison of the ornate estate homes with stunning features, including lots of stone work and columns at the front entrance. Irregular roof lines and wrap around porch added to the charm of this southern legacy. The large bay window on the front of the three story house encompassed the former drawing room, now featured as one of the smaller dining areas of the club. The second floor was mostly offices or storage space, and the third floor held an enormous ball room previously used by the initial owners back in the eighteen hundreds to host scores of parties. Club members were now encouraged to use it for large private events such as weddings or graduation parties. When Allison attended lunch there several years earlier, most of the patrons were in business attire. As they arrived tonight she noticed how formal many of the night time members were dressed.

The Palmetto Club was a members only establishment similar to a country club but without a golf course. It was located in a house built in 1895 in downtown Morgan right in the middle of the cultural district, having been transformed from an estate house into a prestigious facility encompassing private dining rooms, a cocktail lounge, banquet rooms, and a large ballroom. Unique ornamentation and distinctive appearance of the house were owed to the Queen Anne architectural style from the eighteenth century. Some of the features included a tower room, dormers, bay windows, and corbelled chimneys.

The private dining establishment was unmatched in the fine food category, with attention to detail not merely in the private chef's gourmet food but in the surrounding atmosphere as well. They had a strict dress code, enforcing collared shirts and jackets for the men; no jeans were allowed, explaining Jack's attire for the evening. Allison had attended a luncheon there one time as a guest for a non-profit presentation regarding the need for volunteers in an upcoming neighborhood transformation project. She had to take a moment to recall her dining manners from her course she took in college on etiquette. Allison was secretly pleased to be in the exclusive dining facility and was eager to put her etiquette skills back to good use again, especially in the company of such a fine looking escort.

They were shown to a private table set for two set in the smaller back room of the house, typically used for more intimate settings. Tables were covered in a white table cloth, small votive candles, fresh flowers, and a full table setting of silverware, porcelain plates, and crystal glasses. The hostess gently laid the cloth napkins in their laps after they were seated and handed them each a customized daily menu, based on the chef's preference with seasonal offerings.

Trying not to stare at Jack constantly, Allison looked around and admired the interior design of the room. A brick fireplace was centered along the opposite wall, providing warmth and dancing light across the dimly lit room. The walls were a light oak wide-paneled wood, leading up to plaster ceiling tiles that were intricately carved into large two dimensional squares. The carpet appeared to be a more modern plush touch with an antique design incorporated into the floral pattern. "This room is beautiful," Allison stated.

Jack replied, "Yes, it is. Look at the lights in the wall sconces. I bet they didn't have ceiling lights back when this house was first built." The wall sconces looked as old as the house but flickered strong with the electricity running through to each bulb.

The waiter appeared at their table dressed in all black with a crisp long white apron tied around his waist hanging to his shins. He carried a water pitcher and filled one of the goblets on the table for each of them and said, "Good evening. My name is Zack. I'll be taking care of you this evening. May I offer you a beverage or a cocktail before supper this evening?"

Allison was not a frequent drinker, so waited to see what Jack ordered. "What types of white wines do you have available?" Jack asked. Allison was surprised that he asked specifically for white wines. She did not care for red wines so wondered if he knew this about her.

"We have Pinot Grigio, Chardonnay, Moscato, and Riesling. All of them come from a local winery that is a short distance from here," the waiter replied.

"We'll start with a bottle of Pinot Grigio, please," Jack ordered.

The waiter nodded and left as Jack asked Allison quietly, "Does that sound okay to you?"

"Yes," she replied, "I like most white wines as long as they're not too dry."

"I thought as much," he said explaining, "since you had a sweet tooth for the bakery. Most ladies that enjoy that much sugar like the sweeter wines." Well that explained his reasoning behind it, putting Allison's paranoid mind to rest momentarily.

Allison smiled at him asking, "So do you know the ladies pretty well then?"

Jack shook his head no, laughing, "Far from it. I know my wines."

Allison was curious to know more about Jack since she only had a few encounters with him that did not focus around her termination from Remco. "So tell me, Jack Roman, what did you do before your uncle died and you inherited his company?"

"You might not believe me," Jack said, "but I was sort of a detective, like I told you when I first met you. I worked with law enforcement agencies to track down hard to find criminals."

Allison slowly comprehended what he was saying. "You were a bounty hunter?" she asked with a look of pure astonishment on her face.

CHAPTER TWENTY-NINE

"I guess you could call it that," Jack said. "I prefer private investigator." He grinned at Allison as the waiter arrived with the bottle of wine and a chiller to place on the table. He uncorked the wine and allowed Jack to sniff it. Then he poured a small amount into a crystal wine goblet for Jack to sample. As Jack swirled the wine around in the bottom of the glass, Jack noticed the residue on the glass and took in the aroma of the grapes. He took a small sip and let it sit in his mouth for several seconds to fully appreciate the flavor.

He swallowed and said, "Very nice, thank you," indicating to the waiter to pour wine into Allison's goblet.

After filling both glasses, Zack asked them if they had decided on their appetizer or dinner order. Allison had not even so much as looked at the menu, so she had no idea what the options were. She had been too busy admiring the room and her date.

"Can you give us a few minutes?" Jack asked him, noting Allison's frantic look of bewilderment.

"Take your time," Zack replied.

"I hear the bourbon chicken coated in a pecan crust is excellent," Jack offered. Allison perused the menu, trying to take in all of the fancy terminology for the exquisite dishes. The chicken did sound appealing.

"Did you want an appetizer?" she asked Jack. "I see they have brie cheese with fruit, and I love brie cheese. We could share it if you like."

Jack glanced down and read the description of the appetizer. "That sounds great," he said. "Let's get it." The waiter came back a few minutes later and took their appetizer and dinner orders, both of them having decided on the bourbon chicken as their main entrée.

"So you were a bounty hunter, or should I say, private investigator?" Allison asked as she sipped her wine and studied Jack's chiseled features. She could get used to looking across a table at this view every night. "I bet you had some interesting people that you apprehended," she added.

Jack recalled some of the more intense cases that he had been involved with in the lower part of the state, where he resided until he relocated to Morgan. "I think people forget that cameras and computers are everywhere these days," he said. "It made my job easier when they used credit cards in their own name or shopped at the same store repetitively. Many criminals are not the brightest."

Allison enjoyed learning about Jack's previous line of work

and did not hesitate to jump into the more personal side of his life. "How did you and Austin manage to inherit this large company from your uncle? Did he not have any children?"

Jack answered her, "Uncle Cliff and Aunt Rose never had children. Our mom was his sister. We came to visit them here in Morgan every summer until our parents divorced. Our dad left when we were eleven and he's been out of the picture since then. Uncle Cliff and Aunt Rose helped mom by paying for our boarding school and then college in Charleston, South Carolina at MUSC. Mom died of cancer a few years ago, followed by Aunt Rose's death a few months later. When Uncle Cliff passed away, we didn't know he had listed us as his heirs, but I guess we shouldn't have been surprised."

"So you haven't seen your dad in all these years?" she asked, knowing she was diving into a deep personal matter again but unable to stop herself.

"Actually," Jack said, "he was one of the first people I ever tracked down. I wanted to know where he ran off to that he had to leave a wife and two young boys." Allison listened attentively as she paid close attention to each word Jack spoke. "I found him in Las Vegas driving a tour bus, but he had a gambling and alcohol addiction. He didn't recognize me when I rode on his bus one day. He looked about twenty years older than his age. I didn't introduce myself. His life had turned out sad and pitiful. Austin didn't go with me because he didn't want anything to do with our father. Dad died in a car wreck a few months after I found him. They said alcohol had been involved."

"I'm sorry to hear that, Jack," said Allison. "My parents both died as well, in a plane crash. It's hard not having them here to talk to," she confided.

The waiter arrived with their brie cheese appetizer with fresh strawberries, blueberries, mandarin oranges, and small toasted baguettes. A small ramekin of raspberry preserves was on the end of the long skinny platter along with a short rounded cheese knife. Allison looked down at all the utensils and wasn't sure exactly which one to use for a cheese appetizer. She remembered to start on the outside with her silverware and work her way in, so she picked up the small fork on the far left. Jack followed suit, and they served up the brie on the small plates stacked on top of their dinner plates.

"What was your major at MUSC?" Allison asked changing the subject to something lighter, wondering what type of degree would lead to being a bounty hunter.

"Pre-med," answered Jack as he bit off a piece of the baguette loaded with cheese and raspberry preserves. Allison Black choked on her small bite and quickly reached for her water glass.

CHAPTER THIRTY

"How did you go from pre-med to bounty hunting?" Allison asked the burning question to Jack after she recovered from choking.

"Austin and I had always talked of going into medical practice together," Jack explained. "We were going to study pediatrics, but some events happened and Austin dropped out of the program. I didn't want to continue without him; it didn't interest me to go through such a long process by myself. So we both transferred to the College of Charleston where we pursued a degree in political science. Austin started leaning towards becoming a lawyer, but I wasn't sure that was a good fit for me." Allison wondered what events would change someone's goal that drastically but tried not to appear too nosey and left the question unasked.

"So did Austin go to law school?" Allison asked, trying to stay on a safer subject.

Jack nodded, "He did. In fact he graduated at the top of his class and passed the bar exam on the first try. He worked for the state public defender for a while until Uncle Cliff passed away."

Allison then had to state the obvious to Jack, "So you went from pre-med to political science to bounty hunter. That doesn't seem like a natural progression of events."

Jack finished up the last of the cheese as the waiter came to collect the used dishes and placed a small salad in front of each one.

Zack brushed the crumbs off of the table into his hand with a small tool, leaving the linens fresh and clean looking. "Your entrees will be right out," the waiter told them, while removing their appetizer plates and used utensils.

They both took bites from their salad and ate in silence for a few minutes. Jack looked Allison in the eyes and held her gaze for several seconds before he answered. "It's funny how circumstances change your direction," he started. "I was walking in downtown Charleston near the straw market when a fellow ran by me knocking several other bystanders out of his way. I could see a police officer coming towards me, giving chase to the man. I turned and caught up with the offender and held him in place until the policeman arrived. He had been caught stealing and still had a lady's purse in his hands. The policeman thanked me and told me they could use more citizens like me. After that I found out how much money could be made, and I was hooked." The waiter returned carrying their delicious smelling chicken entrées.

Each plate had a pecan-encrusted, succulent chicken breast

cooked to a golden perfection. Young asparagus spears were seasoned in salt and olive oil and placed delicately over the small mound of mashed red potatoes. The dish had been topped off with a sprinkling of parsley.

Allison cut and bit into her chicken, savoring the flavor and moistness of the first bite. "Mmmm," she said, "this chicken is so tender."

Jack also took a bite and agreed, "Yes, it is. Good choice. Everything I've tried here is great. They must have an excellent chef." He chewed his bite slowly, watching Allison as she placed another bite into her open mouth. His eyes stayed fixated on her mouth as she chewed. Allison glanced up and caught him staring at her, causing him to look quickly down at his plate.

He seemed to be genuinely interested in Allison, or at least she had not seen an ulterior motive present itself, yet. She sipped her wine, and decided she would cut to the chase. "What exactly are you and Austin doing at Remco?" she asked abruptly.

Jack set his fork down and picked up his own wine glass before answering, "That's a good question. Neither of us has run a company before now, so we've been trying to get a handle on the whole process for the last few months. As you know, Remco operated on a good old boys' system that we are working on remedying. Austin is looking at the legal aspects of the company while I've been working with the people, getting to know the structure of each department." Allison nodded, listening to his explanation. "I'm really sorry about what happened to you, Allison. As info, we did replace Tomlinson with a new manager recently," Jack told her. Allison gave a small smirk and took another sip of her Pinot Grigio.

"I'm glad to hear it," she said almost bitterly. "Hopefully the company will make a smooth turn around rather quickly." She had crossed her legs when she was first seated, but for the first time all evening she sat back in her chair and swung her top leg back and forth with nervous energy, dangling her new shoe from her toe feeling the heel of it rock up and down with the motion of her leg.

Jack told her bluntly, "I have to say that I'm glad you were fired." Her leg suddenly stopped dead still as Allison sat her wine glass down rather hard and stared at Jack.

CHAPTER THIRTY-ONE

"Excuse me?" Allison asked, sure she had heard him wrong.

Jack Roman repeated what he said, "I'm glad you were fired. After all, if not for that I might never have met you, and we might never have had this wonderful opportunity."

"Oh," Allison replied, feeling somewhat flattered in a backhanded way. Jack finished eating his meal, catching Allison's eye often. Allison did the same, enjoying the asparagus and then the potatoes.

As she finished Jack asked her, "Do you always eat one food at a time? I noticed you ate your chicken, then asparagus, then potatoes."

Allison laughed, "Yes, I do. My mom used to tease me about it. I didn't think other people noticed."

Jack's tone turned deeper, his eyes locked with hers as he told her, "I notice everything about you, Allison Black."

The waiter, Zack, approached and heard her name mentioned and asked, "Are you Allison Black, the owner of that new bacon shop?" Allison looked away from Jack and for the first time noticed other couples had joined them in the room at various tables. She had been so lost in the conversation with Jack Roman that she had tuned out the world around her. Allison saw that many of the ladies were dressed in boutique style dresses or pant suits. The men all had on suits and ties. This was the upper crust of Morgan society and for the first time in her life, Allison felt she actually belonged here.

I need to look into having my own membership here. "Yes," she answered the waiter, "that's me."

"Wow," the waiter said, "I love that place, especially the free Wi-Fi." He appeared to be in his early twenties, probably working as a waiter to pay for his way through college. Zack stood about five foot nine inches tall and had a slim figure and pleasant face. His brown eyes were suddenly full of awe as if he had spotted a celebrity.

Allison had not had such public recognition before now, and it somewhat shocked her that someone would be that impressed with her business. "Thanks," she said simply.

"Would you like dessert or coffee this evening?" he asked, reverting back to his waiter mode as he handed them the small dessert menu.

Allison smiled, "Of course," she said, "this is my favorite part of the meal."

Jack Roman grinned and looked down at the menu. Zack left them to study the dessert menu for a few minutes while he checked on his other nearby tables. Allison spotted the fried Krispy Kreme donut in a raspberry butter sauce, topped with vanilla bean ice cream and pointed it out to Jack.

"Would you like to share? Or should I order my own?" he teased her.

"We can share," she said, "but I get the first bite."

Zack came back over to take their order. Jack ordered the donut for two and a bottle of Moscato for their dessert wine. Allison loved Moscato; it was one of her favorite sweeter wines. The waiter cleared their dinner dishes and returned shortly with their dessert wine. He executed the same process with the wine as he did earlier, allowing Jack to sample the wine first.

"Well, Miss Black, I've done a lot of talking tonight about myself. Tell me a little bit about you. How did you get interested in the baking business?" Jack asked her. Allison hesitated, knowing that he was a private investigator; she wondered how much Jack already knew about her.

"My grandmother was a baker. She loved to do all the specialty desserts, especially around the holidays," Allison told him. Then she picked up her wine glass and sipped the Moscato. It went down smooth, too smooth.

"Did she have an affinity towards bacon?" he asked.

Allison laughed, "No, I came up with that one on my own. I've always loved bacon. Who knew that it would become such a hit around here?"

She enjoyed talking with Jack and getting to know him better. Allison told him more about the concept of baking with bacon when the chef arrived at their table delivering their fried donut in person. "Good evening, Mr. Roman," he nodded his head toward Jack. "I understand we have a rather famous baker dining with us this evening. Is this correct?" the chef asked as he turned toward Allison. He was wearing a white double-breasted chef coat, black and white checkered chef pants, and a short white chef hat. She could tell he enjoyed his job as he was quite heavy around the middle.

As he sat the dessert plate down in front of Allison, she answered him, "I don't know about being famous, but I do own the store Computer Forensics & Bacon Confectionery. It's down the street not too far from here. My name is Allison Black." She held out her hand to shake the chef's hand.

"It's a pleasure to meet you, Miss Black," the portly cook said, smiling while holding her hand in his large warm one. "I am Chef Samuel. Please enjoy the dessert I have created for you tonight. It is a one of a kind, much like your bourbon cupcake with maple glaze frosting and bacon sprinkles, which happens to be one of my favorites." The fried donut had been sliced in two and showed grill marks where it had been seared before being drenched in a butter raspberry sauce.

"It looks heavenly," Allison said.

"Thank you," Jack told the chef.

"I hope you will become a regular here. It would be my honor to cook for you again," Chef Samuel said to Allison. The chef returned to the kitchen as their waiter approached asking if they needed anything else.

"It looks great," said Jack. "I think we're all set." Allison pushed the plate toward the center of the table, so that Jack could easily get a bite of the scrumptious concoction. True to her word, she snagged the first bite.

CHAPTER THIRTY-TWO

The four course meal and a few glasses of wine were settling heavy on Allison's stomach. She was starting to feel sleepy, regretting that last glass of Moscato. Jack's vehicle was warm and the motion of the car was not helping her situation. *It would be so easy to close my eyes and relax.* Allison struggled with staying alert, truly enjoying Jack's company. *Maybe if I close them for a minute.* She was listening to the music playing softly on the radio while he drove them back towards Morgan Country Club Estates.

When she next opened her eyes, she was surprised to find that she was lying on a couch in an unknown room. A warm throw had been placed on her while she slept. She sat up slowly, taking in the dimly lit den that had dark brown leather sofas, several nice pieces of art on the wall, and a leather recliner in the corner in which Jack was sitting. He had removed his coat and tie and had unbuttoned the top few buttons on his shirt. He was watching her from his comfortable position across the room.

Allison stretched and removed the warmth of the throw blanket. "I'm sorry I feel asleep," she said softly, watching his eyes on her as she adjusted herself on the couch.

"You were sleeping so soundly; I didn't want to wake you," Jack said, his voice an octave lower than usual.

She blushed slightly, knowing that he must have carried her in from the car and then watched her sleep. "Is this your house?" she asked, breaking eye contact and looking around. It was decorated with exceptional taste considering two bachelors resided there.

"Yes," he said, "I didn't want to be accused of breaking into your house again."

Allison had almost forgotten about that, but it spurned her next question, "Where is Austin?" Jack rose out of the chair he had occupied and walked over to sit next to Allison on the couch. "He's out of the country, taking care of some shipping business," he told her, lifting up her hand and kissing the back of it. She watched as his lips brushed her skin, creating goose bumps down her arms.

"Are you cold?" he asked, noticing her slight shiver.

"No," she replied.

He leaned closer, wrapping his arms around her, bringing her against the warmth of his chest. He rested his chin on top of her head and told her softly, "I enjoyed this evening with you, Allison." She had wrapped her arms around his torso, savoring the closeness of his body, feeling his breath as he exhaled. He drew away slightly and lifted her chin so he could look into her eyes, his own filled with a deep passion. His head descended, covering her mouth with his own in a sensual assault on her lips. Allison had waited all week to feel those lips against hers, knowing the kind of physical pleasure that would enliven her senses. His kiss deepened as he leaned into her, laying her back against the couch with his strong body covering hers. His right hand caressed her arm, removing all traces of the prior goose bumps. His other arm held her neck as they descended into an intimate position, continuing the onslaught of taking and giving with their lips and tongue.

Allison could feel her body heat rising, along with her heart rate as she experienced the dizzying sensations. She no longer knew if it was the wine or the passion causing her head to spin. She felt Jack's hand move from her arm to her thigh, continuing the caressing movement of his fingers as they slowly eased under the hem of her skirt. Her own hands could feel the sinewy muscles of his back as she clung to him, feeling his every labored breath as the intensity of the moment grew greater. Nothing could stop their sexual momentum.

The overhead light was suddenly turned on as the back door was slammed shut. "Well, what do we have here? Am I interrupting something?" a voice teased from across the room.

Austin! Allison shoved Jack off of her with such force that he landed on the floor in front of the couch as she sat upright.

"Umph," Jack said as he fell on his side, and then pushed himself up into a sitting position on the floor. "Welcome home, Austin," Jack said wryly, clearly not happy about his brother being home early.

"Entertaining are we?" Austin asked and stepped into the room, finally setting his gaze upon Allison. His smirk was erased quickly as his mouth turned down in obvious disapproval. Jack stood up, placing himself in front of Allison, blocking Austin's further view of her.

"I was just leaving," Allison said, standing up behind Jack, slipping her feet into her silver shoes that had been placed in front of the couch while she slept. All signs of their heightened arousal had been quickly doused by Austin's unexpected arrival.

She caught the look of frustration on Jack's face as he approached Austin in the doorway. "Thanks, brother," Jack said as he shoved past Austin on the way out the door. He waited patiently for Allison to follow him and opened the door for her, leading out to the garage. As they settled into his SUV for the short drive to her house, he mumbled, "I'm sorry, Allison. He wasn't due back until tomorrow."

Allison could tell that Jack felt bad for putting her in the awkward situation. She looked down at her watch, denoting the early morning hour. "Well, technically it is tomorrow," she said, trying to lighten the tension in the air. He backed out of the garage and drove past a few houses until he pulled into her driveway.

"I really did have a good time tonight," he said sincerely.

"I did, too," Allison said, placing her hand on top of his hand that was resting on the gear shift. "I'm sorry for falling asleep on you. Wine does that to me sometimes," she stated.

"I'm not," he said. "I enjoyed watching you sleep." Jack leaned over to her, lowering his voice, "But I enjoyed watching you wake up even more." He claimed her mouth once more, offering her a parting kiss that lacked the extreme intensity of moments earlier. As he sat back in the driver seat, Allison reached for the door handle. "I'd like to see you again," he said.

Allison nodded, "I would like that, but you might want to clear it with Austin ahead of time. I don't think he approves."

Jack grimaced, "I don't need his permission. Besides, he's crazy not to approve of you. I like you, Allison. Austin will have to get used to it."

Allison smiled slightly, hoping she would not cause a rift between the brothers, but grateful for Jack's defense of her. "Good night, Jack." She opened the door and let herself out. Jack exited the car and ran around to close the passenger door after she emerged. He walked her to the front of the house. Allison removed the key from her clutch bag and unlocked the door.

"Good night, Allison. Sweet dreams," Jack said as she let herself in the house and then closed the door softly behind her. She could hear Jack's SUV back down the driveway, the engine sound fading into the early morning hours.

CHAPTER THIRTY-THREE

"Good morning, Sunshine!" Brianna DeVoe said as Allison made her way over to her desk the next morning. The bakery downstairs was bustling with business for a Saturday morning, selling as many cupcakes and drinks as quickly as they could make them. Allison had helped herself to a bacon-infused hot chocolate on her way up to the office area. Surprisingly, she was not as tired as she thought she would be after a few hours of sleep. She had passed Gwen in the kitchen when she arrived. Faith and Lorraine did not work on Saturdays. That gave Allison and Brianna time to discuss a few matters in private.

"Good morning," Allison answered back.

"How did it go last night?" Bree asked, not able to wait any longer, and she wanted to hear about Allison's date before they were interrupted.

Allison smiled and said, "The date was great. He took me to The Palmetto Club."

"Oh, is it nice?" Bree asked, not yet familiar with the local places.

"The nicest," Allison answered. "It's an exclusive club you can only get into if you have a membership. It's like eating at a five star restaurant." Brianna sat on Allison's desk waiting to hear more details while Allison logged into her computer for the day.

"The food was fabulous," Allison told her. "I think we should join so we can eat there any time we want." Brianna nodded her head, always game for a good meal.

"What did he wear? Did he like your dress?" Brianna asked her.

Allison told her about his suit and the dress code that was

enforced at the member's only clubhouse. "He looked so nice, Bree, different from his usual jeans but in a good way." She continued to regale the events of the evening, including the food and the chef coming out to meet her.

"I accidentally fell asleep in his car on the way home," Allison said to the enraptured Brianna.

"What?" Bree asked. "Did you drink too much wine?" Brianna knew her friend well.

"Yes, he ordered one wine for dinner and another for dessert. I should've had one glass of each, but he kept refilling my glass," Allison confessed.

"Did he take advantage of sleeping beauty?" Bree asked, teasing Allison. Allison laughed and filled her in on the details, including the embarrassing moment when Austin arrived home unexpectedly.

"You should've seen the look on Austin's face when he saw it was me with his brother," Allison said. "If looks could kill, I wouldn't be standing here right now."

"Well, speaking of kill, I'm ready for us to pull the kill switch on Remco this next week," Brianna informed Allison.

Allison said, "Okay, late Saturday night, early Sunday morning is the best time for implementation. Most of the computer jobs don't run then, in case they need a maintenance window for updates. It will be the perfect time to put in the new program undetected, before the main computer jobs start running again Sunday night. That will give us a good twelve hours or so to make sure it's in place and working correctly."

Bree nodded and hopped down off Allison's desk to go to her own work station. Bree stated, "I'm not as familiar with this older mainframe code, but I reviewed your program and it technically looks sound to me."

"Do you still want to go through with this, even after your date with Jack last night?" Brianna asked her sorority sister.

"Yes, definitely," Allison replied. "After all, Jack wasn't the one that made the mistakes at that company; he simply inherited the mess that his uncle made. I feel perfectly fine helping him fix it, even if he doesn't know I'm helping."

Brianna raised her eyebrows and said, "Then we will plan to keep our weekend open next Saturday and Sunday. I think the new place should be ready to use by then."

Allison nodded, "Yes, I think the safest idea is to work off site in a different building. I wouldn't want to be here at the shop in case someone starts getting nosey, especially in the wee hours of the morning. I don't want people to get suspicious."

Bree nodded her head in agreement saying, "Sounds good to me."

Jane King came up the stairs as soon as they had finished their conversation. Allison had missed seeing her when she first arrived, since she came in through the kitchen and up the back staircase. "Well? How was it?" Jane asked with enthusiasm.

Allison smiled and recounted the events for Jane as she had for Brianna.

When she finished Jane asked, "Was he a good kisser?"

Allison laughed and replied, "Yes, very good."

Jane said, "I knew it. He looked like he would be a good kisser." All three of the ladies were laughing when Gwen arrived upstairs. Allison knew she would have to go through all the details for the third time that morning.

After catching Gwen up to speed, Allison asked Gwen, "So,

how is Ben?"

Jane and Bree both turned to look at Gwen and said at the same time, "Who's Ben?"

Gwen blushed now that the tables were turned and all eyes were on her. Allison answered for her, "Some cute guy that she went to the movies with last night."

"Ooh, do tell!" Jane encouraged Gwen. Allison breathed a sigh of relief, glad for the diversion away from her own personal life.

Gwen relayed to them that Ben had taken her to see the latest movie about terrorists taking over the Super Bowl. The date had gone so well that the two of them were going back out again this evening.

Jane asked Gwen her standard follow-up question, "Was he a good kisser?"

Gwen turned slightly pinker than she already was and answered, "I don't kiss and tell." Allison and Brianna laughed while Jane was left to wonder.

CHAPTER THIRTY-FOUR

Allison stayed up late Saturday night after getting home from the shop. She was testing her code for the program they would be installing on the Remco server. She wanted to make sure her program was flawless so she ran multiple test scripts to ensure the data was accurate for the installation. Wearing her flannel pajama pants and an old sorority t-shirt, Allison relaxed against the arm of the sofa with her laptop settled on her lap and her legs stretched out the length of the couch, with her feet covered in thick furry socks. The television was turned on to the cooking channel, and the volume was set to low to provide a little bit of back ground noise but not enough to break her concentration. Her focus was so completely dedicated to the complex lines of code written in blue on her screen that she jumped when her phone buzzed with an incoming call.

Allison looked at the time stamp on the bottom right of her computer monitor. *1:24am; who would be calling me at this hour?* She leaned over and picked up her cell phone from the coffee table, seeing Brianna's name on the display. "Hello?" she answered.

Brianna responded, "I thought you might be up. Are you running through the test code now?"

Amazed at her friend's intuition, Allison replied, "Yes, how did you know?"

Brianna said, "Well, this time next week we will be doing the install, so I figured you were doing some last minute tests. That was a lot of code you had to write, so when else would you have the time to test it? Besides, you always did your finest homework during the wee hours of the morning when we were in college."

Allison sighed heavily, "You know me well. I was going through the technical script of the code, making sure it was sound."

"How would you like to test it with real production data?" Brianna asked, with an excessively chipper tone for one o'clock in the morning.

"What do you mean?" Allison inquired.

"Well," Brianna explained, "I happen to have the portal open at Remco, so if you want me to, I could grab some real production data to use for your tests."

Allison smirked; she was glad that Brianna was on her team. As a professional hacker, Bree could do some real damage to most any company she wanted to. "Yes," Allison replied, "let me send you the names of the data files I'll need. I see you have your instant messenger turned on, so I'll send the names to you that way. If you could get me a copy of each of the files, I'll give you a raise starting this week."

Brianna chuckled, "Sure thing, boss. Copies of production files are coming right up. Would you like a side of bacon with that?"

Allison laughed for several moments with her sorority sister, thinking that bacon actually did sound good right then because her stomach was growling. She sent Brianna the names of the data files she would need in order to do accurate testing and after a few seconds nervously asked, "Do you see the files on their server?"

Brianna was quiet for a few minutes as Allison heard her typing on her computer through the phone line. "Mmmhhmm," mumbled Bree. After a few more minutes of silence broken by the occasional key stroke Brianna said, "Okay, I found them. I'll encrypt them and send them to you via secure email. I'll keep the portal open for a few more minutes, so let me know if you need anything else right away."

Allison logged into her secure email account and found the encrypted files. She quickly unencrypted them and reviewed the file layout of each one. "These look okay to me," she told Brianna, who was patiently waiting on the line. "Thanks, Bree, I'll run a few tests to make sure it works, but I don't want to hold you up. Go ahead and close the portal connection."

Bree answered, "Okay, I'm logging out of the portal now. It will take me a few minutes to wipe the trail clean so no one will know it was tapped." Allison was eager to use her code against actual data files, ensuring a smooth installation next weekend.

The quiet hum of typing was heard through the line on both ends as each lady followed through with their assorted computer tasks. Brianna broke the silence first, "I'm all done. Good luck with the code testing. I'll talk to you tomorrow."

Allison took a deep breath, stifling a yawn that belied the time of night. "Thanks, Bree. I can't believe our good luck. You were brilliant to think about snagging these files for me. I'm beat so I won't stay up too much longer tonight. Thanks again for your help. Good night."

"Night," Bree said and disconnected the call. It seemed a few minutes had passed, but when Allison looked at the time on her computer it was already after three in the morning. Glancing up she noticed the television channel had reverted to infomercials sometime during the night without Allison noticing.

She could not decide if she was more tired or hungry. Closing her laptop and placing it on the coffee table, she picked up the remote and turned off the television. Then she padded over to the kitchen pantry and stared at the contents, finally settling on a fruit pastry bar. She filled her glass with iced water and ate the snack standing at the kitchen counter. Finishing her low-calorie pastry, she picked up her laptop and cell phone from the coffee table and took both to the bedroom with her along with the glass of water.

Securing her laptop in the safe under her bed, she then plugged in her phone to charge and finally fell into bed. She was glad she had splurged on the mattress and bedding for her king-sized bed, buying the top of the line for comfort and support. The down side to sleeping in such luxury was the unwillingness to give up such extreme bliss in the mornings. The last two days had been busy, but in a good way, sapping all of Allison's energy. She picked up her cell phone and sent a quick note to Gwen that she would be in the shop late tomorrow, eager to catch up on some much needed sleep. Her last thoughts before sleep claimed her were that she was grateful for the opportunity to have her own shop and the ability to get revenge on a company that long deserved it.

CHAPTER THIRTY-FIVE

Allison had not heard from Jack since Friday night when he dropped her off at her house. Since her secret project was consuming her time this week, she had not had a lot of time to stop and think about him or the date. Her own experience with owning and running a new company gave her a new perspective on what Jack and Austin must be going through after inheriting their uncle's company, Remco. *At least I got to pick what kind of business I'm running,* she thought as she drove towards downtown on Sunday. Finding out a company had security flaws, ethics violations, and numerous other issues would be a challenge for anyone, especially for someone in Jack's shoes who had not been in corporate America before now.

Her radio was blaring loudly on her favorite pop music station, playing many songs Allison knew, so she sang along with the words. The blood red Jaguar F-Type made its way smoothly to her parking spot near her shop with her laptop secured in the trunk of the car in her rolling computer bag. She enjoyed entering through the kitchen, so she could snag a bite to eat from whatever had been removed from the oven recently. The kitchen staff was bustling about trying to keep up with the heavy demand of the Sunday afternoon crowd. One of the largest Baptist churches in Morgan was located two blocks down the street, and many of their parishioners frequented the shop after the church service let out around noon.

Allison rolled her computer bag through the hustle and bustle of an active kitchen over to the stairs that led up to the office area. She carried it up the flight of stairs and set it down beside her desk. All of the desks in the office area were solid wood with a modern look and convenience for computer equipment. The stain of the wood was a light pine color, embellishing the grain of the wood. It was quiet upstairs due to Gwen and Jane being downstairs helping in the front of the store. Typically, Brianna did not come into the office on Sunday, so Allison was not surprised to see her chair empty. The chairs were an antique style, yet very comfortable for a typical office chair. They were reminiscent of the old padded leather chairs with the tall backs that bank presidents would sit in while they worked.

As she unzipped her computer bag and pulled out her laptop, she noticed a sticky note in the middle of her desk. In Gwen's handwriting it said, "Please come downstairs." She must have known Allison would by-pass the customer area by coming through the kitchen to her office. She docked her laptop computer and booted up the system, logged in, and then locked her screen before going downstairs to the front of the store.

All of the tables were filled with customers and several lingered around the bar stools at the counter. Many of the patrons were dressed in skirts or suits, having come directly from church. Allison's eyes caught the movement from the new television hanging above the bar area. She saw a flash of Kevin Bacon on the screen as she descended the last of the steps. She took a moment to look around the rest of the store front and saw several other monitors hung so that customers could see a television from any direction in the store. Each one had the same movie playing, showing subtitles because the sound was muted.

Gwen approached Allison with a big smile on her face. Gwen said, "What do you think of the new electronic stimulation?"

Allison grinned and replied, "They look great. I love the Kevin Bacon movie aspect that ties into the theme of the store."

Gwen nodded, agreeing with Allison. "I didn't think you had a chance yesterday to see them installed, so I wanted to make sure you got to see them now that they're functioning," Gwen explained.

"Thanks," Allison said, "I love the whole idea. Have any customers commented on it yet?"

Gwen answered, "Oh, yes, several watched for a minute and then started laughing. You could tell when they put the connection together and started pointing it out to the other people in their party."

Allison noticed that all of the customers seemed to be smiling and laughing, with several drinks or food items on their tables. It pleased her to see the business doing so well and making people happy. She hoped her plans for the upcoming weekend would make many more people happy as well. Allison made her way to several of the tables and asked how they liked the food and the atmosphere. She received nothing but rave reviews. As she approached the customers closest to the front entrance of the shop, two men entered the front door. She glanced up immediately and came to an abrupt stop upon recognition of the new patrons.

Jack and Austin Roman were standing inside the front door, waiting for an open table. Jack caught Allison's eye and smiled and offered a friendly wave. He guided Austin by the elbow over to greet Allison. She walked slowly towards them at the same time and met them half way. Jack was wearing his traditional dark blue jeans that fit him nicely along with a grey button-up Oxford shirt that was unbuttoned at the collar, revealing a white t-shirt underneath. His black cowboy boots appeared to be a type of snake skin. The boots disappeared under the long legs of his jeans. Allison opted for comfortable attire that Sunday, donning her favorite pair of blue jeans and a deep purple sleeveless blouse with a ruffled V-neck collar. Her black wedge sandals provided height and comfort.

"What do I owe this pleasure?" Allison asked as she met up with the twin brothers. Jack casually leaned down and put one arm on her waist, pulling her close for a quick kiss on the cheek. His approach seemed effortless to Allison, who was not yet comfortable displaying affection in public, especially in front of his disapproving brother, Austin. She hoped she did not squirm too much as Jack released his hold. Austin had on dark brown dress slacks and a forest green Polo shirt. His shoes were a dark brown trendy pair of dress shoes that had a European design with an elongated vamp and slightly square toe. Austin's flare for style was much more evident than Jack's, although both wore name brand couture.

Jack answered, "Austin wanted to know what all the fuss was about so I brought him in to try your beer cheese cupcakes with the bacon frosting," Austin looked less than thrilled about being in Allison's shop.

A couple had risen to leave at one of the round two-person tables, so Allison guided them over to sit while she talked. "I'll get a server to come take your order. I hope you both enjoy the food." Her tone sounded rather dismissive without trying to be. She didn't know how to behave in public around Jack, but she knew she did not want to be one of those sappy couples that make out in front of their friends.

"Did you want to join us, or are you too busy today?" Jack asked Allison as she turned to find the closest waitress.

"Oh, thanks, but I have lots of work to catch up on today," Allison answered. Allison opted for a safe distance until she could decide how best to display her affections for Jack. She waved down Angie, getting her attention to come help the newest guests. She looked back at Jack and noticed the look of disappointment on his face. "Maybe some other time," she said, hoping to make up for the lack of socialization.

"Sure," Jack said. "I'll talk to you later."

Allison nodded and replied, "Okay. Enjoy." She walked back to the stair case to retreat to her office, where she could monitor the brothers from her surveillance system on her computer.

Allison Black truly did have work to do judging from the number of unanswered emails she had over the last several days. Several of them had to do with local companies asking about catering services, so she forwarded those emails to Gwen for her to address. She pulled up the security cameras on her computer and spied on the front of the house where Jack and Austin Roman were sitting. They had been served cupcakes and drinks, and she could tell they were chatting back and forth until Austin rose and walked toward the back of the shop. She switched cameras to the one that was located in the hallway that ran beside the kitchen, where the public restrooms were located. Austin disappeared inside the men's room.

She was so busy watching the action on her computer screen that she jumped when Jack's voice startled her as he drew closer to her desk. He had come up the front stairs, but Allison had not heard him nor noticed him until he was almost upon her.

"Hey beautiful," Jack said as he watched her reaction to his presence. She smiled and closed her laptop, trying to appear smooth and not as though she was hiding anything on her computer.

"Hey, did you and Austin enjoy your bacon snack?" she asked him. He slowly came around to her side of the desk and put his hands on her shoulders giving her a mild shoulder massage.

"We did," he said. "I think your cooking has won him over. He was pleasantly surprised at how good your cupcakes tasted."

"Mmmm," Allison said, wanting to close her eyes and enjoy the tension leaving her body as his hands worked magic on the stiff muscles in her neck. "Where is Austin now?" she asked, pleading ignorance on the knowledge of his whereabouts.

"He was going to wash his hands and then head back home. I told him I would catch up with him later," Jack replied, slowly working his fingers down the middle of her back in a slow circular motion. His lips descended, laying soft kisses on the nape of her neck while his hands stayed busy with the massage. The clanging of dishes down below rudely reminded Allison that she was in her place of business and not in a private room where she desperately wished to be at the moment. She gradually stood, letting Jack's hands fall away from her as she turned to face him.

"I have a lot of work to catch up on. Maybe I can call you later this week?" she offered. Jack closed in on her, not easily put off. His arms circled her waist as he blocked her in with her desk solidly behind her.

He claimed a deep lasting kiss from her lips before he replied, "Okay, but you don't know what you're missing." He released her and stepped back, then walked over to the front staircase. He turned and waved, saying, "Don't work too hard." Allison knew exactly what she was missing, and currently work was the last thing on her mind. She watched him regretfully disappear down the stairs.

CHAPTER THIRTY-SIX

As much as Allison was growing to like Jack, she could not afford many distractions this week. Two days passed since the brothers had come into the shop. Allison had not yet called Jack nor had she returned his phone call from earlier in the day. She deliberately avoided him, intent on finishing the programming code tests for the install on Saturday night. Most of the shop's management duties were turned over to Gwen during the day. Brianna was on standby for any questions that Allison might have, but for the most part Bree was not involved in the programming itself. She would be needed specifically during the actual assault on the Remco server.

Allison remembered her college professor, Doc, telling her, "You could try and dummy proof any system, but there would always be a bigger dummy to come along and break the system." As she worked at home to make the program as robust as possible, she kept the lights down low and stayed in the back of the house in the library away from any windows facing the front of the house. Allison wanted to give the appearance of not being home in case any gorgeous looking neighbors were to drive by and wanted to check on her. She snagged several cupcakes and other food items from the shop's kitchen on her way home yesterday in order to have fortification for the self-inflicted lock down. Currently, she was nibbling on some bacon caramel popcorn and reviewing the results of the output from her latest test run.

Being privy to salary files and rankings of employees, it amazed Allison how many people at Remco had settled for less pay than their peers simply because they were unaware of the discrepancy. One of the files she requested Brianna to retrieve for her several nights earlier was the retirement portfolio of all previous associates who had taken a lump sum package deal upon retirement. She found many of the men in the good old boys' club had been paid using a formula almost twice the amount than many women in the company. She also found the same to be true for certain men who had climbed their way to the top without earning a college degree. The college-educated were ranked and paid at a much higher level than those that worked their way up using sweat and endurance.

A privately held company certainly did not have to answer for salary discrepancies the same as a publicly held company. Most topics of salary or rank were strictly off limits among employees, Allison knew her changes in the human resources programs would largely go undetected as most people would not feel comfortable discussing their findings should anyone notice. She paused to take a long drink of the iced tea she had freshly brewed that morning. It had a slight peach flavor to it along with a healthy dose of sugar. The key to making successful sweet peach tea was to use one small bag of peach-flavored tea and two large bags of regular tea, all brewed slowly together and then stirred with a cup of sugar while warm. The same could be said for programming. With enough sweetness and slow brewing, the code could be vitally successful. The most recent system run had produced excellent results, and Allison was happy with the way her testing was going.

After winning two hundred and thirty million dollars, Allison doubted she would ever write computer programs again. She wanted her last hoorah to make a lasting, albeit silent, impression. She was also ready for a long overdue vacation; one that she could enjoy in style. Before she could plan out the ultimate dream vacation, Allison would make sure her new business was running smoothly, like the soon-to-be new program changes to the system at Remco.

Even though Allison was an excellent cook, her eating habits had been dismal of late. That would be one more thing to remedy once her hectic schedule calmed down. She had truly enjoyed the meal at The Palmetto Club and would look into a membership there possibly next week. A message from the manager had been left on her cell phone yesterday, inviting her for a tour of the establishment and all of the available amenities.

Since she had bought her new house already furnished, Allison had not needed to purchase much furniture up front. It had been move-in ready with the exception of a few personal items. She had been in the house for a couple of months now and had yet to stock the wine cellar, which was totally barren of any wine. She also needed a good supply of books to fill her beautiful mahogany bookcases in the stately library. The stone fireplace had not yet been lit, either. Allison had not had much time to enjoy or fill her estate home with her personal touches. Looking up from her laptop computer, she admired the architectural details in the library, from the large windows to the wainscoting around the interior of the room. The windows faced her perfectly manicured back garden, giving her a sense of serenity.

When she moved in, Allison had brought several paperback books and even fewer hardback books that barely filled one shelf of her massive bookcase. She had not had time to read or enjoy any good books lately but vowed to make time in the near future. It was hard to beat a glass of wine, chocolate, and a good book by the fireplace on a cool evening. When autumn approached, she would definitely be lighting up the fireplace and practicing relaxation in this retreat of a room. She could picture a giant globe in the corner and more cushions to accent the leather chairs, as well as a footrest. She placed her empty iced-tea glass on the side table beside her chosen brown leather chair and rose to stretch her back, which was tight from leaning over the laptop for the last few hours.

As she stood, she silently declared more spa days that included full body massages in her near future. She carried the laptop to the desk in the corner and decided a longer break was in order for the approaching evening. Allison walked through the silent house to the kitchen and found an open bottle of sparkling white wine. She poured a generous glass and grabbed the matches from the kitchen drawer. She made her way back to her bathroom and set the wine beside the enormous bathtub.

Taking time to light each candle around the tub and then drawing a hot bath, Allison set the mood for a restful evening.

Her shorts and favorite sorority t-shirt were removed and tossed to the floor near her flip-flops, followed immediately after by her undergarments. Allison grabbed the bath salts and poured a scoop of the lilac and vanilla-scented beads into the rising water. She thought she heard her phone ring but ignored it as she stepped into the relaxing water, sinking down into the warm luxury while resting her head on a bath pillow. She lifted her wine glass and took a long, slow sip, savoring the sweetness of the grapes. After the water rose high in the tub she reached up and turned the knobs off, allowing herself to immerse in the calming nature of the candlelit room.

Allison had been in the tub long enough to drink her entire glass of wine and watch the candles burn down part way, when she thought she heard the doorbell ring. She was not expecting any guests so decided not to leave her peaceful retreat to check the door. She laid her head back against the foam pillow and breathed in the soft aromas floating in the bath water. She had closed her eyes for only a minute when she heard a deep voice from the bathroom doorway.

"I came to rescue the lady in distress," Jack said as he lustfully looked down at her completely naked form in the tub.

CHAPTER THIRTY-SEVEN

Allison's whole body splashed to attention, shocked at the unexpected intrusion of her private sanctuary. "Jack!" she exclaimed, completely embarrassed to be caught in such a vulnerable predicament. "What are you doing in here? How did you get in?" she asked in astonishment as she stood to reach for her towel, wrapping it tightly around her wet body.

"I tried calling you several times," he started explaining, "but you didn't answer. Then I rang the doorbell. I haven't heard from you in two days, so I picked the lock, thinking you might be in trouble and unable to answer the phone or door."

Allison pursed her lips in a disapproving manner. "I'm perfectly fine," she said curtly.

"Why, yes, you are," Jack said cutting off any further reply, letting his eyes rove up and down her towel clad form. Allison was not one to throw caution to the wind, but something about Jack had her tossing all logic out the window. Her body shivered involuntarily from the cool air, reminding her of her vulnerable state. She leaned down to unplug the drain, allowing the water to drain slowly from the large tub.

She turned to look at his face, admiring the fine features of a handsome man while smiling at his boyish grin. "I wasn't expecting you," she said, slightly chagrined. He was clearly enjoying the situation as she became more uncomfortable with his nearness.

She turned the conversation to a safer topic asking, "How exactly did you break into my house? I have a deadbolt on the front door."

Jack took the bait and smiled again. He answered her, "I picked up a lot of skills as a private investigator. Do you want to see some of my other skills?" he asked teasingly.

"No thanks. Excuse me, please," she said as she stepped around him and crossed over into her walk-in closet. Until now she had never noticed the door to the closet as she kept it opened at all times. She closed the newly discovered door, leaving Jack stranded on the other side. Allison hurriedly picked out clothes to wear because she was not expecting to get dressed again that evening. Quickly she threw on yoga pants and an old t-shirt as well as a pair of socks.

She flung opened the door to find that Jack was not there. She padded out into the bedroom and then into the open den area. Not finding him, she called out, "Jack?"

He answered from the back of the house in the library, "Back here."

She strode to the library and found him fiddling with the fireplace trying to light it. In a few minutes, the fire came to life and warmed the room. "Staying for a while?" she asked in a sardonic tone.

He looked up at her from his squatted position, "Maybe a few minutes to make sure you're safe." She could hear the sarcasm in his reply.

"I guess baths are hazardous for my health. Thank goodness you rescued me," she said matching his wit.

"My pleasure," he replied as she flushed at his implication.

She glanced nervously at the laptop she had left on the desk in the corner. It did not appear to have been disturbed, but she was grateful she had closed it before getting her bath earlier. After learning that Jack was a private investigator, she did not want to underestimate him. His choice of the library might have been a coincidence, as most men would have chosen the den where the television was located, but she tried to not put much stock in the decision. Not having a large selection of books to choose from, Allison asked him, "Do you plan to do some light reading this evening?"

"I might," he replied, standing up from his position near the fireplace and walking over to her meager book supply on one of the large wooden bookcases. He read aloud one of the titles, "How to Win Friends and Influence People?" He questioned her selection with a raised eyebrow.

"Don't look at me," she said continuing, "That was required reading by my manager at Remco during a year of leadership training. In fact, most of those books over there are from that book list."

He read another one, "Who Moved my Cheese?"

Allison laughed, "I actually liked that one. It had a lot of good points in it, none of which I can recollect now."

Jack looked up on the shelf above and spotted another title, "Romance of Ages, huh?"

Allison countered, "Who doesn't love a good romance novel?"

Jack continued to mock most of the books in Allison's paltry selection until he grabbed one off of the shelf. "Let's see what this one says." He walked over to the leather couch across from the chair Allison had been sitting in earlier. He lay down and stretched his long legs out on the couch, bringing the book up for closer inspection by opening to a random page in the middle. "Well that explains all that silverware at The Palmetto Club the other night."

What is he reading? She walked over and saw he had picked up her *Etiquette* book from college. He had turned to the chapter that explained how silverware should be placed on the table and the usage for each piece.

"I have a feeling you might need to read that entire book," she told him as she sat down in the chair she had occupied earlier and watched him relax by the firelight.

"I just might," he replied, thumbing through more pages and stopping every now and then. He sat up part way, laid the book on the table, patted the seat in front of him, and said, "Why don't you come join me over here. It's more comfortable to cozy up to someone and watch a fire than to sit so stiff in that chair all by yourself." Allison gave half a smile, not sure whether to trust him or not. She finally rose and sat down in front of him on the couch. He put his arm around her as she stretched her legs out next to his. There was something enchanting about staring at a fire that made her not able to look away for several minutes.

"Tell me about the last big case you worked on as a bounty hunter; I mean private investigator," Allison said, curious to know more about Jack Roman.

Jack spent the next little while discussing a case that involved a motorcycle theft ring where he had been hired by an insurance agency to track down the offending thieves. Allison tried her best to keep her eyes open, but after sometime finally succumbed to sleep in the warmth of Jack's arms. She vaguely remembered feeling him kiss the top of her head while she drifted off to sleep.

CHAPTER THIRTY-EIGHT

Going to the gym was added to the list of Allison's upcoming agenda. Her body ached everywhere from sleeping on the couch next to Jack, causing her muscles in her neck to be tight. Jack continued sleeping on the couch when she arose to take a shower. She washed her hair with shampoo and conditioner, shaved her legs, and soaped down her entire body. Jack was truly one of a kind; he filled a need in Allison's life that she did not realize she had been longing for since college.

Exiting the shower, she rubbed her body down with lotion and put sculpting products in her hair before blowing it dry. She walked to the closet and added yet another task to her growing list. She had a sudden need to fill up the vast space of the half empty closet and decided to go shopping sometime next week. She selected a pair of casual white slacks and a red knit top to wear, neither of which required ironing. With her house guest still residing nearby, she carefully chose a bra and matching panties that were sexier than her standard garb. She artfully applied her makeup and checked her reflection in the mirror before stepping out of the bedroom to wake Jack.

The couch in the library was empty. *Where is Jack?* She heard a noise in the kitchen and made her way down the hall to the large open kitchen area. Jack was currently standing at her stove with a spatula in one hand, holding the handle of a frying pan in the other. The pan was on the lit burner with eggs scrambling inside of it.

"Good morning, pretty lady," Jack said as Allison approached him at the stove.

"Good morning. I thought you were still sleeping," Allison replied as she took in the sight of a man cooking her breakfast. Besides her dad, she could not think of a time when another man cooked her anything in her own house.

"I got hungry. I thought you might be hungry, too," he said. "I found your eggs and skillet, so I'm making one of the things I know how to cook," Jack told her as he stirred the eggs with the spatula.

"I'm starving," she said, reaching up inside the cabinet near the refrigerator to retrieve two glasses. "Would you like some juice or milk?" she asked. "I would offer coffee, but I don't drink it so I don't have any on hand."

He stared at her, "You don't like coffee? I thought everyone drank coffee," he teased her.

"I like hot chocolate, but never developed a taste for the cup of joe that everyone else likes," she explained.

He continued staring at her and said, "But you opened a store that offers all sorts of specialty coffees."

She laughed, "Yes, I did. I understand there's a strong market for that sort of thing."

Jack shook his head and turned off the burner. "I'll take some juice," he answered.

He divided the eggs onto two plates and handed them to her. "Thanks," she said as she placed the plates of eggs on the table. Allison retrieved two forks and the glasses of juice and set them on the table before sitting down. Jack joined her, sitting in the chair beside her.

"Cheers," he said, raising his glass in a salute and tapping it lightly against her full glass. She grinned and took a sip of the juice. Jack asked her, "So what are you so busy working on these days that you can't return my phone calls? I've been worried about you."

She sat her juice down and took a bite of eggs, giving herself some time before forming an answer. "I'm working on a project with Brianna, trying to tie up some loose ends," she said after swallowing the warm, buttery bite of the soft eggs. "These are good," she interjected, trying to change the subject.

"Thanks," he said. "I lived on breakfast in college. I'm

surprised I didn't find any bacon in your fridge."

She laughed and replied, "I ran out the other day after working on some recipes. I haven't made it to the store lately." They ate the rest of their eggs in companionable silence.

He rose to put their plates in the sink. "I'd like to see you again, sooner rather than later," he said.

Allison drew her lips together, knowing that she would love nothing more than to see him every day, but she needed to think of a way to put him off for a few more days until the installation was complete. "I need to finish this project by Sunday," she said. "I've had too many distractions as it is lately."

He wrapped his arms around her in a gentle bear hug and replied, "I understand. I don't know if I can wait until Sunday, but I'll try." He kissed the top of her head and released her.

Allison didn't know if she could wait that long either, but she needed to focus on the immediate task at hand. "I enjoyed last night, even if you did barge in on me," she teased him.

Smiling he took her face in both of his hands. "I did, too. I'll try to be patient next time," he said as he leaned down and kissed her slowly and gently on the mouth. She walked him to the front door to see him out. "I hope you get caught up on your project soon," he said.

"Thanks, I'm sure everything will go smoothly. Have a good day," she replied.

He opened the door and stepped out onto the brightly lit front stoop. "You, too, Allison," he said, emphasizing her name in a knowing way. She watched as he walked his masculine form down the sidewalk to his vehicle parked in the driveway.

CHAPTER THIRTY-NINE

Much of her day passed in a haze of recollection of the previous evening's pleasant interruption. Allison once again stayed home in order to run several more test scenarios without being interrupted. The biggest problem of the day was her own thoughts and memories interrupting her far more than any actual person. By late afternoon she had completed most of her testing, and decided to leave the house in order to clear her mind. Her plan to check items off of her list began with a shopping trip to the local grocery store. Allison had never been into clipping coupons, but noticed when items were on sale or listed as the weekly specials. Now that she wasn't pinching pennies, she could purchase whatever food looked good that day and not think about sales or weekly specials.

Most of her grocery store adventures included a leisurely trip down every aisle to ensure no items were left off the list. Rarely did she run in for a single item and leave with said item. Knowing her cupboards were bare, she grabbed a grocery cart upon entering the brightly lit store. She had been meaning to try a few new recipes for the shop, so she made sure to get all the necessary ingredients while shopping. Not expecting anymore house guests, but leery of being caught off guard, she replenished the eggs and bought bacon along with some canned biscuits in case she had another drop-in visitor. Slowly walking down each aisle she took her time perusing all of the items that caught her eye and loaded up her cart with many purchases.

The trunk of her Jaguar was loaded down with the much needed grocery supplies as she headed toward home to sort and put away each item. Allison quickly checked her email and replied to a few text messages from Gwen and Jane about the shop, before she prepared herself a Panini sandwich from some of her recent purchases. She turned the television on while she sat down on the couch to eat and flipped through channels until she landed on a romantic movie made for TV. It had been months since she sat down to watch a movie of any kind. Within minutes, Allison was caught up in the plot line and comfortably stretched out on the couch. Two hours passed before the show was over, and Allison realized it had gotten dark outside while she lay idly doing nothing.

Feeling the need to do something productive, Allison decided to bake something new in the kitchen. She had an idea for a new blueberry smoothie with bacon flavoring, but wanted to try it out first before introducing it in the shop. She was blending the blueberries in the blender when her phone rang. She turned off the noisy appliance and grabbed her phone, noting the caller ID listed Brianna DeVoe. "Hey Bree," Allison greeted her friend.

Brianna said, "Hi. How's the testing going? I haven't heard much from you lately and wanted to check in on you. Gwen said you replied to her earlier messages, so I assume if you had time to email her everything is going well."

Allison had been pleased with the output from earlier that day and replied, "It's going great. I think I've finished all the testing that I wanted to do. Now we sit back and wait until Saturday night."

Brianna responded, "Woo hoo! I'm glad it went well. I'm all set for Saturday night as well, especially since we already tapped their server this past weekend."

Allison could hear the excitement in Brianna's voice. Spying on a cheating husband by reading his emails was one thing, but doing a major system penetration to a large company was a computer hacker's dream come true. "How's everything going at the shop? Any new interesting computer forensic business this week?" Allison asked, trying to keep up to date with all of her company's aspects.

"We do have a new client," Brianna explained. "The large bookstore in town is having me investigate their systems due to suspected fraud. They are missing a large sum of money and think the office manager moved some funds around until they disappeared. I'll have Joseph, our lead technical guy, scan through her emails and bank statements tomorrow."

Allison was glad they had hired several reputable computer analysts. She also knew that Brianna had some less reputable contacts that could be used for any jobs that required a more stealthy approach, if the need was there. It always amazed Allison what people thought they could get away with in today's technologically advanced world, unless of course it involved a stellar hack job by her best friend.

"I'm betting the office manager will regret taking anything by the time Joseph is done with his trace," Allison said to Brianna.

Bree laughed, "I think the sheriff's office will be paying her a little visit by the end of the week. Are you coming to the shop tomorrow morning?"

Allison told her yes and said goodbye before hanging up the phone. She finished making the smoothie and sampled a small sip of it. *Not bad.* She carried it back to the library to retrieve her laptop she had left in there before going to the grocery store. As much as she wanted to open it and do some more work, mentally she could not motivate herself to do so. She carried it back to the bedroom and plugged it into the charger. Allison then stepped into her enormous walk-in closet and started making a mental inventory of the items she lacked and wished she had. Since she had some time before Saturday night's big install, she decided she would go clothes shopping tomorrow afternoon to help fill in some of her wardrobe gaps. Her first order of business would be to buy some new pajamas in case of any more overnight guests.

CHAPTER FORTY

After consulting with the kitchen staff and introducing the new smoothie drink, Allison joined Jane in the front section of the shop where several customers were seated at tables. Some had laptops, some had tablets and others were there to simply enjoy the food and drinks. It had become quite the hipster hangout for some of the local college kids. Allison remembered studying at a small donut shop at all hours of the night during her college days. She was not willing to keep her shop open twenty-four hours a day like the old donut place, but was delighted that they chose to gather there during the day. Jane was doing a great job of running the front of the store and playing hostess to the clientele. She brought Allison up to speed on the latest town gossip that she had overheard that week.

Gwen passed by them as Jane was telling Allison about the mayor's newest car when Allison noticed Gwen's hand. "Gwen!" she said loudly over the din of the crowd.

Gwen turned and walked back over to Allison and Jane. "Hi Allison, did you need me?" Gwen asked.

Allison picked up Gwen's left hand and studied the diamond ring sitting on her third finger. She showed it to Jane. "Did I miss something?" she asked both Gwen and Jane.

Jane had obviously missed it too and grabbed Gwen's hand from Allison's.

"Oh my gosh, Gwen! Are you engaged?" Jane asked.

Gwen smiled sheepishly and answered, "Yes, Ben asked me last night. I said yes."

Allison and Jane were stunned. Allison was the first to recover. "That was fast," Allison said, but with an approving tone in her voice.

"When you know, you know," Gwen replied and added, "The ring was his grandmother's."

"Wow," Jane said, finally finding words, "When are you guys getting married?"

Gwen could not wipe the smile off of her face, glad that someone had finally noticed her ring. She answered, "We haven't set a date, yet. We're getting used to the idea of finding our perfect soul mate. He told me he didn't want me to get away."

The three ladies were standing in the middle of the restaurant area surrounded by customers at various tables, ignoring them all as they were completely absorbed in the moment of Gwen's revelation. Jane was excited for Gwen and gave her a big hug, then grabbed her hand to check out the diamond again. "This is so exciting!" Jane gushed.

Allison added her comments, "I'm so happy for you. I like Ben, too." It was such a refreshing change to hear good news from a close friend. She usually heard about all the break ups or jobs lost, so hearing about an engagement made happy meter go up.

Jane offered to help her with any planning that she needed and Allison volunteered to take Gwen shopping for her wedding dress. Brianna walked down the front stairs at that moment and wondered why the three ladies were huddled together, giggling like school girls. They quickly brought her up to speed and she congratulated Gwen on the announcement. It gave them all something to look forward to besides work, or in Allison's case, revenge.

Brianna eventually broke up the group by asking Allison, "Can I see you upstairs for a minute? I have something I want to show you."

Allison replied, "Sure." She followed Bree up the stairs to their office space.

Faith was seated at her desk, getting the payroll ready to go out the next day while Lorraine was discussing an advertising segment with a local television studio on the phone. Since Allison and Brianna did not have the area to themselves, Bree motioned for Allison to come look at her computer at her desk. Allison pulled up the chair next to Brianna's desk and watched the screen while Brianna typed in a blank electronic notepad. *When is the last time you saw Jack?* Brianna typed, but then spoke aloud so the other two women would not get interested in their conspiracy, "When did you last read the paper?"

Allison answered the first typed question, "Wednesday."

"It had an interesting article today that I thought you'd like to see," Bree said while typing, *Do you know that Jack and Austin are selling Remco?*

Allison's jaw dropped after reading the question on Brianna's computer. She did not know and she had recently seen Jack, albeit they did not exactly discuss business. *I take that as a no,* Bree typed.

"Interesting," Allison said aloud, pretending to read whatever mysterious article Brianna was referring to.

"I need to run down to that cute boutique this morning. Do you want to join me?" Allison asked Brianna as a way to get them both out of hearing range from other people.

"Sure," Bree said. They grabbed their purses and headed

down the back stairs and out the door.

Before they could get three steps down the sidewalk Allison asked, "Are you kidding me? How do you know they're selling the company?"

Brianna gave a sideways smirk and answered, "I might have tapped Austin's email while I was on the Remco server last Saturday night." Allison stared at Brianna, amazed and in shock that she thought to do something like that. She made a mental note to make sure all of her electronic information was secure before submitting anything over a potentially open line.

"Jack didn't mention it the other night," Allison said, revealing to Brianna that she had indeed seen Jack after hours.

Bree smiled, catching on to Allison's slip and said, "Well if you're seeing him at night, I doubt he was thinking of work."

Allison flushed slightly and shook her head, "No, we did not discuss work." The two ladies were fast approaching the boutique where listening ears would be inside.

"I assume all systems are go for tomorrow night," Bree said.

Allison nodded affirmatively, "Yes, no matter the owners, we need to correct a few past mistakes that were done to innocent people."

Brianna agreed, "I'm ready if you are." They entered the exclusive clothing store and dropped the subject of Remco for the time being, pleasantly distracted by all the pretty dresses and jewelry.

Allison was able to check another item off of her list by purchasing several outfits and dresses to help fill her paltry closet and provide clothing for any upcoming events or dinners. She enjoyed shopping at this particular store because they carried many size four dresses that fit her perfectly. The sales clerk helped to complete each outfit by pairing them with accessories such as scarves and costume jewelry. With her packages slung over her back and across her arm, Allison was wishing she had driven her car down the few blocks so she wouldn't have to walk back with such a heavy load. Brianna was not much help as she herself had made a few purchases and had her own bags to carry. After making it to their cars and unloading their bags, Allison and Brianna made their way back upstairs to the office area of the shop.

Lorraine was off the phone and chatting with Faith when they arrived. "Did you see Gwen, yet?" Lorraine asked the ladies excitedly.

"Yes," Allison said, "we saw the rock on her finger. That's great news."

"I'm so happy for her. She deserves a good guy," said Brianna. Lorraine and Faith continued the discussion about Gwen's hurried engagement until Allison interrupted with a work-related question.

"Faith, did you include the bonus amount for each person for this pay period?" Allison asked her, hoping to surprise some of the crew downstairs with the added bonus she had discussed with Faith earlier.

"Yes," Faith replied, "I expect we'll have some happy employees in the near future." High morale of the employees was always a sign of a successful business, and nothing made morale increase more than a monetary increase.

The next monetary incentive that Allison would supply would not be directly to her employees, but to current and some former Remco employees. She was almost as excited to enact her revenge program as the day she first learned she had the job at Remco some twelve years earlier. As soon as her program was installed, she planned on having a discussion with Jack about his role in the future of the company he was about to sell. It came as a shock that the twin brothers would be willing to let go of a family business so quickly after inheriting it. Her biggest questions were how it would impact her and whether he would stay in the area.

CHAPTER FORTY-ONE

Saturday passed ever so slowly for Allison Black as she waited for the late evening to arrive. She spent her day organizing her closet, washing sheets and towels, and doing some spring cleaning. All of these tasks she knew her maid, Mitzie could do during the week but felt the need to stay busy without going into the shop. She was trying to stay away from the bakery more often to give Gwen and the others a sense of empowerment without the boss always looking in on them. She enjoyed starting the business and providing some recipes, but was eager to turn over the day to day involvement to Gwen and the other managers on a more permanent basis, which reminded her that she needed to find another personal assistant. Gwen loved the shop and Allison felt Gwen belonged there, managing the employees well and having set hours in a stationary place.

Although Gwen was an excellent personal assistant for the extremely short time that Allison used her in that position, she could tell that Gwen blossomed at the store. She would have to talk to Lorraine about putting a help wanted ad in the paper for a new assistant. Ashley Porter, her realtor had secured a place for Brianna that was close to downtown. It was a spacious condo located in an old textile mill building that had been converted a few years earlier to modern and sophisticated units. Ashley had also procured a small out of the way location for their server and computer equipment that Allison did not want on the property of Computer Forensics & Bacon Confectionery. She would be meeting Brianna at this new location later tonight in order to do the hack into Remco from this newly secured site.

Allison had decided to play the part and dressed in all black for tonight's adventure. She wore a black shirt with three-quarter length sleeves, dark black knit pants and soft-soled, comfortable black shoes. Her hair was pulled back into a long ponytail that swung back and forth with each step she took, showing her black and silver dangle earrings. As she glanced at herself in the mirror before leaving the house, she thought, *All I need is a pair of cat ears and a tail to complete the Cat Woman look.* She gathered her laptop, charger and a few snacks to last both girls through the night.

Her blood red Jaguar looked black against the night road as Allison made her way to the private location on the outskirts of town. She had not yet seen the small building, but followed the directions that Brianna had emailed to her the previous day. Ashley had worked with them to create a fictitious company that the building was bought under in case the IP address of the computer server they were using could be traced. Brianna was certain she would not be traceable, but they had completed the anonymous purchase as an added precaution. Since the hours of operation would be somewhat suspicious and Allison drove a recognizable car, the location was off the beaten path and provided a two car garage attached.

She spotted the gravel road on the left as she slowed to make the obscure turn. It was covered by a thick line of trees on either side of the road, causing the already dark path to be even darker. Her car slowly made its way down the long narrow drive until at last she spotted the shape of a building up ahead with a dim light in one of the windows. *Ashley did a great job of finding an out of the way place.* The remote location reminded Allison of a horror movie where victims were kept away from any ears that might hear the occasional scream. The building was an old wooden structure that appeared to have been a hunting lodge at one time. Surrounded by woods, there was no telling what wild life lurked nearby.

Allison pulled her car in front of the garage door and put her car in park. She cautiously opened her door and listened for any signs of people or animals. Upon hearing none, she exited the car with it still running and walked up to the door, glad her headlights were shining to provide the much needed light. She tugged and turned on the manual handle, raising the overhead door and then climbed back in her car in order to pull it inside. She noticed the other garage bay was empty so she had arrived before Brianna. She turned off her car and grabbed her laptop and bag of necessities. She saw a pair of headlights coming up the drive as she walked to the door to close it with her spare hand. She decided to go ahead and open the second overhead door so Brianna could drive on inside without having to exit her car.

Brianna pulled her dark green Jeep quietly into the garage and turned off her car. "Hey," Brianna said as she opened her door.

"Hi," Allison replied, grabbing the overhead door handle and closing it shut. "Turn your lights on for a minute until I can find the light switch in here," Allison told Bree.

Brianna switched back on her headlights while Allison walked over towards the door that led inside the cabin structure and found the light switch. The single bulb hanging down from the center of the garage lit up the area, providing enough light that Brianna could turn off her headlights. She climbed out of her Jeep and opened the back door of her car, retrieving a few bags.

Bree said, "I stopped by earlier today and dropped off most of my supplies, but I had to bring a few necessities with me tonight." Allison noticed that some of those commodities were a pack of toilet paper, soap and paper towels.

"Good thinking," Allison said, nodding to the essential item. "We definitely are not at the Hilton."

"Does this place have running water?" Allison asked with a skeptical look.

Bree laughed, "Yep, thank goodness. We're not that remote. We have running water and electricity."

Allison opened the door leading inside and stopped, astounded at what she saw from the dim light. "Wow," was all Allison could say. Brianna walked in behind her and turned on the overhead lights to further illuminate the entire room. The latest server equipment had been installed including several large databases. The structure had been transformed from a multi-room cabin into one large open area that reminded Allison of NASA with all the terminals and computer equipment around the room. Four desk areas were provided along with comfortable computer chairs.

"The restroom is in the far corner over there," Brianna pointed to the back right side of the room. A large projection screen was on one wall, which was used by the projection unit that hung from the ceiling. Web cameras were installed at each desk that were linked directly to the equipment in case the user wanted to project a computer image or themselves to the large screen or linked remotely to another on-line user. Brianna walked over to the second desk on the left and put her computer bag on the desk, then turned and walked to the restroom to place the toiletries inside. Brianna wore all white, a stark contrast to Allison's black attire. Brianna's skinny white jeans hugged her tall, lanky form along with a sleeveless white tank top and white, cotton tennis shoes.

Allison chose the desk next to Brianna's and placed her laptop on the desk. She held up the bag of snacks as Brianna walked back from the restroom. "I brought nourishment," Allison said.

"Great," Brianna said, "I'm sure we'll be hungry soon. There's a small fridge under the table over there on the right that I filled with drinks earlier."

Allison glanced over at the small refrigerator and noticed a small microwave beside it. Brianna had thought of everything. "I love what you've done with the place," Allison said.

Brianna laughed, "You should have seen it before we started. I think the raccoons had taken over. I had all the equipment ordered and in storage while we worked on cleaning the place last week. Then I had out of town contractors from Atlanta come up and install the equipment this past weekend. I didn't want anyone local to know what was out here. I ran the test from here last Saturday night to make sure the equipment was working."

"I knew I kept you around for a reason," Allison teased.

Brianna said, "I think everything will go smooth tonight, but if it doesn't, I have a few of my tech friends on alert in case we need their support." Allison knew Brianna's tech friends were most likely extreme hackers and that she probably didn't even know their real names. Allison was once again grateful that Brianna was her friend as she would not want to be on the receiving side of any damage her master hacker friend could do. To look at Brianna one would see a willowy hipster that enjoyed sushi and yoga. Most people would never guess she could break into almost any computer system once she set her mind to it. Allison had studied code and logic, but had not ventured deep into the connection and server logic that Brianna had.

A docking station had been provided for Allison's computer, which was then connected to three terminals in front of her. Brianna had her own docking station, with a similar set up. The first order of business was wiping their IP address clear of each machine in order to be untraceable. Each computer is assigned an IP, or internet protocol numerical label that can be traced by a simple on-line lookup. A dummy IP address was created for each computer by Brianna, pointing to the same fictitious company that the building had been purchased under. Once Brianna walked Allison through the steps to make their computers anonymous, they were ready to connect to the Remco virtual private network or VPN as most techies referred to it.

CHAPTER FORTY-TWO

Once logged into the Remco server, Brianna DeVoe could see who else was logged in. Since it was close to one in the morning, she did not expect to see many, if anyone signed in to the company's network. As predicted, all was quiet and no user IDs were present. "All is quiet on the server," Bree said as she turned in her chair to look at Allison. "Are you ready for this?"

Allison smiled and nodded, "I've waited long enough for this; let's do it."

Bree swiveled her chair back around to face her monitors to watch the network activity. "Okay, go ahead and connect to their VPN," Bree instructed Allison. Allison opened the connectivity and navigated to the system area where the programs were installed. "I see you're on-line now," Bree said as Allison sorted through the technical screens, finding the location of the code she would be altering.

Allison quietly pulled up the source code she had written a few weeks earlier and compared it to the current program installed on Remco's server. She made a few modifications to some functions and name structures and then imbedded it within the source file of the benefits program. She compiled the program to make sure it had no logical errors before running it off schedule as a final test to make sure the job did not incur any functional errors. Having worked on the same program for multiple years at Remco, she was fairly confident of her changes. "Okay, phase one is installed," she told Bree.

Brianna was drilling down into some files at Remco while Allison was busy with the first installation. "Did you know that Jack and Austin's birthday is on July fourth?" Brianna asked Allison.

Allison looked up and smiled, "What are you looking at over there?"

Bree smiled and replied as her eyes stay fixed on the screen, "Oh nothing, just some personal information about the new owners, or should I say, soon to be ex-new owners." Allison shook her head. "Do you want to know what their middle names are?" Bree asked.

Allison did want to know, but didn't want to appear nosey, "Bree, I need to concentrate." Brianna appeared unfazed and said, "Sorry, I won't bore you with silly details about Jackson Remco." She emphasized the last part of Jack's first name, revealing part of her findings to Allison.

Allison was not deterred. She found the database file she had been looking for and started making the adjustments to several entries based on her notes she had taken after reviewing the stolen data on the jump drive she had taken the day she was fired from Remco. It took her the better part of two hours to complete the task. She barely looked up when she finished and noticed that Bree was rummaging in the mini fridge for a drink. She was nibbling on a breakfast bar when she came up behind Allison to look over her shoulder. "Want a drink?" Bree asked her, seeing that Allison had come to a break in her concentrated effort.

"Sure, I'll take a Coke," Allison replied, suddenly aware of how parched she was. Brianna went back to collect the said Coke from the fridge and brought it back to Allison.

"How's it going?" Bree asked her.

Allison nodded, "I think I'm done. I finished phase two by updating the database file so I think I'm done."

Brianna walked over to her own work station and looked at the center monitor, verifying that no one had logged in during the time Allison was working. "What do you think Jackson would say if he found out about what you're doing tonight?" Bree asked her, purposefully using his entire first name.

Allison shrugged her shoulders, "I honestly don't know. I don't think he would approve, but since he wasn't there when all the bad decisions were made, and he won't be there in the near future, then I think that's a moot point."

Allison unscrewed the cap on her soda, releasing a hissing sound and took a long swallow of the cool beverage. "So are you going to tell me his middle name?" Allison asked as she turned back to the computer to start the exit process from the Remco server.

"Nope," Brianna said, "I'm going to let him tell you. It'll be my little secret." Bree sat back down in her chair and pulled her legs up under her to sit cross legged. She finished the breakfast bar, took a sip of her drink and watched her screen. "I see you logged out. I'm going to disconnect the VPN connection now," Bree said. Allison stood up and stretched, her body realizing she had not moved for some time. She found the can of cashews and opened it, snacking on them one at a time.

Now that the rush to make system changes was over, Allison was free to look around the room and admire the set up that Brianna had created. "This is some fancy equipment you've got here," Allison noted as she walked around the room, taking it all in.

Brianna had signed off of the servers and was swiveling back and forth in her chair, looking around the room, too. "Yeah, maybe a little overboard with what we were doing tonight, but it will come in handy for some contracts in the future," Brianna explained.

"I'll be right back," Allison said and excused herself to take a quick restroom break. When she returned, Brianna had packed up her computer and shut down the larger equipment. Allison undocked her own computer and gathered her papers that she had scribbled on while doing the installation.

"Even though this place is creepy on the outside, it's a perfect location for any undercover work we might need to do in the future for certain clientele," Allison remarked.

Brianna took a towel that had bleach on it and wiped down all the surfaces of the desks and chairs then went over and wiped the handle of the fridge and disappeared into the restroom. Allison had not thought about removing fingerprint traces, but was glad Bree had thought of that small detail. When Brianna emerged from the back room, she carefully wiped down the door handles and light switches, while turning out the overhead light. A dim emergency light was left on in one corner, the same light that Allison must have seen from the window when she drove up.

Allison glanced down at her watch and noticed it said four fifteen. They had a few hours left before daylight. "Thanks for your help tonight," Allison said. "I know this puts you at a huge risk; one that I wish I could have done without involving you."

Brianna brushed off her gratitude, "You know I would do anything for you. Think nothing of it. Besides, this was the best night I've had in a long time."

Allison smiled, "Well thank you again. I can't wait to see our plan in motion."

Brianna walked over to her car and opened the door. "I think what you've done is brave and much needed by the looks of things."

Allison replied, "Thanks, I think it was way overdue, too. I think I'll wait a few days and see if there is any fall out. If not, I'm going to plan an extensive spa day. Would you like to join me?"

Brianna instantly took her up on the offer, "Absolutely. I'm ready when you are."

Allison put her computer in her car and walked over to raise the garage doors. She watched as Brianna backed out and then closed the overhead door, then backed out her own car. Allison used a towel as Brianna had done earlier and wiped off the garage door handles. Bree had turned her car around so she could drive straight out, but waited until Allison had shut and locked the second door, wiping the outside handle as well. Allison climbed back into her Jaguar and flashed her lights for Bree to lead the way out. Brianna had a remote in her Jeep that she clicked, setting an alarm on the building as they drove down the gravel driveway to their perspective homes. One luxury the building was missing was electronic garage door openers, although Allison was pretty sure she didn't want one to be found in her car.

CHAPTER FORTY-THREE

Allison slept until after noon on Sunday, having turned off the ringer on her cell phone and drawn all the blinds tightly to keep out the sun. She checked her phone as soon as she woke up and noticed there were no notifications from Gwen about the shop or from Brianna. *No news is good news.* She had not been focusing much of her energy on the store lately so she wanted to drop by and make sure everything was flowing smoothly. She donned her favorite blue jeans, a hot pink cotton knit tank top and high wedge sandals that had blue jean fabric straps across the toes and ankles with a brown buckle drawing the skinny fabric strips together at the toes.

She arrived at the shop in her usual fashion via the back kitchen door and said hello to the staff members present. All of them lit up when they saw her; still happy about the bonus amount they received in their checks on Friday. Several of the employees thanked her personally and she reassured them it was well deserved due to their hard work. Allison checked on the front of the store to see how many customers had come in for afternoon delights. Some of the church crowd lingered, but it was not nearly as busy as it probably had been about an hour earlier. The customers all appeared to be happy and well taken care of by her efficient staff. She made her way up the front stairs to the empty office area. She had no notes or memos waiting on her desk which implied no issues had risen over the weekend.

After stowing her purse in her desk drawer, she made her way back down to the kitchen, using the back stairs this time. Her stomach growled as she smelled the sweet smells of cinnamon and bacon. Allison grabbed a hot cinnamon roll off of a pan that had been recently removed from the oven. It had been glazed with a cream cheese frosting and sprinkled with bacon bits. She bit into the lush smoothness of the pastry, savoring the flavors that filled her mouth. "Mmm, this is so good," she said to no one in particular, catching the oozing frosting with her finger before it slid off of the hot roll.

Brianna strolled in through the back door at that moment, catching Allison with her mouth full. "Don't eat up all the profits, Allison," she teased.

Allison tried to smile and managed to make a small grunting sound.

Betty, one of the bakers nearby, overheard the conversation and rebutted, "Allison, you eat as much as you like. You're too skinny as it is."

Allison finally managed to swallow the oversized bite and replied, "Thank you, Betty. It's delicious, but I can only manage one."

Brianna countered, "Don't let her fool you, Betty. That skinny girl can out eat all of us." The ladies laughed as Allison and Brianna turned to head up the back stairs.

"What brings you in today? I thought you might sleep in and take the day off," Allison asked as they climbed the steps.

"I thought the same of you," Bree replied as they ascended to the top landing.

"I'm glad the install went smoothly last night," Allison said standing near Bree's desk, "although it won't be apparent until the next payroll run or ranking review, and even then it might not be obvious to most people."

Brianna said, "Well, we did our good deed for the year, so now we can rest easy." Brianna leaned back in her chair and propped her feet up on her desk, crossing her ankles. At the same time, they heard rather loud footsteps coming up the front staircase.

Allison and Brianna fixed their eyes on the stairwell until

they saw the top of a male head emerge. "Jack," Allison said with a slight smile on her face and then faded when she realized it was not Jack, but Austin.

Brianna stayed in her same relaxed position, not fazed by the interruption. "I thought you might be up here," Austin Roman said with an agitated tone. Brianna raised her eyebrow, thinking it was Jack and that he was speaking to Allison in a harsh manner.

Allison took a deep breath and said, "Brianna DeVoe, may I introduce Austin Roman." She emphasized his first name, giving Bree a chance to make the connection. Brianna did not move from her chair, nor did Austin appear to want an introduction.

He did not glance at Bree, but kept his steely blue eyes fixed on Allison. "I was wondering what kind of trance you've managed to put my brother under," Austin stated.

Allison looked perplexed, "Trance? What are you talking about?"

Austin stood his ground and added, "Just when I have everything arranged with a buyer to unload this company, Jack decides he may not want to sell. Instead, he thinks because of you, we might need to keep the company and try to remedy any issues that the company may have."

"Well that's extremely noble of him," Allison interjected, "but I haven't asked Jack to fix anything at Remco. I was unaware that you wanted to sell the company." She stated the lie smoothly and in fact, she was hoping her changes last night would fix plenty.

Austin stared at her, not believing what she said. "So you didn't tell him to keep Remco and not sell it?" Austin asked.

"Nope," Allison said, "Sell it if you like; I've cut all ties with that company. And as you can see, I've moved on quite nicely." Brianna watched the verbal exchange between the two, much like a tennis match with her head going back and forth as each one spoke. Bree had to admire Austin's appearance in his dark grey suit pants, white button-up shirt with cuff links and opened collar. He had on black dress shoes which appeared to be fancier than most sold in the state of South Carolina; in fact, they looked Italian if Brianna had to guess.

"Well if you talk to Jack, can you please relay your feelings about the issue to him? I'd like to move forward with this venture," Austin said in a defeated conjecture.

"Will do. I assume you can find your way out," Allison replied in a curt tone, eager to end the impromptu meeting.

Brianna lithely stood up and offered sweetly, "Oh, I'll show him out."

Austin turned, seething silently and started making his way to the stairs before Brianna could move out from behind her desk. She caught up with him and glided down beside him in the smooth manner that only Brianna possessed. "Thanks ever so much for stopping by," Allison could hear Brianna tell Austin as she heard the heel of his shoes clatter on the steps in quick succession. Brianna had adopted a slow drawl to her southern accent that Allison had heard her use before when trying to win over rude people. She shook her head, glad to be rid of the intrusion.

It was several moments later before Brianna came back upstairs with a wicked gleam in her eye. "Now that was a pleasant surprise," Brianna stated the opposite of how Allison had interpreted the moment.

"Oh, really? How so?" Allison inquired.

"Well, I always did love a challenge," Bree said smiling as she sat cross-legged in her chair. Allison could almost see the wheels turning in Brianna's head. Bree always saw men as a challenge, recalling many instances in college of Brianna's numerous conquests. "Austin Wesson Roman won't know what hit him," Brianna claimed, already staking him as a prize won.

"Wesson?" Allison asked.

"Yep," Brianna said. "Wouldn't you like to know what Jackson's middle name is?"

Allison shook her head, "No thanks. I do find it interesting that Jack doesn't want to sell the business now. I was kind of hoping he would detach himself from that place."

"Well, it does give you a good excuse to see him again," Brianna said, winking at Allison. "I wonder what it would be like to do it with twins," Brianna murmured.

"Brianna!" Allison rebuked.

"Well not your twin, of course, but I mean twins in general. I wonder if they have the same style."

Allison could merely shake her head. "You are too much," she told Brianna. "By the way, what are you doing here today? It's Sunday," she said to Brianna.

"Oh, I have this new client that I'm going to meet this afternoon. It sounds like an interesting case so I wanted to take the lead on the project." Brianna turned back around and appeared lost in the haze of working on a new potential project.

Allison did not need Austin's visit as an excuse to call Jack, but she decided to use it as one anyway. She selected his name on her cell phone from her contacts and waited for him to answer.

"Hello beautiful," he answered with a chipper tone. His tone was different from the tone that his brother had displayed a few minutes earlier.

"Hi Jack," Allison said, "I had an interesting talk with your brother a few minutes ago."

Jack grew silent on the other end. She could tell he was not exactly happy about Austin talking to Allison. Allison offered, "I thought maybe you'd like to get together tonight and we could discuss it."

Jack hesitated before taking up Allison on her offer, "Sure, I'd love to see you tonight. I'm not sure I want to discuss my brother. What did you have in mind?"

Allison thought for a few seconds and then said, "How about meeting me at Callaway's in the bar around six?" She wanted to meet him on neutral territory, not trusting her emotions to keep her hands off of him if they met in private. Unlike some of her friends, she did not want a relationship based solely on physical attraction, but Jack's unnatural good looks were throwing her common sense to the wind. She wanted to put forth a concerted effort to get to know Jack, and not just his sexual preferences in bed. Besides, she had technically already slept with him twice and wanted to find a place that would keep her awake.

CHAPTER FORTY-FOUR

Allison arrived at Callaway's Steak House a few minutes before six. She did not see Jack's SUV in the parking lot so she had arrived first. She went inside and found a small booth in the bar area located along the far wall. Being a Sunday evening, it was not crowded; in fact, only three other tables were occupied at the time. As she sat down, a young waiter approached. "Welcome to Callaway's. Can I get you something to drink?" he asked pleasantly.

"I'll take your key lime pie martini," she said as Jack approached behind the waiter. He slipped into the booth across from Allison and picked up the drink menu.

"Good evening," the waiter said to Jack. "Do you need a few minutes or would you like to order a drink?"

Jack answered after quickly perusing the menu, "I'll have a vodka martini, slightly dirty."

"I'll put these drink orders in for you," said the waiter and then he left to cross over to the bar.

"Hey pretty lady," Jack said, grabbing Allison's hand that was resting on the table and giving it a kiss.

"Hi," Allison replied with a smile. "I'm glad you could meet tonight," she said staring into his beautiful blue eyes. His hair was slightly ruffled, as always and he wore a white Polo shirt with his dark navy blue jeans.

"I've missed you," he said, asking, "Did you finish the project you were working on?"

"Yes, it's all done. I'll actually have some free time on my hands now," she replied.

Jack smiled, showing off his deep dimples in each cheek, "I like the sound of that." He had implied that her free time would be consumed with him.

The waiter returned with their drinks and asked, "Did you want to order anything off of our menu? We have an excellent prime rib special that includes a baked sweet potato and salad for $18.99." Allison was hungry and loved steak, but her favorite was the filet mignon. She did not need to look at the menu to know that she wanted to order her favorite steak.

She ordered, "I'll have the nine ounce filet mignon cooked medium with a baked potato with butter, bacon and cheese."

The waiter asked, "Did you want to add a salad to your order?"

"No thanks," she said.

Jack answered the waiter next, "I'll take the special, cooked medium."

The waiter nodded, wrote down the order and asked, "What kind of dressing for your salad?"

Jack stated, "Ranch, thanks."

"Excellent choices. I'll put your order in. My name is Wes if you need anything," Wes replied and then walked back toward the kitchen.

"I should've known you would order something with bacon in it," Jack teased.

Allison looked perplexed and then remembered she ordered it for her baked potato. She laughed and said, "I didn't even realize I had done so." She then grew somber and brought up the subject of Jack's brother, "So Austin came by the shop today and asked me if I would talk to you about selling Remco."

Jack picked up his martini to sip it before placing it back on the table slowly. "Oh really," he said, "Why would he do that?"

Allison answered, "He seems to think you're not selling because of me. I told him he could sell the company if he wanted to. I've moved past that chapter in my life and don't care anymore."

Jack seemed to consider her words before he asked, "Do you truly not care, Allison? If you had a chance to make Remco a better company, would you?"

Allison kept her poker face while sipping her key lime pie martini. She had in fact made Remco a better company less than eighteen hours earlier. "I would like to distance myself from the whole situation," she said adding, "I don't want to be caught in the middle between you and Austin so if you want my personal opinion, I'd love for you to sell the company. I'm sure you've already remedied several situations, such as that H.R. guy. Besides, I don't have to be reminded of the past transgressions each time you talk about work."

Jack seemed to consider her words before responding, "It was never my intent for you to be caught in the middle. I did not know Austin would bother you about this whole business. He seems to think you're a liability even though I told him you are not going to sue us." Jack paused and double guessed himself, "You're not going to sue us are you?"

Allison laughed, trying to lighten the heaviness of the situation. "No, you don't have to worry about me. I'm not suing Remco." Jack looked visibly relieved.

Wes, the waiter arrived with Jack's salad and a basket of yeast rolls. "You're steaks should be out in a little bit. Is there anything else I can get you?"

Both of them had briefly sipped their martinis, not ready for a refill. Jack answered, "We're fine, thanks." Wes left and Allison reached up to grab a hot roll from the basket. She split it open with her knife, watching the steam seep out of it. A small container of honey butter had been provided and Allison spread a generous heaping inside of her roll before closing it back together. She laid her knife on her bread plate and took a bite of the piping hot bread.

"Mmm, this is so good. I love their yeast rolls," she said. Jack smiled and cut into his salad, taking several bites and eating in silence.

After finishing most of his salad, he broached the topic one more time, "I'll talk to Austin. I haven't made up my mind about selling Remco, but I appreciate your candid feedback. I want to make sure he doesn't blame you for whatever decision I make."

Allison replied, "Thank you. After all, you're a grown man and are fully capable of making adult decisions on your own. You certainly don't need little old me to tell you what to do."

Jack looked into Allison's narrowed eyes and said, "But I do value your opinion. Don't underestimate the power of a beautiful woman." She could not tell if he was teasing during that last statement or not.

A large party of seven arrived at the bar, laughing loudly and talking all at once. They congregated at the bar stools near the bar, vying for the attention of the lone bar tender. Wes hurried out with their entrees and placed their steak dinners on the table.

"Looks like you got busy," Jack said to him.

Wes looked slightly anxious as he glanced at the waiting customers near the bar and said, "Yes, sir. I'll be busy for the next few minutes, but please flag me down if you need anything else." Wes removed the used salad bowl.

"Thanks," Jack said.

Allison thoroughly enjoyed her perfectly cooked steak. It was seared brown on the outside and had a pink color in the middle, exactly the way she liked it. Jack seemed to enjoy his steak as well. "They say sweet potatoes are supposed to be good for you," Jack said as he took a bite of his potato.

Allison was grateful for the change in subject and quickly jumped on the change in topic, discussing their favorite foods over the course of the meal.

When the bill arrived, Jack was quick to pay for their meals. It crossed Allison's mind that Jack had never once asked her about her recent money windfall or how she could suddenly afford to start a business and live in an estate home. She knew that money was a taboo subject for most new couples and that later on it was one of the biggest rifts between married people. She had assumed that Jack and Austin simply inherited their money from their uncle upon his passing, but she had not directly asked him either. She watched him place a hundred dollar bill inside the black folder that contained the check. "Did you want to do anything else tonight?" Jack asked before standing up to leave, not waiting on any change. He held out his hand, offering assistance as she stood from the booth. She was grateful for his manners and had always loved a man who knew how to be a gentleman.

"You know, I haven't been to the movies in forever," she said on a whim. "Would you like to drive by the theater and see what's playing tonight?"

Jack nodded and said, "Sure, I haven't seen any good movies lately, either. We can take my car if you like." Allison couldn't remember the last time she had gone on a traditional date of dinner and a movie. She certainly had no clue as to what was playing at the theater as she had been absorbed for several months in her business and mission to remedy Remco. They made their way to his car and drove the short distance to the cinema complex. Looking at movies that started in the next few minutes, they agreed upon an action movie that involved spies and car chases.

Full from dinner, Allison passed on the popcorn, not even tempted by the smell. They settled into a half empty theater in the middle row. Sunday nights were work nights for most folks so the movie crowd was rather dismal. It suited Allison fine, as she would rather watch a movie with as few distractions as possible. They checked to make sure their phones were on silent mode as the lights dimmed. Jack reached over and grabbed Allison's hand in his warm strong one. He kept her hand secured in his throughout the entire two hours of the movie.

It was close to midnight when they emerged from the theater into the sparse parking lot. "Do you want me to take you back to your car? I can follow you home to make sure you make it safely there." Jack asked.

"Sure, that's fine," Allison said. Several minutes later she looked in the rear view mirror of her Jaguar to see the two dots of headlights that were Jack. He stayed a safe distance back, but close enough for Allison to notice. She drove through the gate at Morgan Country Club Estates and Allison waved to the guard on duty. He pulled into the driveway behind her as she waited for her electronic garage door to open so she could pull her car inside. Allison parked and exited her car, walking out to Jack as he stepped out of his car, leaving it running.

"I had a good time tonight, Allison," Jack said, wrapping his arms around her in a tender embrace. "I apologize for Austin rushing to see you today."

Allison had wrapped her arms around him as well, enjoying the warmth of his strong body. "No worries," she said. "I'm glad you were able to meet me tonight."

A silver Corvette slowed on the street in front of Allison's house. *Austin.* He momentarily stopped and then peeled away, leaving rubber marks on the road.

Jack shook his head and said, "He's jealous because I'm dating the prettiest girl in town." Allison smiled, liking the term dating, and knew she would have to adjust to this new status. She did not however, want to be the cause of a rift between close twin brothers.

"Jack, I don't' want to cause any problems," she started saying.

Jack interrupted her, "Austin creates his own problems. Please don't worry about him. I have enjoyed getting to know you more." He leaned down and took her lips in a soft, seductive kiss, erasing all doubts that Allison had about their relationship.

She stepped back after they parted and said, "Good night, Jack. Thanks again for tonight."

Jack climbed in his car, held the door open and said, "Good night, Allison. The pleasure was all mine." He grinned big, highlighting his dimples and the twinkle in his blue eyes. She turned and walked back inside as he pulled out of the driveway. She wondered what decision Jack would make about the company, hoping it was the one that kept his brother from hating her.

CHAPTER FORTY-FIVE

After the whirlwind of the last several months, Allison decided to treat Brianna and Jane to a spa day. She booked several treatments at one of the local spas that would last most of the day and included lunch. The three ladies arrived early on Wednesday morning to begin their treatments of massages, facials, scrubs, and seaweed wraps. There was nothing better than a hot stone massage to ease the aching tension in Allison's neck and shoulders. Whether sitting at a computer all day or standing in the kitchen all evening, Allison constantly felt the need to stretch her neck from side to side trying to lessen the tightness. In a relaxing ninety minute session, she could feel the strain from the last few weeks melt away. The hands from the therapist were strong with lots of pressure, gliding over her skin with the help of scented massage oil, creating a blissful feeling of surrender.

Each of the girls had gone into a private massage room with individual therapists. At the end of the ninety minute session, dressed in luxurious plush cotton robes and slippers, the three met in a center lobby reserved exclusively for clientele. They were given water flavored with oranges and lemons to drink in order to release more toxins from their bodies. The therapists worked quickly to transform the massage tables into the seaweed wrap stations. Allison had never had a wrap in her life and was curious to see what changes took place on her body afterwards. After the short break in the lobby, each of them returned to their private room to indulge in a unique experience of having cool seaweed strips placed on their skin and then wrapped in a warm towel. Allison drifted off to sleep for a few minutes while her skin absorbed the healing treatment. She woke as the therapist removed each strip and wiped down Allison's skin.

Wrapped simply in a towel, the ladies were then escorted to the sauna area to relax and enjoy the steam. They discussed the treatments thus far and were looking forward to the provided lunch of salads and light sandwiches. They donned their robes and slippers and were escorted to a privately enclosed garden area that had a small table in the center and four chairs. Three place settings were arranged for the food set out on the table for Allison, Brianna, and Jane. Allison noted how her skin felt smooth and silky after being pampered all morning. She looked forward to the salt scrub for her hair and the facial planned for the afternoon.

A different therapist provided the facial for Allison, which was in a room where all three girls shared the experience together side by side. The chair reminded her of a dentist office chair that leaned far back for better access for the beauty technician. The music playing over the PA system was more like sounds of nature than real music. She heard the occasional bird call or waterfall mixed in with soft melodic tones. The facial scrub felt a bit rough like sandpaper, followed by a cool gel that made her skin tingle. Hot wet towels removed the traces of the mixture and then a creamy lotion was applied liberally over her entire face and neck. Allison hoped no one was taking pictures since her skin was red and blotchy, minus all makeup.

She ran her hands across her face when she sat up, finding it to be smooth as silk. She saw Brianna and Jane sit up as well, each of them wearing a headband that matched her own in order to keep their hair pulled back out of their faces. The last part of the spa treatments would be held in the attached salon. They were guided to three chairs that sat directly in front of three sinks. Each of the ladies had been assigned a hair stylist that applied a rigorous scrubbing of a salt mixture into their dry hair. They were then leaned back in order for their neck to fit in the curved sink, leaving their head positioned directly over the sink. The scrub was washed out with warm water and then shampooed and conditioned. Allison loved the feeling of fingers massaging her head and temples, thinking she should have this done every day. By the end of the day, all three ladies had their hair styled and they donned their street clothes once more.

Busy with all the relaxing and silence of the atmosphere, they had not had time to chat much together. Upon leaving Allison offered, "Since we're splurging today, how would you ladies like to join me at The Lighthouse? We could share a pig dinner."

Brianna raised her eyebrows, not being from the area and never hearing of a pig dinner.

Jane immediately said, "Yes, that sounds like a great idea."

Allison caught Bree's sideways glance and explained, "A pig dinner is six scoops of ice cream with loads of toppings."

"Oh, well then count me in," Bree said smiling.

The Lighthouse was a unique restaurant that had been a staple in Morgan for over fifty years. The man at the end of a long counter took orders verbally and then shouted it loudly to the cooks behind the counter. Different cooks were at various cook stations including fryers, multiple grills, and drinks. The ice cream station was set up in the middle of the dining area, offering twenty different ice cream varieties. The girls each picked two flavors to fill up the six scoop bowl, topped with chocolate, caramel, strawberries, pineapples and whipped cream. As they sat down to eat, Bree asked, "So how was your date last night with Jack?"

Jane looked surprised, "You saw Jack last night?"

Allison nodded, "Yes, it was nice. We ate at Callaway's and then saw that new action movie at the theater."

"And then?" Bree asked hinting that Allison might be leaving out more details.

"And then he went to his house and I went to my house," Allison supplied. Brianna looked disappointed. Jane was smiling, happy for her friend or any friend that had relationship news as she loved to live vicariously through people.

Brianna said, "For someone who's got one of the cutest boyfriends in town, you sure are moving slow." Allison was somewhat startled by the boyfriend term. She had not labeled her relationship with Jack and hearing it from one of her close friends made it seem surreal.

She recovered quickly and answered, "Not everyone moves as fast as you do, Bree. I like to take my time and get to know the guy before we get intimate."

Jane said, "I have to agree with Bree. I don't know how you have the will power to not jump his bones." Allison and Brianna laughed.

Allison responded, "You guys are too much. Since I have your approval, I'll be sure to let you know if and when that next move happens."

Bree whispered loudly to Jane, "She's lying. Allison never tells us her bedtime stories."

Allison tried to switch the subject from her relationship with Jack onto Jane, "Jane, have you been out with anyone lately?"

Jane's shoulders slumped and she looked defeated when she replied, "No, I don't think there are any available men in the whole town of Morgan that would be worth my time these days."

Brianna quipped, "Then maybe it's time the three of us left town for a weekend."

Allison loved the idea, "That sounds great. I need to do some shopping soon. My wine cellar is completely empty." They all laughed at the idea of shopping for wine instead of clothes.

Jane said, "I'm in. I'd love to go to a winery. I've heard of several within about an hour's drive."

Brianna agreed, "I'm in, too. The sooner the better for me before I get started on this new project."

Allison affirmed the decision, "Let's do it, then. What about the large one over the border in Georgia, before you get to Atlanta? I hear they have a great inn attached where we could stay for the weekend."

The girls continued planning their weekend get-a-way to one of the premier wineries in the south. They finished off their ice cream treat and parted for the evening. Allison made her way back to her home to vegetate on the couch and let all the ice cream settle. She turned on the television in the den to watch the cooking channel. She must have dozed off when her cell phone rang, waking her up. "Hello?" she answered sleepily before checking the screen for caller ID.

"Hey," Brianna said, obviously wide awake and extremely alert. "I have news for you." Allison sat up and stretched, trying to fully wake up. She thought maybe something bad had happened with their secret program they had installed several days earlier.

"What is it?" she said sounding worried. "They're selling," Bree said. It took Allison several moments to comprehend what Brianna was saying through her foggy brain.

"Oh," Allison said, "You mean Remco? Jack and Austin are selling? How did you find out?"

Brianna answered, "I checked Austin's email. Remember I tapped it last weekend?"

Oh yeah. Allison had forgotten how resourceful Brianna was.

"Well that's interesting," she replied, actually grateful that Jack decided to agree with his brother and sell the company. Even though her ego had been sorely bruised by Remco, she knew that Jack had nothing to do with those poor decisions. If they were going to continue to see each other, it would be better if her previous employer was not always coming between them.

"I'd thought you'd like to know," Bree said and added, "They also severed all ties with the questionable clients overseas."

Allison replied, "That's great news. Thanks for letting me know."

Bree responded, "Well, good night. I hope you can sleep a

little better now."

Allison laughed softly, "Thanks again, Bree. I'm sure I'll sleep like a baby." She disconnected and lay back down on the couch. Now she was wide awake and the gears were shifting in her head. *I wonder who the new owners will be.* She did not think to ask Brianna if she knew before she hung up. She would find out soon enough as Bree was a flowing fountain of information these days.

CHAPTER FORTY-SIX

Allison knew her secret programming changes had taken effect the next day when she was sitting in the office upstairs in the shop and heard Faith and Lorraine discussing certain recent bank transactions. "It's so odd that I would get a random deposit after all this time from Remco into my bank account. It's labeled as severance," Faith said to Lorraine.

Lorraine pulled up her on-line bank account and checked then replied, "I did, too. Wow, I guess they back paid some of us. I wonder if they had a recent audit or something." Allison smiled knowing that an audit was the last thing Remco would have done.

She glanced up to see if Brianna had overheard the two ladies since she had her earplugs in listening to music on her computer while working. Allison caught her attention and motioned for her to take out her earplugs. Bree slowly took them out and raised her eyebrows in question. Allison put her hand up to her ear and mouthed the word listen, nodding to Faith and Lorraine.

Faith continued, "It's odd after all this time that Remco would give me money after they practically shoved me out the door."

Bree smiled and winked at Allison. Allison smiled back and pretended not to hear the conversation until Lorraine brought her into the conversation, "Hey Allison."

Allison looked up and replied, "Yes?"

Lorraine asked, "Have you checked your bank account lately? Did you get a strange deposit from Remco this week?"

Allison did a good job of feigning any knowledge of any bank transactions. "Let me check," she said, typing on her computer.

She managed to look somewhat shocked and said, "Wow, I sure did. I wonder what that's about." She traded glances with Brianna and quickly looked away fearful that Bree would break out laughing any minute. They both kept a poker face and continued as if nothing else was out of the ordinary.

Faith said, "I don't know, but it was a nice surprise. I guess the new owners are making some positive changes."

Allison almost choked, "Yeah, I guess so."

Faith and Lorraine left shortly to go on a lunch break, leaving Allison and Brianna alone. Gwen and Jane were downstairs, so they were free to discuss the recent events. Bree said, "I guess your changes worked. What all did you do to that benefits program?"

Allison smiled, "I simply added a formula that took the number of years of service for the list of people that were terminated unjustly and multiplied it by one thousand. So if I had been there twelve years, I received a $12,000 bonus check in my bank account last night. It took me a while that night since I had to manually enter each person's employee number that I felt deserved the money."

Bree seemed impressed. She had not been familiar with the exact details of Allison's program, only the breach through the firewall at Remco. "Do you think they'll notice the missing funds?"

Allison shrugged her shoulders, "I'm not sure. I pulled the funds from the retirement accounts of many unworthy managers. Unless those managers watch their retirement portfolio every week, they might not notice immediately. I spread it out so broadly that I don't think anyone will be the wiser, at least not anytime soon."

Bree replied, "So the funds won't be missed from the general ledger accounts."

Allison nodded, "That's right; the operational budget wasn't affected so if they did have an audit, it wouldn't be noticed. I hope the manager jerks don't notice. But if they do, it will take them months to track down the program I installed. That loser Joe that they kept instead of me can't figure out a complex program to save his life. And I don't think many of the former employees will be calling up Remco to ask many questions. Like Faith and Lorraine, they will assume it was a correction from an audit and keep the money."

Brianna laughed, "You are one clever girl, Allison."

They heard footsteps coming up the stairs and turned to watch as Gwen appeared at the top. "You have a visitor downstairs, Allison." Gwen's facial expression did not reveal if it was a good thing or a bad thing so Allison rose and followed her down. She saw the suit and tie and perfectly combed light brown hair near the bar and knew immediately it was Austin before he turned around.

Her first thought was panic. *Does he know about the financial transactions? Does he suspect me of doing it?* Her thoughts were scrambling to find an answer to his unexpected visit.

He turned to face her and for the first time ever, she noticed a rather pleasant look on his face. She had always been exposed to scorn and sneers from him but for the first time thought he could pass for his identical twin, Jack. She wondered if they switched places much as children, deceiving others as to their correct identity. The last time she had seen Austin was on Sunday when he barged up the stairs in an angry fit.

"Hi Allison," Austin said quietly as she approached him.

"Austin, what do I owe the pleasure?"

He got straight to the point, "I wanted to apologize for my behavior on Sunday. I had no right to accuse you of trying to sabotage the sale of Remco."

Allison was shocked. *Did I get an apology from Austin Roman?* "Um, thanks," she replied, at a loss for words on how to accept his apology gracefully.

"Jack explained to me that he had not talked to you about the upcoming sale and that you in fact urged him to sell the company," Austin explained. "I appreciate your encouragement of Jack's decision after the way I rudely blamed you for his behavior."

Allison said, "You're welcome. So you guys have decided to sell then?"

"Yes," Austin replied. I met last week with one of our competitors in Turkey. They have proposed a modest buy out which would maintain Remco's current location here in Morgan. Most of the employees would be retained so it would not create job losses in the community."

Allison smiled, "That's great. I'm glad you found a company willing to do that. And I'm glad that Jack agreed with you to sell."

"I wanted to come in person to apologize and thank you again for understanding," Austin said. He looked like a huge relief had been lifted from his shoulders, not displaying much of the tension and anger he had shown Allison in the past. She caught a glimpse of Brianna coming down the stairs and assumed she must be coming to check out the visitor.

"No problem," Allison said. "I'm glad it's all working out all right."

Brianna arrived and said, "Hi stranger. Welcome back." Her accent was once again thick with a southern drawl as she saddled up to his side, sliding her arm through his. His brows furrowed and his mouth turned into a frown at Brianna's touch, greeting her with silence. It was an odd reaction given Bree's past history of usually winning the male species over within a matter of minutes. Rejection was not in her vocabulary.

Brianna took his icy hint and withdrew her arm from his and decided to retreat. After all, most men reacted to women if some sort of chase was involved. She did not want to appear desperate for attention.

Allison watched the strange exchange as Bree turned and said over her shoulder in a dismissive tone, "Well, it was good to see you again." Allison could swear that Brianna had an extra sway in her hips as she walked back towards the kitchen away from them. Austin watched her go with little reaction to the interruption.

Austin turned back to Allison and cleared his throat before talking. "Well, I hope you have a good day. I don't want to take up any more of your time."

Allison nodded, "Thanks, you have a good day, too." Allison watched as he walked out the front door and then turned to go find Brianna in the back kitchen area.

"I think you're losing your feminine touch," Allison said to Brianna when she found her near the employee's drink machine in the back room.

Brianna lifted her eyebrows and asked, "What was that all about?"

Allison smiled and asked a rebuttal question, "His visit to see me or his rude dismissal of you?"

Brianna answered, "His visit. I'm not worried about his dismissal. He'll come around."

Allison wasn't so sure. "He came to apologize for his behavior Sunday and to thank me for encouraging Jack to sell the company. Of course, thanks to your detective work, we already knew they were selling." Bree smiled, "Well that was nice. He has some redeeming qualities after all."

CHAPTER FORTY-SEVEN

Brianna came bearing the news two day later after reading through Austin's emails. Several managers had noticed the missing funds from their retirement accounts. Funds that were normally withdrawn from their monthly pay check were withdrawn, but did not show on their 401K statement. They were more observant that Allison had given them credit. The Information Systems department would be involved in the mystery to track down the missing funds. "How long do you think it will take them to find your program changes?" Bree asked Allison.

Upon receiving the news, the ladies had taken a stroll outside the downtown shop where they could talk without prying ears. Allison sipped her cup of hot chocolate and squinted as the sun rose higher in the early morning hours. She shrugged her shoulders in a careless manner and answered, "Honestly, I think it will be a while. If they wait for Joe to dig around in the programs it could be months. Todd hasn't programmed in a long time. He's been too busy playing manager to get his hands dirty with some code."

Bree nodded and walked slowly beside Allison before she offered a suggestion, "Do you think we should go back in this Saturday night and remove the code? We would have to breach the firewall again, which could potentially leave another trail, but then your code would be removed leaving them all wondering what happened."

Allison sipped her drink again, keeping her hands warm around the ceramic mug as she looked out around the square. She said, "That might be the best plan. If they sell the company soon, a systems audit will be close at hand. It would be best if nothing appeared out of the ordinary."

Brianna nodded and asked, "What will you tell Jack so he doesn't get suspicious?"

Allison pondered the question and said, "Well, we already talked about having a girls' weekend soon. He doesn't have to know that the first part of the weekend will be in a remote building located on the outskirts of town."

Brianna grinned and patted Allison lightly on the back.

"Well played, my friend," Bree commended.

"Who knew that those old guys would miss a half a million dollars this quickly?" Allison asked under her breath as they neared the fountain in the middle of the Morgan Square.

Brianna stopped walking and turned to look at Allison. "Did you say half a million dollars? Good grief, Allison, I should say they would notice that amount. When you sock it to them, you go all out." Brianna once again revealed that she had not been privy to the specifics of Allison's program.

Allison smiled and walked forward to sit on the low wall surrounding the fountain. "Well, I had to atone for the sins of the forefathers. Besides, if those thirty some odd people had received just a few dollars each, the restitution would have been virtually for naught." Brianna sat beside Allison and looked out over the town of Morgan. Allison finished the last of her hot chocolate in silence while Brianna ran her fingers through the cool water behind her in the fountain.

"Those pigs deserved the revenge you dished out," Brianna said in a definitive tone.

Allison nodded, "Yes they did. I only wish they had not crushed so many people's career aspirations along the way. To be honest, if I hadn't won the lottery, I don't know what I'd be doing right now. I would be pushing my resume on every job search website, hoping for a bite."

Brianna gave a half grin and said, "You'd be working for me instead of the other way around. I would've shown you all my tricks. In fact, I might do that."

Allison laughed softly and watched the sparse traffic go by. "I may be safer not knowing what you do," Allison replied jokingly.

They rose to wander back to the store. Brianna flicked the

water off of her fingers and then waved her hand to air dry it. One of the passing cars mistook it for a wave and honked their horn in response, startling Allison. "Ha ha," Brianna said, "I guess they thought I was waving."

Allison said teasingly, "Warn me the next time you want to flag down passing traffic."

Gwen spotted them when they arrived back and gestured for Allison to come over to her. "I'll meet you upstairs later," Bree said to Allison, not stopping as she climbed the stairs to the office.

Allison met Gwen over at the bar and asked, "What's up?"

Gwen's facial expression was one of worry and distress when she answered, "Did you see Jack outside?"

Allison answered, "No, was he just here?"

Gwen replied, "Yes, he looked kind of angry. He asked for you. I've never seen him look that unpleasant."

"Okay, thanks," Allison said, "I'll go call him and let him know I'm back."

Allison sat at one of the vacant bar stools and dialed Jack's cell phone number. He answered rather curtly, "Hello."

"Hey," she said, "I must have just missed you. Gwen said you were at the shop looking for me."

Jack took a deep breath before answering, "Yes, I need to see you. I'll be back to your shop in a few minutes." Allison stood and paced around the store, nervously clutching her cell phone wondering what had caused Jack's foul mood.

There's no way he could connect me to the changes I installed Saturday night. What else is there? She stared at the door willing him to enter until she saw him jerk the door handle, striding in quickly, making a bee line straight to her.

She smiled, giving it her best effort to diffuse the unknown situation, "Hi Jack," she said. He stared at her for a brief second as she watched his lips twitch.

He finally asked in a soft yet firm voice, "Allison, did you receive a large amount of money from Remco this past weekend?"

She nodded, "Yes, I did. Was that you're doing?" she asked with feigned ignorance.

"No," he said, "I wish you would've told me. I had to hear it from other people that a lot of former employees had large deposits hit their bank accounts this past week."

Aha. He's mad that I didn't tell him first. "Oh, I thought that was your doing. It didn't occur to me that you didn't already know," she stated as a quick excuse adding, "In fact, I was going to thank you the next time I saw you. So if you didn't do it, who did?"

Jack frowned, "We don't know. Do you mind if I see the routing number and any account information from that transaction?" His shoulders slumped some as he lost the edginess to his voice. He had put on his private investigator hat and switched from accusatory to inquisitive.

"Sure," Allison said, walking towards the stairs to the upstairs office. "I'll pull up my account upstairs so you can see that specific transaction," she offered, not wanting to appear the least bit guilty.

He followed her up the stairs and said, "Thanks. I appreciate any help you have to offer."

Allison walked over to her desk and sat at her chair. She said,

"Pull up that other chair if you like. It will just take me a minute to log into my bank account." Jack grabbed the nearest chair and dragged it over to sit beside Allison. Her monitor was tilted just enough that he could not see her screen as she pulled up her account, displaying an obscene amount of money thanks to her lottery winnings. If their relationship continued to grow, she would eventually show him the bottom line, but she was not yet ready for him to know that information. She clicked on the specific deposit from Remco and zoomed in on just the information needed before turning her monitor at an angle for him to see.

Jack removed a small writing tablet from his front shirt pocket and a pen and wrote down the amount, the verbiage and the account number. "Do you know why you received that specific amount?" Jack asked Allison.

Allison replied, "I'm not sure. It's labeled severance and reminds me of the package your brother offered me when I was first terminated. I just assumed you guys went ahead and processed a similar amount. Do you think Austin was involved?"

Jack shook his head, "No, he is trying to figure it out, same as me."

Allison said, "Hmm. Well let me know if you need any further help. I can have Faith and Lorraine call you with their information as well when they return. They also received severance deposits."

Jack gave a half defeated smile and said, "Thanks. I'll talk to you soon." He rose to leave, folded his notepad and placed it inside his shirt pocket along with his pen. Allison watched him go thankful that she was not considered a suspect, simply a recipient of some mystery money. It was quite a change to see the business side of Jack rather than the playful, flirty side.

CHAPTER FORTY-EIGHT

Allison did not hear much from Jack for the rest of the week; hence she did not need an alibi for her Saturday night rendezvous with Brianna. She once again donned all black in preparation for the stealthy adventure in the dark of night. She was confident that no one had found her code yet given that Joe and Todd were not the fastest when it came to debugging a system, plus she had Brianna scanning Austin's email for any triggers that might alert them to recent findings. *I really need to get a different car soon.* Her red Jaguar was darker at night than the blood red color highlighted by daylight hours, but it was a unique car and Allison did not want to be spotted at that time of night. She drove cautiously to avoid any hidden police cruisers.

Her thermos was freshly filled with steaming hot chocolate, enhanced by three miniature marshmallows that by now had melted into the creamy smooth drink. Her left hand gripped the steering wheel tightly while she lifted the container to take a sip, almost scalding her tongue from the heat. She drove directly to the gravel drive outside of town that led her to the modified high-tech building where Brianna would be waiting. As she approached the house, she noticed more lights on inside than last time. *Brianna must already be here.* She put her car in park and while it idled got out and manually open the garage door. She spotted Bree's Jeep just inside the other bay. She parked her car, shut the garage door, grabbed her bags and opened the door to the interior of the building.

She saw Brianna sitting in a chair with a strange look on her face, her eyes shifting left quickly as if something caught her eye. Allison put her bags on the desk she had occupied previously and said, "Hey Bree, what's up?"

Brianna paused, not answering right away when a male voice answered instead, "Hi Allison. I was just having a chat with your friend, Brianna."

Jack! Allison spun around and saw him emerge from behind the desks where the refrigerator and microwave were located. She looked quickly back at Briana with wide, questioning eyes, raising her eyebrows.

Brianna answered one of her unasked questions, "I just arrived a few minutes ago when Jack walked in behind me. We haven't had much of a chance to talk." Allison took the hint and was not about to reveal anything that might incriminate the two of them.

Jack paced on the other side of the room while Allison stood rooted to the spot next to her desk. "Funny thing about computers," Jack stated, "is that they most always leave a trail."

Allison glanced again at Brianna before she replied, "I'm not sure what you're talking about, Jack." Jack stopped pacing long enough to stare at Allison several seconds, boring holes into her eyes as if trying to read her mind. *Have we been busted? Surely not, I think he's just fishing for answers.* Allison's thoughts were running wild with doubt and questions about his arrival.

"You see, Allison, I really liked you a lot, and I knew you were smart," Jack said and continued before she could interrupt, "And smart girls can be vindictive given the right circumstances."

He's guessing. Brianna was eerily quiet, not offering any of her usual pithy comments or opinions.

"Do you remember that night last week when you fell asleep on the couch?" he asked Allison.

"Yes," she replied slowly with uneasiness about his line of questioning.

"Do you remember where your computer was that night?" he asked.

Allison's throat began to have a strange lump in it as she replied again, "Yes, in the library."

Jack stated, "You're not the only one with some computer skills. After you fell asleep, I quickly installed a keystroke copycat program on your laptop, which you left unlocked."

Allison's heart sank, knowing exactly what that type of program meant.

Brianna finally spoke out, "You jerk. You played her." Allison looked at Brianna and had to look quickly away before her emotions overtook her good sense. She did not want to implicate Brianna in any way.

Allison turned back to Jack. "So you monitored my every keystroke since that night?" she asked with disbelief, shaking her head ever so slightly.

"Yes," Jack said. "I really wanted to believe that you were not bitter toward Remco, but Austin called it right."

Allison looked down, not able to keep eye contact with him; certain she could feel his disappointment in her. "What are you going to do?" Allison asked softly, swallowing the words with difficulty.

Jack came closer to her without touching her, "Honestly, I don't know," he answered and added, "I had to come to see if you were going to cause another problem tonight."

Allison shook her head slightly, wary of admitting any wrongdoing. "No," she finally said, "in fact I was going to reverse my changes so any auditors wouldn't find the code."

Jack looked surprised, "Really? You took a big risk coming here again tonight just to undo the code you did last weekend. In fact, I don't know much about the computer language and code you used, but I do know how to read activity on a computer. I could tell you had done something rather high tech, but didn't know what until we had some complaints from some of the managers."

Allison grimaced before asking, "Are you going to prosecute me?"

Jack bit his lip, contemplating her question, "I should, or rather, Austin should, if he knew about any of this."

Allison reeled slightly with the shock of Austin not knowing. *Jack didn't tell Austin?* She was more confused than before, "I thought you said Austin was right about me."

Jack started pacing again before he answered, "He was, but that doesn't mean he knows I tapped your computer with a keystroke copycat program or that you committed any crime. Honestly Allison, I had been racking my brain trying to think of a way to rectify the wrongs that my Uncle Cliff had done. You provided the solution, although not exactly in the manner that I would have used. Except now we have a bunch of pissed off managers that are wondering where their money went. I don't know how to explain that one to them. I can't exactly tell them that my girlfriend stole it and gave it to her friends."

Girlfriend?

Allison's eyes widened at the term considering what had just transpired. She had been caught in a lie that could destroy her freedom, not to mention the impact to her best friend, Bree. The lack of trust between Allison and Jack was a glaring red flag that the relationship was doomed. He had invaded her private domain and breached the inner sanctuary of her personal laptop.

She had barely begun to contemplate the consequences of her actions when Jack said, "Can I watch while you back out your changes?"

Allison looked quickly at Brianna, whose face must have mirrored her own in stark wonder. "Excuse me?" she asked, certain she had misunderstood him.

"I want to see how you did it. After all, when the auditors do come in to review Remco, I want to make sure all the evidence has been removed so as not to affect the sale of the company."

"You've got to be kidding me," she said, her tone almost in a monotone sound of disbelief. Allison looked around to see if any hidden cameras had been installed that she missed earlier.

Brianna quipped, "We've come this far. We might as well entertain him."

Brianna turned toward her computer and logged in to the Remco server through the firewall. Allison opened her laptop and set it on the desk while Jack rolled a chair over to her desk. Brianna quickly viewed the log on screen and noticed that no one was currently logged into the Remco server.

As Allison went through the motions of logging in, Brianna said, "I see you logged on now."

Allison kept her back straight, not speaking as she navigated through Remco's production system until she found the program she had installed. She selected the backup copy of the original program from her hard drive and overlaid the one she had previously installed. Since she did not have to enter information about individuals to ensure payment this time, she had the program replaced in a matter of minutes.

"The next payroll run should run as scheduled with no interference this time," Allison said aloud.

She logged out of the system and then Brianna said, "All clear." Brianna then deactivated her connection to the Remco server.

Both ladies turned and faced Jack in silence. Jack looked at Allison and then to Brianna. "That's it? In less than five minutes time, you've removed all traces of your changes?"

Allison nodded and took a deep breath letting out a long sigh, "Yes, that's it. Since the job logs are only kept for three days, there is no tracer from last Saturday night that would point to anything having run differently." Her fate was now in the hands of a man with whom she had betrayed. Brianna rolled her chair over and grabbed the laptop off of the desk Allison had been using. Bree sat Allison's computer in her lap while clicking and typing for several silent moments.

As she finished, Bree announced, "Now that's it." Allison and Jack stared at her for a minute with eyes glazed over in confusion. Brianna explained, "I removed the keystroke copycat program that your boyfriend installed."

Allison replied, "Oh, thanks."

Jack grimaced and backed his chair away as he stood. "Thanks ladies. Now all I have to do is come up with a feasible explanation that will satisfy the managers who are missing funds."

"You could tell them they should be lucky they still have a job at all," Brianna quipped.

Jack turned up one side of his mouth contemplating her suggestion. "Right, well, good night," Jack said and walked toward the door.

Allison called out, "Are you going to tell Austin?" and then added, "I mean, should Bree and I be worried?"

Jack looked at Allison with his ocean blue eyes, revealing no emotions on his gorgeous poker face. "If you're going to take on the Wonder Twins, Allison, be prepared for ice and fire." He turned and left quietly, shutting the door firmly behind him. Minutes later, they could hear the sound of his vehicle as it started to life and drove from the back of the house around to the front, fading away in the distance down the long gravel driveway.

"I can have us out of the country with new identities in less than twenty-four hours," Brianna said quickly, breaking the silence of Jack's parting.

Allison had been staring at the door unable to breathe. *What have I done?* She had jeopardized everything she had worked for over the last several months, including her friendship with Brianna and her relationship with Jack, not to mention her new business that currently employed dozens of innocent people.

Brianna had wheeled back to her own computer and was furiously typing away. "Which name do you like better, Sally or Jennifer?" Brianna asked her.

Allison Black turned around slowly, "Sally, I guess, why?"

Brianna replied, "I'm creating your new identity, Sally Deen."

Allison stood up abruptly, glanced back at Brianna and said, "I don't need a new identity. I'm not going anywhere." Brianna stopped typing and watched her friend snatch her computer and toss it carelessly in her oversized bag and then stride purposefully towards the door. Allison jerked open the door and slammed it shut behind her. Her car peeled out, spinning gravel as she gave chase to her lost dreams.

CHAPTER FORTY-NINE

Her dash clock showed 2:34 a.m. Her sporty F-Type was racing down road when Allison spotted the taillights of Jack's dark SUV ahead of her. He had not yet turned into Morgan Country Club Estates but was quickly approaching the neighborhood. She watched as his left turn signal flashed off and on in the dark of night and then disappeared in the turn, her car not far behind. He had cleared the guard's gate when she turned, but she quickly drove up right behind him as they neared her house. She flashed her lights and kept tailing him as he drove past her driveway and closed in on his own. Not wanting to wake the neighbors, she resisted the urge to honk the horn, instead opting to pull into his driveway directly behind him.

Jack opened the garage door with his automatic opener, but did not pull his car into the garage. He stepped out of the driver's side and with a pinched expression, took a deep breath while waiting for Allison to approach. She had thrown her Jaguar into park and flung open her door, taking quick strides to meet him face to face.

Allison had never been one for confrontation, but her emotions were in a state of unrest, needing immediate answers. "Jack, we need to talk," she began.

Jack cut her off, "No, Allison, we had our talk. I need to sleep. It's late and it's been a long day." Allison stared at him in open fascination, wondering how anyone could sleep after the events that had just taken place.

She said, "Excuse me if I find it difficult to rest when my

future lies in your hands. I need to know if you're going to press charges against me or not." Jack ran his hand over his face slowly, and then looked at Allison's troubled hazel eyes.

"Allison, I really like you. In fact, I haven't had feelings this strong for anyone, ever," Jack said and then paused.

Allison jumped in, "But?"

Jack took a deep breath, "But I honestly can't believe you stole funds from my company. Austin and I were working on a plan to rectify the past mistakes before you took it upon yourself to become some kind of vigilante."

Allison's hackles were raised, her voice growing louder as she said, "Do you mean that by rectifying mistakes you and Austin would break into my house and force me to sign a legal agreement? What kind of plan is that?"

Jack's voice rose to match hers as he responded, "First of all, you can't prove that anyone at Remco broke into your house. Second, at least Austin was offering you recompense the legal way." He mumbled an addition, "Even if I didn't agree with his delivery tactics."

Allison huffed, staring up at Jack and replied, "You and I both know Austin was behind the break in, even if I can't prove it. And his offer was only for me, not the thirty-two other former employees that deserved it."

The outside flood lights came on, the back door opened and Austin came running outside. "What is going on out here? I can hear the two of you going at it from inside the house," Austin said loudly as he approached them.

Allison crossed her arms and took a deep breath, turning away from both of them. Jack looked at Allison then turned back to Austin, taken aback to see him barefoot, wearing only boxers and carrying a baseball bat.

"Are you going to beat us to keep us quiet, Austin?" Jack asked his twin.

Austin pursed his lips and said snidely, "I didn't know it was you and Allison until I got out here. I thought maybe you were in trouble." Jack rolled his eyes. Austin lifted his chin in a short nod toward Allison and asked Jack, "Lovers spat?"

Allison turned around and faced Austin, "Oh, please," she said, her eyes cold. It finally clicked that Austin was not wearing much clothing. She looked him up and down, admiring his general physique even in her agitated state. His ruffled hair made is resemblance to Jack uncanny. Jack took notice of her admiration of his brother and stepped between them, breaking her gaze.

"Allison was just leaving," Jack said, his back to Austin facing Allison.

"Allison's not going anywhere," Allison rebutted, cocking her head to one side and placing her hands on her hips. Austin shook his head and turned his back on them.

He walked toward the garage and said, "Whatever. I'm going back to bed. Jack, you might want to get a muzzle for your girlfriend."

Allison spat her words at his back, "I'm not his girlfriend!" Austin disappeared into the house with a final wave.

Allison did not miss the fact that Jack didn't tell Austin what had happened earlier, but it didn't mean Jack wouldn't tell his brother later. She lowered her voice, keenly aware that others might be listening, "Look, I'm sorry that I didn't tell you about my plans. It wasn't exactly a conversation I could have with the new owner of the company. It's not like I crippled the company financially. So what if a few hot heads lost some of their retirement dollars. They stepped on good people to get to where they are and had it coming." Allison felt vindicated as she stated her opinion to Jack.

Jack stared at the ground for a few minutes, fiddling with the car keys in his hand. "I'm trying to make things right here," he said in a low voice. "I don't need you going behind my back to make a point. You could have brought your concerns to me, as your friend, not just an ex-employer."

Allison took another deep breath and closed her eyes. She glanced over at the garage, cautious now of being overheard. "Are you going to tell Austin?"

Jack looked up and away, not making eye contact with Allison. "I don't know. He deserves to know what happened, but I don't think he'll take it as lightly as I did," Jack replied.

"This is taking it lightly?" Allison asked somewhat sarcastically and then changed her tone, "I understand if you need to tell him. After all, he is your brother. I would appreciate some kind of notice before you do so I can get some things in order."

She turned to walk back to her car and stopped, then turned and looked at Jack one more time. "For what it's worth, I really like you, too, Jack. I'm sorry I messed that up." She climbed into the driver's side of her car, closed the door softly and reversed down his driveway. Jack stood several seconds in place before entering the house, not bothering to move his car inside the garage.

CHAPTER FIFTY

Allison slept fitfully on her couch that night, waiting with baited breath for the sheriff's office to come knocking on her door. When no one arrived by mid-morning, she finally called Brianna's cell phone number. The operator's automatic voice answered telling her the number had been disconnected. *Great.* She had a feeling that Brianna would go underground rather quickly instead of waiting to see if Jack pressed charges. Someone in her line of business could not afford to be exposed. Brianna was as smart as they come and Allison knew she would land on her feet safely. Allison had tried to right so many wrongs and help get justice for those that deserved it, but she had failed to protect those closest to her.

After not getting through to Brianna, she dialed Gwen's number. "Hello?" Gwen answered on the first ring.

"Hey Gwen, it's me, Allison. Do you think you could hold down the fort for me for a few days? I need to take care of some personal business."

Gwen did not hesitate, "Sure, no problem. Take as much time as you need."

"Thanks," Allison said, "Oh, and Brianna will be gone for a while, too. If you get any new computer forensic assignments, please have one of the tech guys take a crack at them for us." Gwen answered,

"Okay, will do," Gwen said.

Allison then asked her to pass along the message to Jane that both she and Brianna would not be able to go on the upcoming winery   tour.

Gwen said, "I'll let her know. Take care. Call me if you need anything."

"Thanks, talk to you later," Allison replied. If anything did go down today, she did not want to be at her place of business in the public eye.

Allison showered and dressed in simple linen pants and a cool button-up striped blouse. She slipped on her sandals and styled her hair in a simple ponytail. She grabbed her purse and her car keys and left the house, constantly looking in her rearview mirror. On a whim, she drove to the nearby town that had many car dealerships lined up along a stretch of road known to the locals as the motor mile. Her first stop was the BMW dealership. She parked her Jaguar F-Type in a parking spot near the customer entrance and made it to the second car in the lot before a sales person appeared. "Good morning," said the tall, lanky man. He appeared to be in his late forties, nicely groomed and impeccably dressed.

"Hi," Allison said, shading her eyes from the blazing sun even though she wore sunglasses.

"Can I help you find anything?" he asked as he casually walked closer to the car she had been walking near.

She glanced around the lot and decided that one new car might not be enough. "I'm looking for a new vehicle or two," she said vaguely until her eye caught the first type of car she had been looking for across the parking lot. "Over there," she pointed towards a brown metallic convertible.

"That's our M6 Convertible. It's a very nice ride," he started explaining as they walked toward the indicated car. "The color is called Mojave metallic. It comes with a beige full merino leather interior and 20 inch alloy wheels. Of course, you can always build your own model and have it delivered straight to this dealership." She peered into the driver's side window of the beautiful car with the black soft top.

"It's a beautiful car," she said.

He offered, "Feel free to open the door and sit inside." She checked the handle and found it unlocked.

She sat inside on the cool leather seat and admired the wood paneling and classic dash board. The salesman patiently waited outside the car until she finished looking through the interior of the luxurious car. As she climbed out, he asked, "Would you like to take it for a test drive?"

She nodded, "Yes, I would love to."

"I'll run get the key," he said, and then jogged back toward the showroom. He returned just moments later and said, "If you don't mind, I'll ride with you and share some of the additional features on this model."

Allison replied, "Sure, that's fine." She settled into the driver's buttery soft seat while the salesman entered the passenger side. Allison saw the button to start the car and pushed it, causing the car to purr to life.

She slowly put the car into drive and pulled forward as he spoke, "The M6 is one of my favorite lines. It has night vision with pedestrian detection and has USB, Bluetooth and Smartphone integration."

Allison asked few questions during the test drive since the salesman answered many of them ahead of time. She found out his name was Luke and that he started selling cars several years earlier after a large layoff at a nearby textile mill. They returned to the lot and Allison parked the car where she found it. She turned off the engine and exited the car, followed shortly thereafter by Luke. She glanced around the lot again until she spotted the SUV models several rows away. "I'd like to look at that SUV over there," she pointed the way once again. "Which of the SUVs has the biggest engine in it?" she asked as they walked the short distance.

Luke answered, "The X5 xDrive50i has 445 horsepower with a twin turbo V-8 engine."

Allison said, "I'd like to test drive one of those, please, Luke."

Luke nodded eagerly and said, "I'll go get the keys." He returned quickly and they were off on test drive number two.

Allison enjoyed the feel of the vehicle and liked the space gray metallic exterior color with the ivory white leather interior. Luke rambled on about the features while Allison drove through a few nearby neighborhoods. She returned the car to the lot and Luke asked, "Is there any other model you would like to see?"

She shook her head, "No, I think I like the two that I drove."

Luke smiled and asked, "Which one are you leaning towards?"

"Both," Allison said.

Luke chuckled as they walked into the showroom. "It's a tough decision. They are both really nice cars. You can have them built with any features that you like" he said. Allison Black smiled, knowing it wasn't every day that a customer walks in and buys more than one car on the spot.

Making herself very clear, Allison touched Luke's arm causing him to turn and looked him in the eye stating, "Luke, I want to buy the M6 convertible, as is. And I want to buy two X5 models, so that's three cars total. And I'm going to pay cash today." Luke blinked with his mouth slightly open.

After the shock wore off, Luke hurried to gather the necessary paper work, making the transaction as painless as possible. Allison casually asked Luke what type of car he drove.

"Oh, I drive a Ford F150. It's not a BMW, but it gets me

where I'm going."

Allison pondered this for a minute and then asked, "Do you mind if I buy it from you? I would pay you cash." Luke dropped the pen in his hand onto the floor. He recovered slowly and picked it up asking,

"Why would you want my truck?" Allison smiled, "I need a good pickup truck for errands and things." She silently added, *And I need a popular vehicle that would be less conspicuous around town.* The Ford F150 was one of the most popular trucks on the market and every other male in the state of South Carolina seemed to drive a pickup truck.

Luke said slowly, "I've never thought about selling my truck, but I guess I could."

Allison replied, "Great. I'll pay you $35,000 in cash."

Luke shook his head, "Ms. Black, my truck isn't worth over $23,000 if it was new, and it's seven years old."

Allison said, "Well then, it looks like you're getting a pretty good deal."

It took the good part of an hour to sign all the proper paperwork and cut a large check. Allison arranged for the SUVs to be delivered as a surprise to her intended recipients, Jane and Gwen. She decided to drive the M6 home, leaving the Jaguar at the dealership, to be delivered to her house later. After the formal paperwork was complete for the dealership, Allison and Luke stepped outside to complete the sale of his personal truck. She asked him to bring it by her house by the next day, giving him the address and code to her garage for him to leave it inside. *Hopefully, I won't be in jail tomorrow.* After the dealership, she made her way to a local cellular phone company and bought two cell phones with a prepaid limit on the number of minutes and data usage. She did not have to register her name or link it with her existing phone records, enabling her to have untraceable phones, at least for the time being.

Driving in her new BMW with the top down, Allison Black made her way to the bank and withdrew a large sum of cash to have on reserves. She did not want to be in a bind if her bank accounts were frozen due to any future litigation that might happen. She placed twenty-five thousand dollars in a large manila envelope along with the second cell phone she had purchased earlier. The cell phone contained one contact number which was the new number from the first secured cell phone she had purchased. The rest of the cash she placed in a second large envelope and tucked it tightly into her open purse. She then drove to the sports club and rented a locker for one year under the name Sally Deen. She put one of the keys to the locker in an envelope and left it at the front desk for Sally Deen to pick up at a later time. Inside the locker, she placed the envelope with the cash and cell phone and secured the lock, taking the spare key with her.

She then drove home, packed a large suitcase and a small carryon bag, which contained her passport and laptop. In case of impending incarceration, she wanted to have emergency supplies packed in her car for a quick get-a-way. She didn't feel the need to completely go off radar as Brianna had done, but she didn't want to be backed into a corner without a backup plan. Her heart told her that if Jack had not turned her in by now, she could be safe, but her head dictated a logical approach.

CHAPTER FIFTY-ONE

Allison received two phone calls back to back that evening, one from Gwen and one from Jane. They were both shocked and excited about their new BMW vehicles that were delivered that afternoon. She thanked them for their friendship and extra hours at the shop and told them she had wanted to do something special just for them. Their names were listed on the titles, which they should receive in a few weeks as soon as the paperwork was processed. The elation in their voices was clear and made Allison smile to know she could continue to do good deeds in the midst of her turmoil.

Sitting at one of the barstools at her large granite kitchen countertop, she thumbed through a catalog she received in the mail, numbly looking at passing photos of furniture and decorative items coming into style for the upcoming autumn season. Her cell phone gave a quick buzz, indicating a text message had been received. Allison had to read the text twice until she understood who it was from. *Brianna!*

The text only contained an unknown phone number and the phrase "secure line." She ran quickly and grabbed her new cell phone that she had purchased earlier that day and called the number listed.

"Hello?" Brianna DeVoe answered on the first ring.

"Oh gosh, Bree, it's good to hear your voice," Allison gushed.

"Hey Allison, I'm glad you got my text. I didn't realize you had another phone. I halfway expected a phone call later tonight after you purchased one," Brianna said, impressed with her smart friend.

Allison replied, "It was one of the first things I purchased today. I didn't know if you had some resources already in place, but if not, I have an extra phone and some cash for you at the sports club on Freemont Street. It's in locker twenty-one. There's a key at the desk for Sally Deen that will fit that locker."

Brianna gave a small chuckle, "Sally Deen, huh? I thought you would like that name as your alias. Thanks for thinking of me. I'm leaving the country in a few hours but wanted to check in on you. Any word from the twins today?"

Allison took a deep breath and answered, "Nothing so far. As of last night, Jack had still not told Austin about our little adventure." Brianna was quiet on the other end of the phone. Allison filled in the conversation gap, "I'm really sorry about all of this Brianna. You shouldn't have to leave everything behind because of me."

Brianna was quick to answer, "I knew the risks and was very happy for the reward. I'm a big girl and can take care of myself. Don't start thinking you made me do something I didn't want to do. Besides, I need a little vacation. We've been way too busy the last several months. If anyone asks, you can tell them I needed some personal time to find my chi."

Allison swallowed the lump in her throat and said, "I'll keep the envelope at the sports club there indefinitely. Go get it if you need it. Call or text me if you need anything. Sally can be our shared nickname."

Brianna said, "Thanks Allison. And don't worry about me. I'll check in as I can. Who knows, you may decide to go on an extended vacation, too."

Allison replied, "No vacation, yet, but soon hopefully. Take care, Bree."

Brianna signed off, "Bye."

Allison stared at the small cell phone in her hand, now quiet in the vast space of her open kitchen area. *So this is what it feels like to be rich and lonely.* She now knew the exact meaning of the expression about money not buying happiness. Although, truth told, she was pretty sure that Jane and Gwen were very happy with their recent gifts. Allison stood up, determined to get her mind off of recent matters by watching one of her favorite movies. She grabbed a bag of popcorn from her cabinet, took off the cellophane wrapper and put it in the microwave to pop. She then walked over to her drawer of DVD movies and selected a humorous chick flick movie from the stash she had collected over the years. She placed the disc carefully in the player and pressed play, then walked back to her bedroom to change into comfortable clothing.

As she stepped back into the den in her flannel pajama pants and t-shirt, the movie options were just coming on the television screen. She picked up remote and selected play, almost missing the knock at the front door due to the loud popping sounds coming from the microwave.

Oh great, now they come as soon as I change clothes. Allison padded in her sock-clad feet to the front door and opened it, surprised to see Jack on the front porch, alone. She peered behind him before narrowing her eyes, taking in the scowl on his face.

He said, "I'm alone. May I come in?" She shrugged her shoulders and pushed the door wider, turned her back on him and assumed he would follow her into the kitchen. She heard the front door click softy shut as she found a bowl in the cabinet next to the microwave. She carefully removed the hot popcorn bag and tugged at the corners until a hot cloud of steam emitted from the opening. She dumped the golden fluffy kernels into the bowl and carried it into the den just as the song from the movie blared to life loudly on the TV screen, signaling the start of her movie. Jack jumped at the sudden noise, causing his arm to flail up, hitting the passing bowl of popcorn. The bowl arced out of Allison's hands in a spiraling motion, delivering a popcorn shower upon them both.

"Umph," Jack grunted as he reached out to catch the bowl before it hit the floor, landing on one knee while extending his arm out as far as he could, grasping it with his fingertips just in time. Allison wanted to laugh, but her overloaded senses kept her stoic, standing in place while Jack stood back up with his prized catch. Popcorn was scattered all over her floor, coffee table and couch.

"Sorry," Jack murmured, placing the empty bowl on the coffee table. He knelt back down to pick up the loose pieces of popcorn, tossing them into the bowl.

Allison said, "Don't worry about it. I can clean it up later." Jack continued picking up the pieces, scooting around on his knees as he made progress. Allison rolled her eyes and started picking up the pieces that had landed on the couch, tossing a handful into the bowl.

Allison spoke as they worked together to pick up the remaining pieces of her dinner, "I thought maybe you would have the police with you when you came tonight." She looked down, keeping her head low as she waited silently for his answer. Jack sat back on his heels and studied the top of Allison's head for several moments. When he stood up, he dumped the handful of kernels into the bowl and rubbed his hands together briskly, removing the residue from the popcorn.

Taking a deep breath, he began speaking, "I told Austin about the programming hack that you did to Remco." Allison looked up quickly with large brownish-green eyes and caught his deep blue ones looking back at her. "His reaction was not the same as mine," Jack continued. Allison slowly stood up and then sat down, perched on the edge of the couch. Jack sat down on the matching loveseat and wrung his hands together, looking down as if his hands held the next words.

Allison impatiently waited for him to continue, staring as his hands moving restlessly. Jack said, "He just laughed. He told me that I was too trusting. Somehow Austin knew you wouldn't let it go and had been expecting you to retaliate." Allison lowered her head, and stared at the carpet under the coffee table.

Jack spoke quietly, "I came over to let you know that neither he nor I will be pursuing charges against you. After talking it over, we decided that what you did may not have been the most ethical way to handle the situation, but the monetary rewards were well deserved by all the recipients. We will tell the affected managers that there was a computer bug that is now fixed and compensate them for their losses. There's no need to let them know where their money went. Nor are we going to tell the former employees where it came from. They can assume it was a severance gift, as denoted on the deposit."

Allison glanced up at Jack, her mouth slightly open in shock that there would be no legal backlash for her actions. She nodded slightly and mumbled, "Thank you, Jack."

Jack continued, "The sale of the company will be complete by the end of this week. Luckily, your changes did not affect any of the budget numbers that the buyer reviewed so no red flags were thrown. Hopefully, the transaction will go smoothly and Austin and I can step away from this company without looking back."

Allison asked, "Is that what you want?"

Jack nodded, "Yes, I'm not cut out for a corporate world executive. Austin has not enjoyed his stint either. He's ready to practice law again."

Allison nodded, "And what about you? What will you do, Jack?"

Jack gazed at Allison's face, taking in her long blonde hair flowing freely down her back and her soft pink lips. "Well," Jack said smiling slightly, "After the sale of the company, Austin and I will be quite wealthy, so I feel it's only appropriate that I start dating one of the richest girls in town."

Allison's cheeks grew red, slightly embarrassed by his brazen tone. "How do you know I'm one of the richest girls in town?" she asked, tilting her head to one side in wonder.

Jack stood up and crossed the short distance to sit beside her on the longer couch. He picked up her hand with his left hand, using his right hand to run through her hair, tucking her hair behind her ear. "I know you won that big lottery several months ago," he said, surprising her with the information. Allison's hazel eyes grew wide, shocked that he guessed correctly as she had not told him about her winnings.

"How did you know?" she asked as his smile grew wider, showing off his white teeth and deep dimples.

Jack answered, "The same way that Austin knew where to find you that first night you were terminated."

Allison drew her eyebrows together. "Huh?" she asked, perplexed on how he could relate the two things together.

"Remember the lawyer, Charlie Ponder?" Jack asked. Allison nodded. Jack continued, "Austin had a GPS tracking device attached under your car before you were escorted from the building that day. He had Mr. Ponder follow you. He backed off once he saw you were scared and hiding in that church parking lot, but resumed his pursuit once you were in a public area. After your visit to the lawyer's office, he tracked your car to the lottery office. Once you started spending money, and they had announced an anonymous lottery winner, he put two and two together."

Allison sat speechless, her mouth gaped open. *All this time I thought I was an anonymous winner.* She spoke, "Please don't say anything to anyone. I don't want the public to know that I won. Who knows what kind of crazies will be knocking on my door?"

Jack laughed, "You mean like me?" Allison smiled, enjoying the feel of his hand rubbing the back of hers. His closeness was a comfortable feeling that she had missed.

She jerked upright remembering Brianna. "Did you tell Austin about Brianna's role in the hack?"

Jack shook his head. "Nah, I figured one fall guy was enough to take the blame. Why involve her?"

Allison breathed a sigh of relief, "Thanks, Jack. She is innocent, only doing what I asked of her as her employer. I designed and wrote all of the code that I used. Besides, I think she has a thing for Austin and I wouldn't want for her to start things off in a bad light."

Jack cocked his head to the side and said, "Really? She has a thing for Austin? Hmm, who would've guessed?"

Allison said, "Yeah, too bad she went underground so quickly. I don't know when she will be back in the country. I think she was afraid that you guys would prosecute her so she left town rather quickly."

Jack seemed surprised, "Really? That seems rather drastic for a hipster such as Brianna."

Allison laughed, "I think Bree is more than just a hipster. She deserved a vacation, so I think this gave her the excuse she needed to enjoy a relaxing, uninterrupted time away from customers and demanding employers."

Jack relaxed back into the sofa, bringing Allison with him as they cuddled closely. He inhaled deeply, breathing in her scent while wrapping his arms around her. For the first time in over a week, she was able to relax, sinking into his warm embrace. "I do have quite a bit of money," she said.

Jack laughed, "So I guess we'll need a pre-nup if we continue this relationship."

Allison answered slyly, "That depends on how much money you get after the sale of Remco."

Jack chuckled deeply and said, "Let's just say we will both have plenty to use however we want."

Allison's lips turned up as she pondered all the ways she could use her money for good. "You're not just dating me for my money are you?" she asked with a teasing grin on her face.

Jack raised his eyebrows in a conspiratorial manner, "No, I'm dating you so I can eat all the bacon that I want."

They both laughed and Allison started thinking of more creative ways she could serve Jack bacon. Her thoughts were running the gamut, jumping from cooking to money to love. After months of planning and executing the biggest computer hack job that Morgan had ever seen, she could truly start enjoying the finer things in life. The first on the list would be a kiss from the man that she loved with all of her heart. She pulled his head in close for a tender touch of the lips, cherishing the love of a man that knew of her flaws and loved her anyway.

ABOUT THE AUTHOR

Dodi Williams lives in South Carolina with her husband and two young sons. She is a full-time data analyst, a part-time avid baker and a part-time hopeful writer.

www.ingramcontent.com/pod-product-compliance
Lightning Source LLC
Chambersburg PA
CBHW070549130626
46556CB00001B/81